MW00749084

HOW ONE BECOMES
SARAH MEAD

Copyright © 2021 C. L. Craven

All rights reserved

No part of this book may be reproduced, or stored in a retrieval system, or transmitted in any form or by any means, electronic, mechanical, photocopying, recording, or otherwise, without express written permission of the publisher.

ISBN-13: 978-0-578-83990-5

For Melissa, Nicole, and Nicolette.
This book exists because of your friendship and support.

CHAPTER 1

S arah's feet pounded the dark red bricks, and through her frog-like running shoes, she noted each divot and curve of every brick she landed on. She allowed herself to become annoyed again at how much she paid in property taxes so the city could pave in brick this street which tourists didn't even visit. This was the only thing that kept her mind distracted from the certainty that with each stride, another strand of hair was giving way to gravity.

She had been losing her hair for the last twenty-five years. Alopecia areata. Until recently, she'd been lucky. Regular shots of steroids injected into her scalp had been keeping her hair anchored in place. Over the last few weeks, though, it was as if her hair, which had been hanging on only by hopes and prayers, was staging a revolt and mocking her efforts to save it. What had remained quarter-sized bare spots scattered around her scalp and were easy to conceal with some creative styling were quickly becoming whole bald patches the size of her fist. Soon she would lose it all, and she refused to watch that happen.

Sarah ran down the middle of the street to avoid the flooding sidewalks, which she felt a particular kinship with this morning as the five-foot-high mounds of snow piled beside the walkway gave way to the fifty-degree February heatwave. The pristine, pretty snow was melting first, leaving behind jagged piles with a layer of road sludge on them, which resembled an alien mineral form more than it did snow. This was precisely how she viewed her femininity in the wake of losing her hair. She understood that she was being unreasonable about the whole thing, for there were far worse things one could lose, but that didn't change how she felt.

Sam, her boyfriend, had been the one to suggest she cut it off. He couldn't bear watching her suffer each day as another long chocolate-colored strand came out in her hand as she brushed it. "It's just hair," he had reminded her again and again. But was it? It seemed to Sarah that whenever anyone said, "it's just" whatever, it was anything but just that.

A car passed by Sarah; its driver sped up but paused to give her the finger before he sped away. He had honked at her as well, but Sarah wasn't aware, nor would she have cared if she had been. Running in the center of the quiet street, unaware of how many drivers she pissed off, was one of her simple pleasures in life. Taking up space in the world as a Deaf woman and not changing her behavior to appease hearing people, choosing instead to force them to adjust to her.

She started her run before Sam was awake. She had gotten up for morning prayer, and when she rose from sujood, a fistful of her shoulder length hair came loose as she unwrapped her headscarf. With that, nerves that left her hands trembling replaced the usual sense of peace and certainty she felt after each of her daily prayers, so she set out for a ten-mile run—five miles longer than her regular weekday route—to wrestle her anxiety back into submission.

Despite her best efforts to be quiet, Sarah always woke Sam when she got up for morning prayer. He was glad to let her keep thinking she was a master of stealth and quietness even though she might have been the loudest person he had ever known. Sam got out of bed the moment he heard the condo door close and saw the tangle of his girlfriend's hair in the bathroom trash. It was by far the biggest bunch she'd lost so far, so he prepared his barbering kit. He knew what Sarah would ask of him when she returned from her run, and he wanted to do whatever he could to ease the heartache he knew it would cause her.

Sam pulled the t-shirt he'd slept in over his head and tossed it aside, and without giving it a second thought, he grabbed a handful of his hair and started cutting away haphazardly with his scissors. He'd kept his hair styled the same way since he began testosterone therapy, and his hair had started thinning. Wearing it combed back in a modern pompadour allowed him to hide his growing bald spot easily, and as he cut away the length it shocked him to see just how much his own hair had thinned. He smiled at the thought that he was giving Sarah a run for her money in who would lose all their hair first.

When he'd cut enough to be sure he wouldn't clog his clippers, he plugged them in and got to work. He wanted to be sitting in the living room playing his video game and carry on like nothing at all was out of the ordinary when Sarah found him without the hair she'd often mocked him for being so vain about. When she saw the expanse of the bald spot he'd been hiding, they would have a good laugh at the situation they both found themselves in. Sarah often lovingly mocked Sam over his sorry excuse for a beard, which she referred to as his "ten chin hairs." Sam came from a family of men with lush facial hair. When he dreamed about transitioning in his twenties, the glorious beards of the Kane men were what he imagined for himself, and not the fact that where their beards grew, their hair began failing them all in their early twenties.

Sam finished with his clippers and chuckled as he studied himself in the mirror. "Ten chin hairs and now, ten head hairs. Sarah's a lucky girl," he said to his reflection, which he half expected to point at him and laugh. Sarah was the only person allowed to joke about the things that made Sam a man—or the lack thereof—because she was the only person who did so without ever questioning the validity of his maleness. And Sam was the only one allowed to make bad jokes about Sarah's hair falling out, mostly because he was the only one who knew. Sam thought about this unique arrangement of mocking in the shower as he rehearsed in his mind a dozen variations of how he would propose to Sarah after he had finished cutting her hair.

Sarah jogged into her condo building to find Mrs. Kostas sitting in the lobby earlier than usual. Every day, the old woman dragged a chair from her dining room out of her first-floor condo and into the lobby where she sat for hours, as though she was the building greeter.

"Good morning, S," she signed to Sarah, her fingers too arthritic to spell out her full name.

Sarah always wondered if the old woman was lonely, and this practice gave her some human contact or if she was bored and appreciated the change in scenery.

It was a mix of the two, plus Mrs. Kostas had a bit of the crush on the mailman, and she enjoyed bringing in all the packages delivered to other residents, shaking them, and trying to guess what people had ordered. Mrs. Kostas was a rather adept nosy neighbor.

"Good morning, Mrs. K," Sarah replied.

She forced a smile as she blew right by the old woman, who was clearly eager for their morning chat. Mrs. Kostas had been the only one of the nineteen residents of the building who had bothered to learn any sign language, so Sarah made a habit of stopping to talk with her each day. But today, Sarah had no time or patience for small talk. She made her way to the stairwell, feeling a little nauseous at the thought that the next time Mrs. Kostas saw her, she'd be bald, and she'd have to talk about it.

Sarah took the stairs two at a time. When she reached their condo door—the only one in the hallway with no seasonal decoration—she stopped, drew in a deep breath, and held it for a moment, steeling herself before bursting through the door to get on with the worst thing she could imagine having to endure.

Sarah startled at the sight of Sam, whom she didn't immediately recognize, and he sucked in his lips to keep his mouth from turning up in a grin when he felt her eyes on him.

"Have a good run?" He signed to her without looking in her direction.

"Oh, you think we're not going to discuss this?" Sarah said and then patted the sizable bald spot on the crown of his head. "Jesus, Sam, you had a comb-over!"

"Technically," he began, "it was a comb-back, and a heads up would have been nice." He grinned at her as he waved his hand in a circle around his head.

"Been a little busy with my own balding, Sam," she smiled at him, struggling to not break into full-on laughter.

"Yeah, saw that in the trash. It's time?" He asked the corners of his mouth turned down in part concern, part empathy.

Sarah nodded, "It's time."

Sam rose from the couch on one leg, favoring the other which was still healing from surgery, and hooked his finger in the waistband of Sarah's leggings and pulled her toward him and onto his lap as he collapsed back into his seat.

Sarah focused her attention on the TV screen, not wanting to look at Sam because she refused to start crying before anything even happened. He was playing his favorite game, in which he played as a wizard who wore tiny blue swim trunks and rode around the game world on a giant fluffy cat. She understood why Sam loved playing games as a wizard, bending the world around him to his will and changing reality with ease. She'd kill for a little magic like that of her own right now.

Sam put his game controller down and gently pulled off Sarah's microfiber skullcap to inspect the day's new loss and see what he had to work with. Though he'd told Sarah she should simply shave her head, it was the very last thing he wanted to do to her, as he imagined it wouldn't be unlike him being forced to walk around without his chest binder on.

Sarah looked away as she felt more of her hair come out as her hat came off.

"I can't believe you don't have an opinion on this," she said, frustrated.

"I do have one; it's just not the one you expect," he reassured her. "It's the same as yours about my top surgery. I don't need to understand why you need to do this to support you. If this will make you happy, then I'm glad to do it for you."

"Happy? Really?"

"You never know, it might end up being the best thing you ever did," he raised an eyebrow hoping he'd convinced her that easily. "Alright, you ready?"

Sarah held her breath and nodded. She stood from Sam's lap and fought the urge to vomit as she rushed into the bathroom, paying no mind to Sam, who didn't follow her. He had to ride his cat back to his camp to save his game.

Grateful for the delay, Sarah held herself up on the bathroom counter and leaned into the mirror to inspect her hair. She'd been hoping until this very morning that she wouldn't need Sam to shave it. She'd hoped that the loss would stop or that Sam would become a wizard himself and alter genetics and gravity so that just cutting her hair short would be enough to make it stop its mass exodus. She knew the length had no bearing on whether it fell out—nobody went bald because they had heavy hair—but she still held onto her admittedly ridiculous hope. This morning's loss was tremendous, though, and right at the front of her hairline. Sarah understood this had become a total loss situation, and she was grateful to at least have Sam to do this awful thing for her, so she didn't have to bear having her stylist—whom she'd not seen in months since her small bald patches first began growing—shave her head. It was time for her to trust Sam's words that she would make a gorgeous bald woman.

Sarah studied the contents of the barbering kit Sam had neatly laid out as though it was a menu of all the terrible and intimidating choices available to her. What would Sam do? Use the scissors and make the process a slow but less painful burn? Or maybe he'd start right off with the burgundy pair of the aptly named balding clippers and rip the bandage right off. Sarah spotted the monogrammed straight razor she'd gotten Sam for his birthday two years before and prayed that it wouldn't be the first and only tool at his disposal. No matter how ridiculous she knew her feelings were, the fact remained that the razor, in particular, felt like something that should never touch a woman's head.

Finally, Sam appeared in the mirror behind her, and he looked at her with the poorly concealed smirk that Sarah knew meant he was more excited to do something than she was. Being a barber and on his feet all day, he'd taken medical leave after tearing his calf muscle and having surgery to repair it. He'd been going stir crazy, having nothing productive to do for weeks. Sarah imagined he felt the way she did over summer and holiday breaks at the university when she got so desperate to teach *someone something* that she often ended up lecturing Sam or an unsuspecting friend on Deaf culture and history.

Sam tugged on Sarah's shoulder until she turned around to face him, and when she did, he put his hands around her waist and lifted her up onto the counter. He leaned into her and kissed her deeply. Sarah responded in kind and was so lost in her lust for him that she didn't even notice that while he was kissing her, he also cut off her ponytail.

Sam pulled away and held up the hair like it was the pelt of a small creature he'd just hunted.

"So, you really are a wizard?"

"Distraction is key," he told her with a proud smile. "You sure you don't want this for a wig?"

"I don't want a wig," Sarah insisted, and when Sam still didn't appear convinced, she repeated herself. "I *don't* want a wig."

Sam dropped the hair to the floor behind him without another word about it and pulled forward the stool they kept stashed in the corner. He patted it, and Sarah sat down. Sam cradled her cheeks in his hands and kissed her. He stared at her with his wide green eyes, which, depending on the mood, either made Sarah think of a cute leprechaun when paired with his red hair and short stature or made her feel compelled to undress him and get him in bed. Today it was the latter.

Sarah had been trying—and failing—to trick herself into believing that losing her hair did not differ from being Deaf. Briefly, she wondered if, somewhere in the world, there was a community of bald people that made the proud distinction between being Bald and being bald, as there were Deaf people and then there were deaf people.

Sarah closed her eyes and saw her father's mouth forming the words he'd said so often when she was young; *she might be deaf but look at what a pretty girl I have*. Regularly bathed in shame for her deafness as a child, her pretty hair, pretty eyes, and pretty face had been her saving grace. In the last twenty-five years she'd been free from her father, she'd put tremendous effort into convincing herself that this was not true, that she was much more than just a pretty girl. Some days this was easier to believe than others. Each day she spent with Sam, it became slightly easier to accept as true, as he told her, over and over, that what her father said was bullshit. On an intellectual level, Sarah believed him, but fifteen years of daily conditioning had taken its toll on her.

"You know," Sam began, carefully weighing his next words, "this doesn't have to be a bad thing. You'll be a stunning bald woman. So rock it, make it your thing."

"Let's just get this over with," Sarah said, allowing herself one last look in the mirror before closing her eyes. She didn't want to watch, and she definitely didn't want to see Sam's reaction as he revealed his bald girlfriend. Mostly though, she didn't want to have to see the blinding glare from the globe bulbs above the mirror reflecting on her new huge bald patch. She couldn't imagine how bad the shine would be by the time Sam was through.

The thought that he'd better not screw this up—though there was not much he could have done wrong—occurred to Sam, and he widened his stance just in case his healing leg gave him trouble. He whipped the scissors around so fluidly that they seemed to be a natural extension of his fingers. While he appreciated how painful this was for Sarah, he was grateful to be working on someone's hair. He loved his job, and he missed it terribly.

Sam couldn't work until he could stand all day and walk on both legs again. His surgeon told him that being on his feet all day would severely impact his healing time. Sam was also an athlete and being sedentary was simply not in his nature. He was an equestrian and going to see his horses at their boarding barn without being able to ride them was torturous. He would have the stable hand fetch them, one at a time, from the pastures in which they spent their day, and he secured them in the crossties and meticulously groomed them as he did before each ride. First the curry comb, then the stiff brush, then one more pass with the soft brush, so their coats shined.

Perhaps he imagined it, but the horses seemed disappointed upon reaching the end of their grooming ritual without being saddled up and instead returning to their pasture. At least Claude, his Irish Sport Horse, had found new ways to entertain himself during their time together, stretching his neck to the side and using his muzzle to knock Sam's crutches to the ground. When Sam would pick them back up and move them out of his reach, Claude would stomp his hoof on the concrete until he moved them back.

How Sam injured his leg had provided Sarah with endless amusement when people asked about what happened. The assumption was that he'd hurt himself during some impressive equestrian feat, but when asked, Sam answered honestly. "I tore it walking down the stairs." People waited expectantly for the good part of the story, and Sam continued, "That's it. I was going to get the mail and *pop*."

Sam had his share of impressive athlete stories, like when he still took first place in an event despite having broken a rib earlier in the day, but he was never one to boast. His humility was one of the things Sarah loved the most about him. She thought of him as a Muslim who was unaware of it, as his beliefs and morals were perfectly in line with Islam even though he insisted he was an atheist. Sarah adored the man the rest of the world didn't get to know. The one who did silly things to make her laugh and honestly believed "stunning" and "bald woman" could be used together in a sentence about her. He was exactly who Sarah needed.

Sarah opened her eyes when it occurred to her that Sam was not doing her hair, and she found him staring at her.

"Stop looking at me and just get on with it," Sarah pleaded.

"Okay, but I don't think you want me to do this without looking at you," Sam said, trying hard to contain a smile.

"Right, like that would make it any worse," Sarah laughed as tears filled her eyes again.

Sam was careful to not let any of the hair he cut drop onto Sarah's shoulders. He thought it was the least he could do, spare her from the reminder every few seconds that she was losing a part of herself. He worked as quickly as he could, trying to concentrate on his task and not on Sarah's body shaking as she cried.

Until the moment she entered the condo after her run that morning, Sarah's primary concern had been what Sam's reaction would be. His profession, paired with his sense of vanity, worried Sarah the most. Him being a barber, it seemed reasonable that having good hair and having a girlfriend with equally good hair would be a requirement for him. He had certainly been obsessed with his own hair. He had an entire budget devoted to his haircare, and he always took great care to ensure he appeared neat and clean-cut, never letting a hair stray out of place. So, until that morning, she thought his rejection of her would be her biggest problem. Now though, she'd seen how easily and carelessly he'd parted with his own vanity, just for her. The only thing that remained for her to worry about was the simple fact that in a matter of minutes, she would be a bald-headed woman and how unnatural that felt.

All her life, Sarah had worn her hair long, hanging past her shoulders, and each time Sam cut a strand, the sudden sense of being lighter surprised her. She wondered if she would feel like a whole new person without the weight of her hair and then allowed herself to wonder if this might be a welcome change.

Sam finished with the scissors and placed them on the counter. He reached for his clippers but stopped when he saw Sarah's shoulders bouncing as she sobbed into her hands. He'd wanted to tell her, so many times, that letting herself be sad about this loss was okay, that she didn't need to liken it to her pride in being Deaf, but he hadn't for fear of seeming like he thought he knew better than she did how she should cope with something. He was glad to see she was finally allowing herself a modicum of vulnerability about the situation, but he felt her sadness in his bones and just wanted to make it stop.

He raised her head to meet his eyes and gently told her, "We can stop. We can scrap the plan and stop right now and go get a wig. It's okay to not do this. It's okay to be a little vain."

"No," Sarah quickly responded. "I need to do this."

Sarah was right. Sam didn't understand. He knew it had something to do with her father and what an asshole he was, but he also knew better than to ever bring him up unless Sarah did first. He knew that it was only because of her hair falling out that Sarah had been able to leave the cult started by her father, that much she had explained to him long ago. What he didn't understand was why she felt she had to continue suffering because of something she'd been free from for twenty-five years. It's not as though she would ever see her father again and feel some kind of bald-headed sense of victory over the man.

Desperate to get Sam off the subject, Sarah looked up at him, at his hair. "This is sexy, you know. You should have done this a long time ago."

"I was happy living in denial, thank you very much," Sam joked. "They skip this part in the *So you're trans, here's exactly what to ex-pect* guidebook."

"Oh, there's an instruction book, is there? I wonder if they have one for bald women too. How to get that perfect bald-headed shine and whether you still use shampoo or is soap good enough now?"

"I mean, how else are we supposed to be indoctrinated by the trans agenda? And God knows there's an angry bald feminist agenda for you."

"Shave your head, burn your bras, renounce men. Easy." Sarah's hands moved through the words she signed so fluidly one might think this was the mantra by which she lived.

"I don't think bra burning is for you. Might be a little uncomfortable." Sam joked and cupped one of Sarah's large breasts in his small hand.

Sarah was grateful again for Sam's gift of distraction, for as they swapped jokes, he had started and finished using the clippers on her head, and the warm vibration of the blades had been nothing more than a background distraction.

"One last step," Sam told her and smiled. "And I was right. You're beautiful."

As Sam massaged oil into Sarah's scalp, she forgot all about her apprehension and her fear, partly because she still hadn't dared to look in the mirror, but mostly because in this moment with Sam, she had somehow never felt more attractive or more wanted by him. Was it possible that he actually believed what he told her about being a stunning bald woman?

She watched him work and gathered that heads were much harder to shave than legs by the way Sam held his tongue between his thin lips in concentration, or, she thought, maybe it was just because she sat on the stool topless. Sarah focused on her conflicting emotions instead of what was happening because she didn't want to cry anymore. On the one hand, the warmth of Sam's fingertips touching her skin felt electric and made her want to knock the razor out of his hand and wrap her legs around his waist. On the other hand, the only reason she could feel his warm fingertips was because they were touching her now-bare head. But when she felt Sam's hot breath evaporate off her scalp and she shivered, the feeling of the former won her over, and she did not care much why she was feeling his touch.

Sam tapped Sarah on the shoulder, and she startled out of her fog. "All done," he said, "have a look."

She stood, reluctantly, her feet nested in mounds of long hair, and took a sharp breath in when she glanced down and saw just how much of her was now on the floor. She turned around to face the mirror slowly, fearing what she'd see.

For so many years, Sarah had kept the same very specific hairstyle and enduring the mocking of her friends for being so boring because of it. They didn't know, for Sarah had become skilled in disguising her bare patches. The moment she met her own eyes in the mirror, she surprised herself when she let out a quick chuckle as she wondered, *who's boring now?*

She raised her hands to her head as though she couldn't see herself unless she felt her head. She hadn't imagined how she would look. She couldn't. But for the first time, she noticed for herself features others had always complimented. Her big dark blue eyes and the curve of her pronounced cheekbones, the diamond earrings she always wore, which Sam had given her for her birthday five years ago, twinkled when the light hit them, and she wondered if they'd always done that. She saw her slight double chin, which she'd never really noticed before, that appeared and disappeared as she moved her head around. She'd imagined her head would feel and look rough as Sam's face did after he shaved, but somehow it felt smooth and fragile. Sarah looked beyond herself in the mirror and met Sam's gaze, who looked to be staring at her in awe with a dumbfounded look on his face. He was, in fact, dumbfounded that he was seeing the most gorgeous woman in the world for the very first time even though he'd seen her every day for five years.

Sarah turned to face Sam and pulled his shirt over his head. She wrapped her arms around his shoulders and her legs around his waist, as she had so many times before, forgetting about his healing calf muscle. They seemed to move in slow motion as they collapsed to the ground, laughing, and they made love in the doorway and again in the shower after Sarah washed away all the tiny dark hairs off their bodies.

CHAPTER 2

L oathing was not quite a strong enough word for what Ruth Mead felt towards her twin brother, Abraham. She thought about the day, two years ago, that the police chief of Red Ranch, Arizona, called her and told her that her niece, Mina, had been hospitalized with third-degree burns all over her torso. And Ruth thought about how it had taken her two full years to convince her niece to come with her, to leave behind the cult Abraham had so skillfully and carefully grown. Her teeth ached, and the thumb on her left hand twitched as they did when she unwittingly clenched them whenever she thought of her brother.

"Going to visit your niece, Dr. Mead?" her driver asked, jolting her out of her hatred of Abraham.

At the mere mention of Sarah, Ruth's face went from an angry scowl to the smile a proud mother wore for her child. She thought of Sarah as her own daughter, as for the last twenty-five years, Ruth had essentially been Sarah's mother. She had no children of her own and was very happy to claim her niece. She couldn't be prouder of the woman Sarah had become. A woman much like herself who knew better than to be duped by the archaic and misogynistic ways of the "Christianity" their family practiced and preached. Like Ruth, Sarah had always been too smart to fall for it.

"Yes," Ruth answered, "a surprise visit."

She swallowed the lump in her throat that held the surprise—likely an unwelcome one—she had for both Sarah and Sam. She'd told them she was coming to town to visit. She hadn't told them it was only briefly, en route to Arizona to get Mina, and only so she could ask them to give Mina and her son a home.

Ruth had done well by Sarah. She had rehabilitated her niece, re-modeled her, she liked to think, from all the damage caused by Abraham. It was a shame, Ruth thought, that he would never get to know the woman Sarah had become in spite of him.

Ruth visited Sarah and Sam often and even more so now after she'd retired, and her husband passed away. She hadn't wanted to retire; she didn't feel that she had finished her career as a surgeon yet. But she'd had breast cancer two years ago, and the chemotherapy caused neuropathy in her fingers from which she had never fully recovered, and her fingers no longer served her as a surgeon's must. So now she traveled and did needlepoint in her endless and futile effort to regain full feeling in her fingers.

Ruth propped her elbow against the armrest in the back of the SUV that took her to Sarah and Sam's condo. She felt a minor annoyance with the thought that she should have allowed at least enough time for Sam to do her hair. Every decision Ruth made was always about practicality, as nothing upset her more—aside from her brother—than impracticality. Having to return soon just for a haircut was impractical, but her fondness for Sam and the trust she had in him was about anything but practicality.

Ruth had liked him immediately upon meeting him five years ago, shortly after he and Sarah started dating, but it wasn't until she began chemo two years ago that she came to consider him one of her dearest friends.

Ruth and her husband, Hank, had been visiting Sarah and Sam, as they did every year to watch the Super Bowl and overeat chili cheese dip with Fritos. It was just before the half-time show when Ruth sneezed and then pulled out a fistful of her hair as she brushed it away from her face with her fingers. Sam noticed the hair in her hand and the unexpected tears in her eyes, and he stood from the couch where he sat beside Sarah and nodded for Ruth to follow him.

Sam had done the difficult job of ushering a woman into cancer by cutting off her hair when it started to fall out many times throughout his career. In fact, he'd become somewhat known for it because he always made it an entertaining—some might even say enjoyable

—experience, and he never charged for the service. He loved join-ing his customers in their brief and desperately needed moments of happiness and laughter as he took them on what he called a "hair adventure" of all the ways in which one should never wear their hair, including a mullet, a bowl cut, and a flat top. Sam had never had cancer, though his kindness surrounding it often led his customers to assume he had. He was all too familiar with loss so unexpected and devastating that it changes the very core of who you are and how you see yourself.

Ruth and Sam returned to the living room well into the second half of the game, both of their bellies aching from laughter. Ruth donned one of Sarah's running skullcaps to keep her head warm and felt grateful for the practicality of no longer having to watch her hair fall out. After chemo, her once auburn hair grew back in a stark, snow-white, and when her husband told her she was more striking than Judi Dench at the Oscars, she kept Sam as her barber and wore her hair in a feminine crew cut because Hank liked it. Plus, it was practical, and everyone knew how Ruth felt about practicality.

When she took her place back on the love seat beside her husband to rejoin the Super Bowl viewing, he plucked the hat off of her head and smiled. "Beautiful," he signed, waving the fingers of his right hand around his face, and he kissed her. To Sam, he signed, "Great, thank you," and Ruth chuckled, as she always did, at the sign for "great" as she thought it looked like someone high-fiving God, whom she did not believe in but appreciated the sign nonetheless.

Ruth rode in the back of the car, grateful for these memories and the brief distraction from the crushing guilt she felt concerning Mina. For two years now, she had been calling her niece every week, planting the seeds of escape in Mina's mind. She told her of places she had never been herself but that she knew would thrill Mina and her son. Places like Disney World and SeaWorld filled with childhood joy and wonder that little Noah would never know if Mina didn't leave.

Finally, a week ago, Mina called her aunt.

"We need to leave here," Mina told her. "Thomas is going to kill me if I stay, and Noah needs a mother."

Ruth covered the microphone on her earbuds, so Mina didn't hear her heartbreak upon the realization that her niece, whom she had let herself forget about for so long, only cared about herself to the extent of being alive for her son. She wanted so badly to tell Mina that yes, Noah needs a mother, but the world needs you too. But she knew Mina was too far gone, too broken, at least right now, to accept that truth.

Ruth had told neither Sarah nor Sam that she was going to get Mina, or that she was about to ask them to let her and her son live with them. She knew that their home, the love that swelled within it, was right where Mina needed to be, where she would be able to heal. Still, she also knew the understandable bitterness that Sarah harbored for her father, his cult, and anything associated with it. Even her sister. Ruth couldn't risk giving them time to come up with a practical reason—of which they could indeed find many—to say no to her.

When Ruth spotted the rainbow-colored lamp posts of Boystown, the neighborhood Sarah and Sam called home and Ruth's favorite area in all of Chicago, she took out her phone to text Sarah that.

"In your neighborhood. Be there soon!" Ruth texted and got no response.

When the car turned onto their block, she texted again, "On your block, hope you're home!"

CHAPTER 3

"**S**o, you like bald Sarah then?" Sarah joked to Sam, who still couldn't take his eyes off her as they redressed themselves.

"I mean, I like any version, but *damn*. If I'd known that would lead to *that*, well, I'd have suggested it years ago."

Sarah pushed him away from her, playfully, finally able to return his smile. Sam stood from the bed and bent to kiss Sarah atop her head. His hot breath and the sensation of his chin stubble against her skin gave her a shiver, and she laughed to herself at the thought that they could very easily have sex for the third time in two hours and was mildly disappointed to remember that they couldn't, they had errands to run.

"Don't move. I'll be right back," Sam told her.

Sam left the bedroom, limping as quickly as possible, and Sarah did as she was told and waited on the bed. *Oh, I bet he's getting donuts. Yeah. He better be getting donuts. We've earned them,* she thought, and she let out a short and disappointed breath when he returned, holding something other than the long teal box from the donut shop around the corner.

Sam balanced on one leg, slowly lowering himself to his knee, and Sarah thought he looked like he was about to break into some sort of routine.

"Do you remember the day you first told me you were losing your hair?" he asked.

Sarah nodded. How could she forget? It was an awful day which Sam had turned into a wonderful one.

"You told me it was alright if I left and didn't want to see you anymore because you knew nobody wanted a bald girlfriend."

The memory brought tears to Sarah's eyes for the third or fourth time that day. She had fully expected Sam to leave and never come back after pulling out a fistful of her hair in the middle of them having sex. But he didn't go. He comforted her, and for the first time after months of dating, he took off the tank top he always wore, which turned out to be a chest binder. "Now we're even," He'd told her, and they carried on in bed like nothing at all had happened.

"Well, you're right," Sam continued. "I don't want a bald girlfriend."

Sam picked up Sarah's hand and kissed her knuckles.

"I want a bald wife," he said, both of them crying now. "Sarah, I love you, and I want to be your husband. Will you—"

Sarah didn't wait for him to finish. She nodded her head so vigorously it hurt and nearly knocked Sam over with a hug.

"This is so much better than donuts!" Sarah signed through her ecstatic sobbing.

"Uhh. Okay. I mean, I hope so..." Sam said to himself, unaware that Sarah had been hoping for donuts but now wishing he had, in fact, gotten donuts.

"Yes," Sarah said, "I will. Yes."

The two held each other and kissed through their shared tears.

"Cool. Now can you help me up off the floor?" Sam smiled as he wiped the tears from Sarah's cheeks. "I think I'm stuck down here."

Sarah laughed and pulled him up by the hand to her. He held her, and his hand grazed her head.

"Oh my God, it's a miracle!" Sam joked. "It's so nice to do that and not get my hand slapped or pull out any hair."

The flashing light of the doorbell interrupted their post-proposal bliss. Sarah pulled away from Sam, and it occurred to her that as happy as she was with her decision in that moment with Sam, she'd eventually have to leave the house, see other people out in the world. She'd have to go to work, explain herself. Sarah wasn't ready for that; she'd never told anyone she had alopecia. She wanted to be able to enjoy it for a little longer.

"Expecting anyone?" Sam asked.

"Don't think so," Sarah signed and then immediately remembered her aunt Ruth telling her she needed to talk to both of them. "Oh, I bet it's Ruth. She texted a couple days ago; said she'd be in town."

Sarah checked her phone and there they were, six missed texts outlining Ruth's arrival in the city and then their condo. The most recent text read, "On your block, hope you're home!"

Sarah adored Ruth. She was a mother to her but also a friend who never did any of the annoying motherly nit-picking crap her friends and colleagues with *real* mothers often complained about. So, she was glad Ruth was in town to visit and a bit annoyed by her timing. Sarah wanted Sam, again, and donuts and Ruth's presence dashed her hopes for both.

The two stood in the open doorway after Sarah buzzed Ruth into the building, and tears began to swell in her eyes. She just wasn't ready for anyone's reaction to her decision, not even Ruth's. Sam noticed the tears, wiped them away with the back of his index finger, and kissed Sarah's head.

"Don't worry, Sarah, it's just Ruth. She'll probably think it's great and want to do it herself."

They both laughed because they both knew he was right. Ruth was the least judgmental person either of them knew, and she was simply enamored with the two of them. They stepped into the fourth-floor hallway when Sarah felt the subtle vibration of the old elevator arriving on their floor, and she held her arms open to embrace her aunt as Ruth stepped into the hallway and came towards them. Ruth locked eyes with Sarah, and after a moment to take her in, she raised her hands and covered her mouth in surprise.

"Oh my God," Ruth signed, "Sam finally proposed! Look at that ring!"

That had not been what Sarah was anticipating Ruth noticing first, as even she, in just a few brief minutes, had forgotten that she now wore an engagement ring on her finger. Ruth carried on, not even seeming to notice Sarah's lack of hair, and she pulled Sarah's hand toward her so she could get a closer look at the ring as they walked back into the condo.

"Oh honey, I'm so happy for you," Ruth signed, crying now, "and it's about damn time, Sam."

Ruth hugged Sarah once more and then embraced Sam before returning her attention to her niece.

"I love it," Ruth signed, pointing to Sarah's head. "It suits you, honey. And remember, I told you, being bald was the best part of cancer for me. Saves you so much time and money."

"What money? You've never paid for a haircut in your life," Sam said.

All three of them laughed, and just that easily, as though she wasn't seeing Sarah without two feet of hair for the first time, Ruth made her way into the condo and made herself at home. *Now, if everyone can react this well,* Sarah thought, relieved Ruth hadn't made a thing of it.

Ruth put her purse down on the entryway table and took off her long wool coat. She looked at Sam and smiled.

"You've finally decided to give up the fight and embrace the male pattern baldness, I see?" Ruth joked. "So, who's bald in support of who, here?"

"You know, either of you could have told me. Just a quick, dude, you're bald, give up!" Sam said. "Letting me walk around, looking like I'm in denial. Some family you all are."

"Aww, well, I didn't want to make you lose hope, Sam." Ruth playfully mocked him.

Sam reached out and ruffled Ruth's short hair. "You decided to grow your hair back? Rock the old lady look again?"

"Nah, I'm just lazy" Ruth smiled as she rubbed Sam's cheek with her thumb. "Maybe I should join your little bald club, eh?"

Sarah adored the relationship Ruth and Sam shared. Sam hadn't been in touch with his family since they disowned him after coming out as transgender, and Ruth filled in as a mother for him in the same way she had for Sarah. Sometimes it was hard to believe Ruth was related to Sarah's father at all.

"Well, I'll get right to it," Ruth started, instantly changing the tone of the conversation. "Sarah, you remember your sister Mina?"

Sarah nodded her fist; yes, furrowing her brow at what seemed like a stupid question. She may not have seen or spoken to her sister in over two decades, but she certainly remembered her. Sarah put the girl out of her mind to ease the guilt she felt for leaving her behind when she made her escape. She hadn't really thought of her much at all. It wasn't as though Mina had tried to be in touch with her, after all.

"I'm getting her away from her husband. And your father. She asked for my help, and God, someone needs to help her. I'd like to bring her here to live with you two. Mina and her son, he's two." Ruth alternated her stare between the two of them, not giving them the chance to say no.

Ruth was nothing if not spontaneous, but this was out of character, even for her, and both Sam and Sarah stood, wide-eyed and speechless.

"I'm sorry, you what?" Sarah signed, her arms moving with a force that clearly indicated her suddenly foul mood. "My sister, from the cult that thinks I'm basically Deaf Satan? That sister? The one I haven't even spoken to since she was what, five? She wants to live with us? The Deaf and now bald Muslim and the trans man?"

"Well, *want* is kind of a stretch. She wants to live with me, but they belong here. And I...well I didn't exactly tell her about Sam." Ruth stumbled over her words.

"And why would you? No explanation needed here. We're everything the crazy Christian cult loves," Sam offered the rare opinion of Sarah's family and snorted a laugh.

"Mina's not like that; she's not like your father," Ruth explained.

"Really? Then what's she like? What's her reason for letting twenty-five years go without even acknowledging I exist?"

"She couldn't, Sarah. You don't understand what her life has been like. That bastard's going to kill her if she stays, and you know your father. He'll let him if it means his image gets to stay intact." Ruth's face wore the contempt she felt for her brother.

"Right. So, you want us to take them in, let her come here and shit on us because our father is a bastard? We're happy, Ruth. We've got a life. We're getting married, for God's sake. What's she going to do in six weeks when Sam has his top surgery? Spray holy water at us and have an exorcism? And does she even sign? Am I going to need an interpreter in my own house?" Sarah's fury was radiating from her arms as she signed so wildly that both Sam and Ruth took a step back.

"Please, just think about it. Consider what good you could do for Mina. Look at how much you two love each other. You could show her what life is supposed to be like. I know this is the right place for her, so please," Ruth pleaded. "I have to go. I'm meeting her at the airport in the morning, and I still have some last preparations to make. I'll be back tomorrow."

Neither Sam nor Sarah said a word as Ruth left the condo and walked back down the hall to the elevator.

"What the hell was that?" Sam asked the second he heard the elevator door slide shut.

Sarah laughed and shook her head, "Just Ruth being Ruth."

Sarah and Sam were on very different levels of acceptance because while Sarah was still at a firm no, the next thing Sam said was, "Where we gonna put 'em?" As though they'd already decided.

Three hours later, Sarah sent her aunt a text. "Fine. They can stay. For now." She was still furious at the suddenness of Ruth's request. She and Sam had just gotten engaged for God's sake; this was not what not next in the line of things to do. But she and Sam had discussed it, and Sam was right, as he usually was when it came to helping people. Mina was her sister whether or not she knew her, and if her life was bad enough to take her kid and flee the state, it was the least they could do.

Technically, they did have room for Mina and her son. Their condo had three bedrooms. One of them was a makeshift library and office for Sarah, and the other a disorganized storage space that housed all the crap they both had nowhere to put after they'd moved in together.

The speed with which they prepared the two bedrooms would have impressed even those professionals with shows on HGTV. Sam went out to rent a storage space, while Sarah recruited some students from around campus to help pack and move things. She ordered two bedroom sets from Ikea and thanked God for rushed delivery and assembly.

The one benefit to all of their rushing was that Sarah didn't have even one thought about her hair or how anyone reacted to her. Nor did she think about Mina and all the guilt that came with her last memory of her as a little girl; five-year-old Mina standing beside their father, his hand clutching her head like a carnival claw machine, waving to the taxi that drove Sarah away from the cult forever.

After spending the entire day packing and arranging, the pair fell asleep on the couch together out of sheer exhaustion and around two a.m. Sarah jolted awake, worrying about Sam's guns. For reasons Sarah never quite understood and never asked about, Sam insisted on keeping guns. He had once said something about it being because he grew up on a farm. They lived in Chicago, though, not in the wild west, and Sarah wondered why he needed guns. With just the two of them living in the condo, Sam didn't store them in the safest manner. The two Sam didn't carry were in drawers somewhere, and the one he did was always in his bag, which he stowed in any number of places throughout the condo. Sarah had never seen a reason to store them differently as she didn't even want to look at them, and anyone intent on using the guns on her or Sam would have to get past two locked doors in the lobby, down two hallways of nosy neighbors, and of course, past Sam and his gun.

Sarah poked Sam in the shoulder until he woke.

"We have to put your guns somewhere," she said as Sam tried to follow her signing through one open eye.

"You want my gun?"

"No, we need a safe or something. They can't stay where they are, not if we're going to have a kid in here."

"Shit. Can't it wait?"

"No, we need to check it off the list." Sarah insisted, and Sam knew nothing else mattered once Sarah mentioned her dreaded list until she completed the task.

They both got up slowly and began their trip to the twenty-four-hour superstore, where they not only bought a six-gun safe—the smallest the store offered—but a cart full of toys that were their best guesses as to what a two-year-old would play with.

"Does he have teeth?" Sarah asked Sam, holding up a chunky plastic teething toy.

"Every kid needs a good LEGO set," Sam said with a grin, clutching a LEGO set of Apollo 11.

"Only if you want to kill him. Look at the age recommendation, Sam, he's two, not 16," Sarah corrected him and now thought of how much easier it would be if the child was 16.

With their cart full of toys, they stopped in the bakery area for some cake as Sarah felt they had earned a cake.

Back in the car with their safe, cake, and toys, Sarah told Sam that she couldn't help but notice how everyone—all five of the other people out shopping before dawn—stared at her. Sam laughed as he studied her head.

"You've got a pretty strong five o'clock shadow going on there. And the patchiness makes it look kind of like a puzzle," Sam told her, trying his best to not laugh harder.

"Keep laughing, Sam. You'll look awfully weird when I shave your eyebrows off in your sleep." Sarah said, her face not giving way to a smile at Sam's joke even the slightest bit.

"Look. People are gonna stare. They already do. They stare at me because they can't tell what I am. They stare at you because you're pretty and you sign. They stare at us because we're an unlikely couple. Just add this to the heap of reasons."

"Should I get a wig? I should, shouldn't I?"

"You should do whatever makes you feel good. If you want a wig, then yes, get one. Hell, get seven." He stopped to kiss her knuckles. "If you want a wig because you're worried about what people think, no, don't get one. Fuck 'em. I meant what I said. You're stunning. Give yourself some time to get used to it."

Somehow Sam had mastered always being able to say the right thing. If Sarah bought a new pair of pants only to come home and realize they fit funny and asked Sam if they made her hips look too wide, he didn't miss a beat before giving a full dissertation on why she did not look wide, or why it didn't matter. He had the perfect response to everything, and this was no different.

Sarah hesitated, searching for a fault in Sam's logic but found none.

"You're right. Plus, if people keep staring, I'll just show them one of your guns."

"You've finally figured out why I carry. *Keep your eyes off my woman, buddy!*" Sam said and then held his hands like a gun.

They drove home as the sun was just starting to rise. Sarah's nerves had eased, and now she could about the entirely new problem of Mina, the stranger, moving in.

CHAPTER 4

Mina woke to her son's tiny hands peeling the bloody bedsheet away from her face, glued there by the blood seeping from a cut under her eye. She had lost count of how many mornings she'd woken to find herself in this state. Thomas found cause to hit her most evenings, and last night was no different. She couldn't recall why, but she remembered his ring and how it sliced her cheek open. This was the first time her son had ever found her this way, though, and it would be the last. She focused on him staring at her, his hands now bloodied, as he stared at her with a look of unknowing concern children have when they're worried but don't know why. She brushed the sleep from his eyes with a swipe of her thumb and tried to smile at him despite the pain that burned in her cheek.

"Good morning, my love." She stroked the boy's hair, a curly mess from a good night's sleep. Mina hoped speaking to him as though everything was normal would abate the fear he felt from seeing her hurt and bloody.

"We're going to take an airplane ride today, way up in the clouds. Doesn't that sound like fun?"

He shook his head vigorously and kissed his palm, pressing it to his mother's face, mimicking the silly way she often kissed her fingertips and pressed them to his cheek. As he waited beside her on the bed, she lay knowing she was failing him.

It had taken Mina so many years to have her son, Noah, whose name described precisely what she felt in his presence—comfort. His wide caramel-brown eyes had a way of keeping her composed on her worst days. Each time she looked at him, she saw all the promises she'd made to him before he was born. Promises of a life in which he would never have the opportunity to grow into a man like his father. Promises of a mother he could be proud of and that he understood loved him without question or condition. Mina had promised herself many times that if she was ever fortunate enough to have a child, he would never see the truth of what she endured. If she had a daughter, she knew there would be only a few short years before she learned to fear her father. If she had a son, she wondered how long it would take him to realize he had complete control over his mother by the simple act of raising a fist to her. She knew keeping these promises would mean taking Noah away from any family he knew. As terrible as they were to her, they loved him, and they were his family.

Mina willed her body out of bed when she heard the church bells chiming. She had given up on prayer long ago and only attended church services when Thomas or her father demanded she did, but this morning she found herself praying as she looked out her bedroom window toward the house of a woman she used to know. The woman who had once been both her only source of joy and her greatest torture. She prayed that she would be able to forget the life she had here. She prayed for some kind of sign that she was doing the right thing. It occurred to her that perhaps the fact that she had to pray for the ability to forget her life was all the sign she needed. It was well past time for her and Noah to leave, and she forced herself to imagine what life might be like tomorrow.

Before she was a mother, she didn't lie in bed thinking of a new life on mornings like this one. Instead, she hoped that she could die and not have to live another day of this hell. Before she was a mother, she had only herself to think of, and she did not think very much of herself. But on this morning, she pulled her aching body, purple with fresh bruises, out of the white sheets, because on this morning, she had every reason to. This was the last morning Mina would spend cleaning and mending herself from the previous night's beating. This was the first and last time Noah would ever see his mother bloody and broken at the hand of the man he called "Bapa."

Mina gave Noah some toys inside his little wooden playpen and got into the shower, careful not to look at her body as she passed the mirror. She didn't want to see the camouflage of new and fading bruises, nor did she want to catch a glimpse of the woman she'd become. Mostly though, she didn't want to see Thomas's glare stalking her, as she did each time she looked at her reflection, as though he lived in her mind and manifested each time she dared to think of herself. She unraveled her long hair from its bun, and it brought the ever-familiar ache of being pushed and pulled around by a man's hand in her hair, as though it was the reigns controlling his horse. She stood in the shower, the water as hot as she could stand it, and rubbed the soft white washcloth over her face, shocked by the amount of dark red blood on it. She didn't bother to look to the mirror that clung to the tiles behind her.

Out of the shower, she toweled her hair dry, gently, so she didn't cause herself any more pain. It seemed so heavy hanging down her back as she automatically reached to tie it back into the same bun she wore every day, the bun every woman in Radiance was required to wear. This, they were told, would keep them from "competitive vanity," which, on better days, Mina couldn't help but giggle at the image of women in an Olympic-style race to don their makeup and best hairdo. Mina was the only woman in Radiance that had been allowed to wear makeup—simple red lipstick because that was what Thomas liked. She often wondered if his fondness for it was because the red resembled blood, something Thomas loved seeing more than anything.

Something gave Mina pause as she began to tie her hair into a neat bun. She'd suddenly become a woman possessed by spite and gathered it into a ponytail with one hand and reached for the straight razor Thomas kept in the drawer as a threat with the other. She sliced through it at the back of her neck with the sharp blade and placed it neatly beside the sink—something for Thomas to remember her by. Mina smiled as she tucked what remained of her hair behind her ears, pleased with herself for having done something so hasty and without the usual careful consideration and weighing of consequences.

She brushed her teeth and spit blood-stained toothpaste into the sink. She reached for the faucet to rinse it away but stopped herself. Today it would stay there. A small reminder that she'd lived here.

That she'd lived.

Mina walked down the barren hallway of burgundy walls with Noah on her hip. Every wall in their home was empty. They had no happy family portraits adorning the walls, no art hanging. No sign that people with lives and feelings lived there because, Mina supposed, people with lives and feelings did not live there. Noah existed there, and Mina suffered. Thomas ruled there. They once had some small sculptures and vases displayed here and there, but they had all broken, one by one, as Thomas tossed her around and into them.

In the kitchen were members of the house staff that Thomas employed, dutifully waiting to be given the day's instructions. Mina didn't regard them with words, she only waved her hand at them, and they quickly fled the kitchen.

Two maids, a chef, a butler, and two groundskeepers. All fellow residents of Radiance. The contempt Mina felt for them had been slow-growing, but by now, it was a raging fire of hatred. Such loyal and good servants they were, that they had mastered the art of selective vision. They chose to never see the things Thomas did to her, to never see what the man who would become their leader was really made of. They chose to never help her. They chose to not even look at her, instead always holding their gaze to the ground and speaking to her without ever seeing her. How many times had they cleaned up her blood, swept up tufts of hair torn out by their boss, heard her cries for help, and carried on as usual? This was what they were paid to do, of course, but still, they were monsters, all of them.

With the staff out of sight, Mina put Noah in his highchair and prepared some oatmeal for him. They usually had a breakfast of fresh fruit and yogurt. It was easy, and the monotonous slicing of fruit allowed Mina a brief escape, but today Noah would need the hearty meal.

"Eat your breakfast, my love," Mina said as she put the bowl in front of Noah, not realizing that she hadn't given him a spoon.

Mina didn't eat. She couldn't. Nerves had her entire body buzzing, from her fingers to her teeth, and her stomach turned on itself at the thought of eating. She only downed a glass of water, savoring the pain and the moment's distraction it brought as she gulped the icy liquid.

As Noah ate his thick, warm oats by the handful, Mina wound a loose strand of her foreign feeling hair around her finger.

As Mina waited for Noah to eat, her two cats entered the room and began their daily ritual of winding themselves around her ankles until she picked them up. She didn't look down at them, but she didn't shoo them away either. She had spent the last two days ignoring them because she knew she would have to leave them behind, and she couldn't bear the thought of what might become of them. Mina knew they would die, that Thomas would take his rage out on them in her absence, but she had a choice to make. Their lives, or hers and Noah's. While she wouldn't have chosen herself alone, Noah would always come first. Always.

When Noah finished his breakfast, she wiped his chubby face and stared at him for a moment, wondering if she was doing the right thing for him. Was a fatherless son better off than a boy whose father would teach him violence made him a man, made him Godly? Did violence make him a man? Was it inevitable? It often seemed that way to Mina.

She put Noah in a diaper, for today was not a day to practice toilet training, and though it was a hot spring day in Arizona, she dressed him in his fleece pants, a long-sleeved red shirt, and his puffy coat. She needed to protect him from unknown weather and everything else that remained a mystery on the journey ahead. Immediately too hot, Noah held his arms to his side and began waving them, wishing his mother would get the sweater off of him.

Carrying the boy on her hip, Mina took a slow walk around their home. For the fifth or sixth time, she checked that Thomas was indeed not home, and with each room they entered came a flash of the shameful secrets that room held. The broken and poorly repaired chair in the dining room that failed to bear her weight when she was shoved across the room and onto it. The remnants of blood spattered on the corner of the library wall where her forehead collided with it. The bedside table she'd cowered behind so many times, hoping that for once, this inanimate object would protect her from another violation in the bedroom. So many secrets within the walls.

Mina hadn't wanted to be paired with a man, at least not when she was and not to Thomas. She'd wanted a life, a career. The community that her father presided over practiced homeschooling. During Mina's time in school, she'd trained to work in the community beauty shop with a woman who had been a hairstylist before arriving in Radiance. Women weren't permitted to cut their hair in Radiance, aside from their initial Embracing Ceremony when they first came to Radiance or after that, when they were being punished for something. In the ceremony, their heads were shaved in a show of sacrifice for the community and submission to the men of Radiance. Thomas and her father made a whole thing of it, complete with Bible verses and a rebaptism of sorts.

The contrast of the Embracing and the punishment had always stood out in Mina's mind. The former being beautiful and something every woman was eager to do, while the latter—though Thomas carried it out with equal showmanship— was something every woman lived in an ever-present fear of, for none of them knew exactly what "offense" would earn them this punishment. Fortunately, punishment was rare.

The beauty shop served as a place where women could have their hair curled or braided for special occasions, such as after a month of being shared among all the men of Radiance, and they returned to their paired mate. Mina loved being able to give the women the temporary gift of a break in the monotony, a reason to feel special for just a few hours when there was usually no reason at all for a woman to feel special.

Mina wanted to be productive; she wanted a job but understood that her one and only real job was to give life, to carry the future generations of Radiance. A job she had failed to do for twelve years until she became pregnant with Noah. Mina had a talent for doing hair, though, and she wanted to put it to use.

Thomas wasn't a handsome man. He wasn't ugly, but his character had seeped into his appearance. He was tall and slender. Almost frail looking. Delicate. But he was deceivingly strong, at least when compared to Mina. He had the long fingers of a pianist, and his veins all stuck up in startling blue along his hands and arms underneath his pasty skin. He was well-groomed and spoke slowly and eloquently with a hint of a Southern drawl. He had started balding young, so he kept his head shaved, which Mina thought made him appear even more ghostly. He had perfect posture and a kind smile for everyone but her. She tried not to let the fact that she was not attracted to him in the least color her opinion of him in the days before their pairing ceremony as they got to know each other. This turned out to be an easy feat. Thomas made no effort to hide what a wretched man he was even during their pairing ceremony. He held her wrist instead of her hand as Mina's father performed the ceremony and spent the entire time staring her down in a way Mina would later realize had been his first of many challenges to her. Challenges to try him, test his patience and forgiveness, and see what would happen.

Mina stood frozen in Thomas's bedroom. The pair slept separately, as everyone in Radiance did, to keep them from being averse to mate sharing. She tried to take in every detail of him left behind in the room. She didn't want to remember him, but she didn't dare forget him. His scent lingered in the air—cedarwood and juniper. When they were first paired, Mina could close her eyes and inhale his fragrance and almost feel attracted to the man. Now the scent only made her heartbeat quicken, and her insides feel knotted with fear.

Mina took one last look around her home, where she had been a prisoner for fourteen long years.

This is it, she thought, *we're nearly free.*

She put on her oversized sunglasses to hide her black eye and ugly gash and reached into her purse, took out her keys, and put them on the mail table, right beside the catalogs Thomas still had to look through. She took one of the hoodies Thomas wore on his daily jog and put the hood up to disguise her hair that would surely draw stares once she left the house. She chose a freshly washed one, so she didn't carry his scent with her. Mina took a deep breath, closed her eyes, stepped through the front doorway, and walked away with Noah clinging to her hip. She didn't let herself look back as she walked faster and faster.

A few days before, Mina spoke with her aunt Ruth and told her what she'd hidden for so long. Ruth left the family years before Mina was even born when she realized there was no place for a woman like her in a family like theirs, and she lived in New York City with her husband. Mina always wondered what happened that caused Ruth to estrange herself from their family and had finally gathered the nerve to ask for her help.

Mina hadn't seen Ruth in years, not since just before her pairing ceremony, but she had always been the one person Mina could count on to offer the love and concern that her father never had for her. Ruth made sure to call Mina at least monthly, just to chat about benign things, though Mina always wondered if her real motivation was to make sure she was still alive.

"We need to leave here," Mina told her aunt over the phone, and she admitted to her the ugliest parts of her life, things Mina suspected Ruth was aware of but just never knew how to help her. "We have to get away. I can't raise Noah here."

Mina told Ruth that she didn't know what she'd done to provoke him—this was a lie, Mina knew exactly what she had done—and that in the past couple of years, Thomas had only grown more brutal and frequent with his beatings. She told Ruth that he had lost any sense of restraint he'd once had. Ruth didn't judge or question her; she only said, "Of course I'll help you, Mina. Of course I will."

In the days following that conversation, Mina didn't allow herself to wonder how Ruth would help her or how they would get away. As frightening as her daily life was in Radiance with Thomas, the prospect of leaving, beginning a new life she knew nothing of, was inconceivable.

The only instructions Ruth gave Mina were to wait for her call, and when she called, Ruth told her to meet her at the airport in Flagstaff before noon. Mina didn't pack anything. She couldn't without Thomas asking questions. What does one pack that could prepare them to start a whole new life anyway? Mina hoped it would seem as though she and Noah had simply vanished, leaving behind all their possessions. She imagined Thomas having to grasp at excuses when people asked after her and Noah and stumbling over his words when he had to tell a lie he hadn't carefully prepared for.

Ruth told Mina that they would have a home in Chicago, living with her sister. Mina had long since forgotten about Sarah. She used to think of her occasionally when she was still a child and felt lonely, as none of the other children dared play with Abraham's daughter. All she knew now of her sister was that she was who had given her the name Mina. Mina knew her actual name was Rebecca, though she couldn't recall ever having been referred to by the name. She didn't know how Sarah had arrived at "Mina" from "Rebecca" but she had been known only as Mina for so long that she didn't suppose it mattered.

She had asked her father once, when she was ten years old, where her sister had gone to and if she would ever come back.

"Sarah had her Embracing Ceremony when she was fifteen," Abraham explained to her, "and God never gave her back her hair because her heart was impure, so she couldn't stay here. She won't be back; put her out of your head."

Mina had never wondered about the truth of what her father told her; she simply accepted a woman having hair as a sign of purity and God's favor. She did what she was told and put Sarah out of her mind and instead became preoccupied with the fear that God would do the same to her when it came time for her Embracing Ceremony.

Ruth told Mina that living with her sister would be different from anything she knew and was used to, that it would take time for her to adjust, and that she would likely question the choice Ruth made for her. But Ruth promised that in time, Mina would see that this was the very best place for her and Noah. She promised her that eventually, she would be happy, and it would become their home.

If Mina was honest, happiness was the farthest thing from her mind because she couldn't recall what joy felt like. She just wanted to feel safe. She feared what she'd find in Chicago. Her whole life, her father had preached about the danger, the sin that corrupted the big "Godless" cities, and Mina had never been to one to see for herself if the threat was real. She'd never been outside of Arizona, or even the twenty-mile radius surrounding Red Ranch, the town in which Radiance was founded.

The promises Ruth made were what Mina tried to concentrate on as she made her way to the airport with Noah. She walked two miles away from Radiance, so quickly that her heels had blistered, burst, and now bled, and then called the one and only cab company that serviced the area. When the cab arrived, Mina dropped her phone on the side of the road. She wouldn't risk Thomas finding her, tracking her with it. However that sort of thing worked. The terror of being caught overwhelmed her. What if this cab driver knew Thomas or her father? What if he'd driven them before? What if he took her back to them? Mina knew she was being unreasonable and paranoid, but paranoid becomes your usual mode of operation when you live each day with the strong possibility of being beaten unconscious.

Along the ride, Mina kept her head down and practiced calling Thomas her husband. She couldn't imagine Sarah thought about Radiance or how it operated anymore. No woman is a "wife," only "paired" with one man responsible for providing for her and any children she bears. A practice Mina understood made the idea of sharing the women for maximum child-bearing probability more palatable to the men who all viewed women as their property. Women were a community resource of sorts, not unlike the various shops within the community, which were managed by one man but shared freely among community members. Mina didn't want to have to explain how she'd not only been raped by Thomas hundreds of times but by all the men in the community as well. "My husband, Thomas," Mina repeated in her head over and over as she rode in the back of the cab.

When they arrived at the airport, Mina went straight to the place Ruth told her they would meet but barely recognized her aunt. She saw no one that resembled Ruth as she remembered her from over a decade ago. Only a handful of men wandering alone, a couple of women her age with children, and an old woman wearing a suit with closely cropped white hair standing with her arms folded over her chest. It wasn't until Ruth spotted her and called her name that Mina remembered to breathe.

The two women stood and looked at each other for a moment before Ruth wrapped Mina and Noah in a hug, and Mina wept. That hug was the first kind touch Mina had felt since the day of her pairing ceremony when one of the women she worked with at the salon hugged her before she was given away to a monster.

Ruth didn't try to remove Mina's sunglasses as she gently wiped the tears from her cheeks with a pink silk handkerchief. She knew why she wore them. The edges of a black eye had crept out from behind the cover of the oversized frames. Noah reached for Ruth. He must have felt her warmth radiating through his mother, and for the first time in his young life, Mina allowed someone else to hold her child. They didn't speak while they waited to board the plane. They just sat, Ruth's hand over Mina's on the uncomfortable armrest of the airport seat. When they were called to board, Mina stood and took one last look around, as though she was surveying the countryside from atop a hill. Ruth smiled at her encouragingly and linked arms with her as they boarded the plane that would take Mina and Noah to their new existence.

Mina had never flown anywhere. She'd been confined to her small community for all of her thirty years, except for the times she'd been in the hospital. Settled on the plane, Ruth rested her hand over Mina's again and reassured her with gentle pats. Though the two spoke regularly, they were both now at a loss for what to say.

Ruth looked different than Mina remembered her. Older but maybe happier too. The last time she'd seen Ruth was fourteen years ago, just before her pairing ceremony. Ruth had come to give Mina the chance to escape. She told Mina that she would take her to New York with her and that Mina would never have to endure any of this. Ruth had practically begged her to come with her, but Mina still knew what hope was then. She was ignorant to just how evil one man could be, and she felt it was her duty, as Abraham's daughter that hadn't run away, to at least try. Ruth told Mina she would always be there for her should she ever need her, and she left after unsuccessfully begging Mina to leave one more time. Ruth kept her promise. She had been there each time Mina needed her. Still, Mina insisted on keeping that need to a minimum, and their relationship existed only through casual phone conversations when Mina could sneak them. Mina didn't want anyone to know what she'd been enduring because of Thomas. She didn't want Ruth to know how much she hated herself for not taking Ruth up on her offer to leave when she had the chance.

Mina remembered Ruth with long and dark red hair, and now it was mostly silver and cropped short. Uncomfortable with the silence, Mina attempted to make small talk.

"You've changed your hair," Mina said and regretted it as the words left her mouth. Of course she had; people tend to get haircuts over the course of fifteen years.

Ruth ran her slender hand with well-manicured nails over her hair and thought for a moment, trying to recall what she'd looked like the last time she'd seen her niece.

"I did," Ruth said with a smile. "I had cancer two years ago. After my treatment ended, I kept it short. Hank liked it this way."

"How is uncle Hank?" Mina asked, wondering why he'd not come with Ruth to the airport and feeling ashamed she didn't know Ruth had cancer.

"Oh honey…" Ruth began and paused, her face changing to what almost resembled pity. "Hank passed away. A year ago. He had a stroke."

Mina was embarrassed and angry, not at Ruth, but at Thomas, at her father, for forcing a life on her that required she be so selfish that the person who loved her the most didn't feel she could burden her with their own devastation.

"Oh," Mina said, too embarrassed to meet Ruth's gaze, "I'm sorry."
Ruth pulled her phone from her purse and handed it to Mina, a woman's photo displayed on the screen.

Mina studied it for a moment and smiled, pleased to know that God had seen fit to give Sarah back her hair. She handed the phone back to Ruth, and the two returned to their uncomfortable silence while a thousand questions floated through Mina's mind. Why was Ruth sending her to live with Sarah? If she lived alone now, couldn't she and Noah live with her? What was Sarah like now? Did she look like a new person too? Would she let Mina practice her hairstyling so she could eventually get a job and support herself? The only thing Ruth told Mina over the phone about her sister was that she was a college professor and a Muslim. Mina wondered what happened to Sarah to make her want to convert to what Mina knew only as the religion of terrorists? Would Sarah hate her? Would she be able to like Sarah? Mina tried picturing her sister wearing the outfit, whatever it was called, that Muslim women had to wear, and the thing covering her hair, and she couldn't.

Noah had fallen asleep when Ruth tried talking to Mina again.

"Mina, honey, I want to prepare you for all this," Ruth began. "I don't want anything to come as a surprise. Sarah is different from how you probably remember her. She's happy, she's done quite well for herself and, well, you've been so sheltered—"

Mina interrupted her aunt, "Ruth, I don't expect her life to look like mine. We wouldn't be going there if it did, would we? Will she let me sleep and eat in peace? Will she beat me? Force us to be Muslims too? Maybe I won't like the way she lives or understand her, but I suspect that goes both ways." Mina shouted in a whisper.

The truth was that Mina didn't care what Sarah did or didn't do. Sure, there were things she wished she could understand about her sister, but her only thoughts about her were of memories of her. Mina was five years old the last time she saw Sarah, and she imagined her looking exactly the same, only taller. She'd always remembered what a pretty girl Sarah was with her big hazel eyes and long, wavy brown hair. All Mina wanted was for herself and her son to be safe, and she trusted Ruth enough to assume they would be.

What Mina felt most strongly was sadness. She was overwhelmingly, profoundly sad. Outside of her life with Thomas, she had a full life. The women she'd had to leave behind without a word, they were her sisters, and their children were Mina's children too. She'd been forced to run for her life by a horrible man, and the unfairness of it struck her, thousands of feet in the air.

Ruth realized Mina was in no mood to talk, and she couldn't blame her, so she stopped trying and let the girl's mind wander. There were so many things Ruth wanted to know, to ask, but she didn't dare. She knew why Mina kept her sunglasses on, she'd seen the edges of that bruise, but she noticed other scars too. There were purple burn scars that ran upward on Mina's neck, and Ruth wondered how far they stretched underneath her clothing. At least the boy seemed happy and untouched, Ruth thought.

Ruth tried to keep her hatred for her brother from consuming her, so she never let herself think of him or what he'd done to Sarah and allowed to happen to Mina. He was a civil engineer, turned architect, turned religious zealot, and now Ruth couldn't think of him as anything more than a monster. Abraham founded his community on the idea of being fully self-sustaining and closed off from the rest of the world, where men ruled, and walls and gates kept the women and children locked in. He'd bought up hundreds of acres, and true to his word, he created his own little enclave. He built fifteen houses to start, all hidden behind a big concrete block wall in the middle of the desert outside of Sedona. They supplied their own power, composted their own waste, and Abraham had strategically recruited residents with a man for every purpose a community could need. A doctor, a plumber, a butcher, a barber, and a lawyer. Ruth and Abraham grew up in a strict Baptist home. While Ruth drifted away from religion in her teen years, Abraham craved it and the sense of power he believed the

Bible gave to men, and he reveled in his bastardized faith.

People had always been quickly captivated by Abraham, he had a manner of speaking that could mesmerize a person even if they disagreed with every word he uttered, so the role of the leader, The Father, as he fancied himself, came naturally and easily to him. Forty years and several hundred community members later, Abraham had his very own cult full of equally delusional and zealous men and their submissive women.

Ruth had long understood his view of women. Their father had been an abusive bastard and beat all three of them, particularly their mother, and Abraham was no different, though he'd never been able to find a woman to marry him. But it wasn't until Sarah was in her twenties and confided in Ruth that Abraham had raped her that she understood just how far gone her brother was. But by that time, Abraham had forbidden Ruth from entering the community, and she'd never been able to confront him or ensure Mina was safe. So instead, she put all of her efforts into making sure Sarah became a healthy, happy adult, and she'd done very well by her niece. They were two separate families now—Ruth, Hank, Sarah, and now Sam, and Abraham, Mina, and all of his people. The task of moving Mina from that into her side of the family was a daunting one.

When they landed, Mina became instantly nervous, her heart pounding in her throat. Sarah wouldn't be meeting them at the airport. A car service was picking them up, and Mina wished that Sarah had come to greet them so they could meet on neutral ground. She imagined her arrival at Sarah's door would be that of a distant relative showing up out of nowhere for a surprise visit and expecting to be hosted indefinitely. Mina assumed Ruth had told Sarah about her, why she was coming at least, but she didn't know how much Sarah knew. How much she even wanted to know. Was she doing this because she wanted to or because Ruth had asked her when there was no one else? Mina also wondered why she was being sent to live with Sarah, a stranger, instead of Ruth, but she didn't question it. If nothing else, Mina excelled at doing what she was told and never questioning.

They got off the plane, Noah in Mina's arms and Ruth carrying Mina's oversized purse. They hurried through the airport, and Mina tried to take in all the accents and languages she heard. So many people existing in their own little worlds, leaving loved ones, picking up old friends, greeting visiting relatives. Hugging, crying, kissing, holding on. She wondered, were any of these people abandoning their lives? Were any of them running from their pasts into something unknown?

They walked out into the sun, and it was much warmer than Mina imagined it would be for February in Chicago. Noah started crying, so Mina took off his puffy jacket. She looked into his big green eyes and wiped away the tears from his fat pink cheeks with a slow swipe of her thumb.

Mina wasn't aware, but she'd stopped walking and was standing, frozen, in the middle of the sidewalk. Suddenly she wanted to turn around and beg the plane to take them back home. She couldn't do this. She didn't know how. She'd watched the bad made for TV movies about women that had run from their abusive husbands. They always left under the cover of night when their conveniently traveling husband was conveniently out of town. They always had one friend devoted to helping them become someone else who knew their secret. They changed their hair, started wearing glasses, learned self-defense, and how to shoot a gun. They took a new name and assumed a new life in some remote town.

That wasn't Mina. She had no friend who knew where she'd gone. And nothing about her had changed except for her now-missing ponytail—which she regretted—and the kind of fear she felt. She had been afraid of existing for almost fifteen years because no matter what she did, she couldn't be the woman Thomas demanded. She'd remained a woman who deserved beating. Now she was afraid she didn't know how to be anyone else.

Ruth came to Mina's side and gently put an arm around her. She guided her niece to the car that waited for them—a black SUV with darkened windows all around. A man stood outside it wearing a black suit, a white shirt, and a narrow black tie. He opened the rear door when the women neared the car.

"Ladies, good afternoon," the man said with a slight nod of his head.

Ruth motioned for Mina to get in first. She gave her Noah to hold while she climbed in, and Mina noticed someone had put a child's car seat in the back for Noah. Mina suddenly felt more welcome, knowing someone had thought to provide for her son. She hoped it was Sarah.

They drove away from the airport and sat in silence. The vast differences between Red Ranch and Chicago astounded Mina. She'd never seen a place so flat before, and the houses all looked like they'd come from cookie cutters, all exactly the same but in varying shades of brick. Ruth told her the neighborhood's history and explained that most of the two-story houses they drove past were called two-flats, with one family living on the lower level and one on the upper. Mina worried when she saw hundreds of people out walking, but none of them resembled her people. There were no groups of young mothers out with their children, and she saw no churches anywhere.

As if reading her mind, Ruth said, "Don't worry, Mina, you'll fit in here. You'll find people."

You'll find people, right, Mina thought, and as the houses rushed past her window, she wondered if she had ever known how to do that.

CHAPTER 5

S arah had very few memories remaining of her father. She hadn't seen him since the day she left for boarding school when she was fifteen, and as for speaking to him, she couldn't actually recall that ever happening. He'd always talked at her, looking down at her like he was addressing a pest on the floor. Sarah had never been a particularly adept lip reader, so she only picked up a word here and there. She was sure she wasn't missing much in conversation, though.

She remembered the day she left Radiance. A taxi had come to the main gate to take her to the airport, and she sat in the back, fingering the first of many bare patches on her scalp, simultaneously thanking God for it and cursing Him for everything else.

The catalyst for Sarah's escape from Radiance was the first clump of hair that fell out. Her father was in her bed the night her hair began to fall out. She laid there with her eyes closed, like she always did, begging God to kill her or at least allow her to lose consciousness. And as always, her prayers went unanswered. As he jerked around on top of her, Abraham ran his knobby fingers through her hair and pulled out a fistful of it.

He leaped off the bed, so utterly shocked and almost certain that he heard God talking to him, that he fell over his pants that hung around his ankles. In his haste, he threw the clump of hair, and it landed right on

Sarah's face. Any other teenage girl, Sarah imagined, would be devastated, probably sobbing. But Sarah understood it to be God finally, after three excruciatingly long years of torture, answering her prayers.

She'd opened her eyes just in time to see the horror come over her father's face as he jumped off of her, and she knew it was all over.

Abraham understood what happened that night to mean one thing. He had been wrong in understanding how God wanted him to grow his community, and not even a week later, Sarah had a brand-new suitcase in her hand, and she was fighting the urge to smile and cry tears of joy as the cab driver took it from her and loaded it into the back of his car.

She was free. She didn't know how she would survive on her own, but she didn't care. She was free from her father and Radiance. The rest, she imagined, she could figure out. Abraham had done his eldest daughter the courtesy of contacting his estranged sister, Ruth. He told her that Sarah would be living at a boarding school in Connecticut, and Ruth was at the airport to greet Sarah when she got off the plane.

Ruth had never met her niece before. She hadn't even known she was an aunt until Sarah was five years old, and Abraham called to tell Ruth that their mother had died. Ruth studied ASL ravenously in the days between Abraham's call and Sarah's arrival, and when Sarah stepped out of the jetway, they immediately knew each other, and Ruth signed, "Welcome home, Sarah."

Sarah held on to the image of driving away from little Mina, only five years old at the time. She looked behind her as the taxi drove her away from Radiance and saw the little girl, only five years old, standing next to their father, his hand clutching her head. Sarah tried not to allow herself to be consumed by guilt for leaving behind her little sister. She imagined that Mina would now have to fill in the role she'd left, but Sarah had learned long ago how to compartmentalize.

That one image was the only thought she'd ever given to Mina, and in hindsight, Sarah felt terrible about it, but twenty-five years removed, what could she possibly do? She couldn't even be sure Mina remembered she had a sister, and if she did remember, Sarah was sure the girl's mind had been corrupted, ruined by the cult and its zealots.

"Is it too late to change my mind?" Sarah signed to Sam as they approached the fiftieth stop sign in as many blocks. "This is going to be awful. We might as well have invited a stranger off the street to move in. Hell, that would probably be better. Less chance of them being a religious nut."

Sam leaned over and grabbed the steering wheel, his jaw clenched.

"It'll be fine. Just drive and freak out later, okay? Nobody will be living with us if we die on the way to the store."

Sarah hated driving with Sam in the passenger seat. He always complained when she tried to talk as she drove, as she not only took both hands off the wheel and drove with her knee but turned her head to look at him as well. Sarah was always happy to remind him that statistically, deaf people were better drivers than hearing people. However, that was probably only true when they weren't trying to talk to their passenger. It had been a long few weeks of Sam being unable to drive because of his leg injury.

Neither of them had slept well the past two nights. The first night, they'd not slept while preparing the house for its new residents. The second night, nerves kept them tossing and turning. Just as suddenly as Sarah had woken two nights ago thinking about Sam's gun, Sam woke early on the morning of Mina and Noah's arrival worried about food, which was typical of him. He realized that they didn't have a lot of food, and what they did have, Mina and her son likely wouldn't want. Both Sam and Sarah were vegans and managed their diets without any awful substitute foods that so many vegans eat. The fake cheese that didn't melt and the soy "meat" that tasted like a wet gym sock. But they imagined that going from normal food—whatever that was—to their version of vegan would be too great a change for Mina and especially for a little boy, so they set out to buy the rubbery and odd-smelling substitute foods for them.

The day began with what turned into a five-hour trek to the grocery store due to a half-marathon blocking their route of choice and various construction projects blocking every alternative. Driving fifty feet and stopping, honking, cursing at cab drivers and cyclists who didn't believe traffic laws applied to them—a typical day of driving in Chicago when the summer construction began in February. On the way to the store, the two argued about everything there was to pick a fight about, except the one thing that worried them both. Mina. In two days, she'd become the elephant in the room. Both Sam and Sarah knew that taking in her and Noah was the right thing to do, but that didn't make it any more appealing.

They both felt terribly out of place at the chain grocery store, neither of them having shopped in a non-specialty store in years. Sarah tended to shop where people knew her and therefore didn't condescend to her because she was Deaf. Sam had always been amused that most of the customers at his store of choice were fellow queer people. But here at the Jewel Osco, cisgender straight women shopped for their husbands and two point five children. But unlike Sarah, Sam reveled in being the minority. He was a people watcher and loved any opportunity to observe and learn from those he didn't understand. Sarah wanted to crawl under a rock as Sam said "hello" or "good morning" to each person they walked by. She was surprised when many returned his greeting with a smile. Sarah had grown used to an often much lonelier world in which, instead of risking their discomfort, strangers simply turned and walked away upon seeing Sarah sign.

"What kind of food would make them happy?" Sam asked after their cart had remained empty for ten minutes.

"How the hell would I know?"

"You ate food growing up, didn't you?"

"My nanny was from Ecuador. Ask me what Ecuadorans eat, and I'll give you a long list."

Sam's nostrils flared, and he rolled his eyes.

"I don't know, Sam, let's just get something so we can leave, please."

Eventually, they gave up trying to figure out what Mina and Noah would like and just got what seemed easy. A bunch of frozen meals, a bag of "Chickn" nuggets, and some vegan frozen pizzas.

If all of this hadn't been so sudden, Sarah never would have believed it was actually happening. Ruth said a lot of things that never came to be because she was a flake. A kind, generous, and loving woman, but always a flake. Her husband was Ruth's anchor, seeming to keep her wild imagination rooted in doable reality. When he died, Sarah grew used to Ruth making a dozen grand plans of trips they could take, planning visits, and if Sarah was lucky, one or two out of the dozen came to fruition. Sarah loved Ruth like a mother, but she understood that when it came to being able to count on her, Ruth was only reliable for the most important things. Concrete plans were not within her skill set.

Sarah remembered Mina, but only vaguely. She'd not seen so much as a photo of her sister since the day she left for boarding school. Mina was barely out of diapers the last time Sarah had seen her, and therefore, she existed as someone distant and not having any significance in her life. For that, Sarah felt guilty. She'd come to feel guilty about many aspects of their nonexistent relationship in the last two days. The complicated mess that was Sarah's family felt like something she'd need charts and graphs to explain, so she never discussed it with anyone. She let people assume they were dysfunctional for all the regular reasons, that she was an only child, and that her father wasn't the leader of a massive cult. Sam was the only person who knew the truth.

Sarah was born from rape to a fourteen-year-old girl, a member of the cult, as Abraham didn't believe he should elevate any one woman to the role of his mate. He raised her as his prized child until she was three years old, and he learned she was profoundly deaf. Sarah was cast aside as damaged goods, and a nanny—the only person ever employed by her father from outside the community—was hired to raise her. Abraham showed no interest in her again until she grew into a pretty girl. Abraham raped the same woman eight years after Sarah was born and conceived Mina.

Sarah had gotten lucky. Because she was Deaf, Abraham had no plans of pairing her with a male follower. She'd been allowed to leave after the night that still haunted Abraham—his daughter's hair coming out in his hand. Given the precious gift of exile, Sarah built a normal life for herself with Ruth's help. Mina had no such good fortune, and she was stuck, a cult member for life. Until now.

It had been twenty-five years since Sarah had seen her sister and at least fifteen since she'd even thought about her. Now a thirty-year-old woman who may as well be a stranger and her toddler son were coming to live with them. Sarah wasn't proud of feeling the way she did about someone she knew she should naturally and automatically love, but there wasn't much she could do about that. She couldn't very well produce the proper feelings for someone she didn't even know. Sarah wasn't particularly proud of how she thought of Mina's faith either. Sarah had been raised a Christian, of the most zealous and conservative variety. When she left Radiance, she left behind faith, but in college, that changed.

Her three suitemates were Muslim women. Sarah attended college in Washington, DC, and after 9/11, she witnessed firsthand how quickly their lives changed. Overnight, they went from carefree college students to getting death threats shouted at them. These women that had quickly come to feel like her sisters had suddenly become dangerous suspects in the minds of so many. Sarah wanted to help them because she knew them to be good people, but she knew nothing about their faith, aside from their prayer habits, and that two out of three of them covered their hair with a scarf. She set out to understand Islam and found that it was the one and only faith that was nearly entirely in line what everything she already believed to be right and true. And so, in her mission to help her friends, Sarah became one of them and had been met with nothing but love and openness by her new Muslim brothers and sisters. Even after she and Sam got together, not one person from her masjid had a cross thing to say about him, about them. The Christianity Sarah knew was one of judgment and hate, and "do as I say, not as I do." The only hatred and cruelty she had ever experienced had come from Christians. After enough painful experiences, Sarah easily wrote the lot of them off as hateful and hypocritical people that she wanted nothing to do with. Sarah believed Mina would judge everything about her life, and she didn't want one of *them* living in her home.

The worst part, though, was Mina's son. Neither Sarah nor Sam ever wanted kids. They didn't like them, weren't comfortable around them, and definitely didn't want one in their life, with their constant messes and germs, crusty noses, and diapers. Nothing about their condo was child-friendly either. They had fragile decor, nice furniture, and Sam hung nude boudoir photos he'd taken of Sarah in their bedroom and bathroom. Now the living room looked like Santa had come and dumped his bag of toys at the wrong house.

Sarah wanted to help Mina; she just didn't know how she'd be able to. Ruth had Skyped them on her flight to Arizona and told them a little more about Mina. She told them she'd been given to a man who worked for their father when she was just sixteen, and in the four-teen years since then, Mina had endured what amounted to torture. Her husband beat her, and nobody did a thing to help her.

Sarah knew Sam wouldn't even think twice about killing anyone that hurt her. She couldn't fathom fearing Sam. He was everything good and safe to her. Ruth didn't share details—Sarah wasn't sure she knew them herself—but she told them that Mina feared for her life and had finally asked for help. Ruth told them, "I think you'll be good for Mina, both of you. She needs love and safety and someone to care enough to give her a chance. I know you two are the right people. Look at what you've got together. Show her that."

They'd already told Ruth that Mina and Noah could stay but to compliment the love and respect Sarah and Sam had for each other —which they were quite proud of—was one way to ease any remain-ing hesitation they had about Mina's arrival, and they were sure Ruth knew that. Not only did they love each other, but they also loved the image others held of them as the perfect, loving, and supportive couple. And people weren't wrong. They were perfect together.

Sarah stood in the dining room and nursed a cup of tea, staring out of the large door-wall in a fog. She had so many fears and assumptions about Mina now that she couldn't focus on just one, and they all wres-tled to win the spot of her biggest fear.

Sam entered the room and stood behind his fiancée and let out a sigh as he rested his head on her shoulder.

"So, no wig, then?" He asked. "Drop the bald bomb *after* the queer, Muslim, transgender bomb?"

Sarah pulled away and turned to face him, so appalled by the ques-tion that all she could do was stare at him with a severely raised brow. Just hours before, Sarah had expressed regret at the timing of shaving her head—she wasn't used to it herself yet and was just beginning to believe that she had made the right choice. Sam had told her not to worry about it, that she was beautiful, and to just give it a few days to feel normal. And now he was asking if she wanted a wig. Though it was an innocent question in Sam's mind, Sarah took it as a suggestion, and it stung, so she did all she could do and bit back.

"You going to get a wig and take off your binder, so Mina doesn't have to play *what's your gender?*" Sarah asked and immediately regretted the cruelty of her reaction.

"I'm not gonna put on a damn dress and some makeup just to make her churchy ass comfortable here. This is our house, she can cope, or she can leave," was Sam's response.

The truth was that Sarah had considered getting a wig for their initial meeting. Not for Mina's comfort, but so she wouldn't have to deal with any bullshit Mina might utter about her hair. But she'd decided against it, instead hoping that her baldness, paired with her deafness, would make Mina as uncomfortable in their home as Sarah felt having her there.

Mina and Ruth were scheduled to arrive late in the afternoon, and after their contentious shopping trip that morning, the couple spent the afternoon in nervous anticipation and preparation. Sam shaved Sarah's head again to rid her of the blackish-brown stubble, and Sarah was upset that this time it felt a lot less sexy and a lot more like a chore. Sam changed his shirt at least a dozen times, searching his vast collection of graphic tees for one that couldn't possibly be offensive, which was a daunting task as most of his t-shirts were sure to offend someone. He arrived at one with a cartoon sloth on it, wearing aviator sunglasses with the words "Hello Ladies." Sarah wasn't sure how that choice would be inoffensive to a conservative religious woman, but she had her own problems. Her nerves made each attempt at penciling in her eyebrows look like she'd scribbled them on with marker and would be guest-starring on Sesame Street. She didn't know what to wear either. Did she dress as usual, in clothing that enhanced her already-large chest, or did she try to tone it down? As it happened, Sarah didn't own any clothing one might consider toned down, so cleavage it was.

Ruth sent a text, "Just got off the plane," around four p.m., so Sam arranged for takeout from their favorite cafe to be delivered by five. The two sat in silence, Sam reclining with his leg propped up on the arm of the couch, his head resting on Sarah's lap, while she mindlessly played with the velvety stubble on his head. Ruth sent another text forty minutes later. "On your block!" Neither Sam nor Sarah spoke, instead sharing their uneasiness in glances, as they slowly made their way to the building's front entrance to wait for the car to pull up. It arrived, flashes on and double-parked, and they headed outside to greet them. Sarah sighed and thought, here we go.

CHAPTER 6

R uth got out of the car, holding a little boy, and walked right to them, all smiles, as though nothing at all was different about the day. One look at Mina's son told Sarah he resembled his father much more than he did Mina. He had pale skin and light brown hair with sparse eyebrows, where Mina was olive-skinned and had strong features and thick hair like Sarah. Sarah did her best to focus on Ruth and not stare at Mina, but she couldn't help but notice what a beautiful woman she'd grown into. More than that, she was struck by how eerily similar they looked. They could have been twins. Sarah's cheeks were high and prominent, Mina's were more so, and they had the same painted red, full lips. They even had the same subtle cleft in their chins. She wore dark leggings and a white blouse with a light red flower pattern and bright red flats to match her lips. Then there were the big dark glasses. Mina looked like a model, a star, and Sarah had to admire her style. She took a deep breath and walked over to greet her sister.

Mina stood clutching her purse to her chest—Ruth held Noah, and Mina needed something to hold on to tightly—and stared up at the drab beige box of an apartment building. It looked straight out of the seventies with its ugly green awning over the front door and the rows of glass blocks all around the building. Mina had been searching up and down the street for anyone that could have been her sister, and despite seeing at least ten women outside, walking, playing with their kids, and doing garden work, she didn't spot anyone she thought could be Sarah. She did wonder why a short bald-headed woman and a person whose gender she couldn't identify walked toward her. Mina shot her aunt a look as if to ask, *who the hell are these people?* And she felt a wave of anxiety come over her when Ruth's smile hinted that this bald woman was her sister.

Of course, bald women weren't unheard of in Radiance, with that being the punishment of choice whenever a woman did something Thomas disapproved of, but none of them looked like Sarah did. They were always ashamed and stayed away from the rest of the community until enough hair had grown in to cover their heads, while Sarah looked almost proud, or at least not ashamed. It was then that Mina once again recalled why Sarah had left Radiance in the first place—God was still punishing her for being a bad person.

Sarah looked nothing like she'd imagined. Mina was a foot taller than her sister and while she was thin with what she'd always felt was a rather unfeminine body, Sarah was large chested and a little heavy, with curves that made her look like the Greek sculptures Mina remembered seeing pictures of. And despite being bald, Mina thought Sarah was still beautiful. Mina felt sorry for her. She tried not to judge Sarah for her low-cut shirt that put on display parts of her body Mina would never dream of leaving uncovered in public, or the privacy of her own home, for that matter. Making Mina even more uncomfortable was that she still couldn't determine the gender of the person with Sarah. It had the small frame of a woman, the thin fingers and delicate features, but dressed like a man, was balding like a man, and had a short and neatly groomed beard.

"Mina, I'm so happy you're here. Welcome," Sam said, interpreting for Sarah as she signed a greeting that surprised him with its warmth.

Sam spoke again as Sarah signed. "Mina, this is Sam, my fiancé, and this is home," Sarah motioned to their ugly condo building.

This caught Mina off guard, and she had to stop herself from pushing Sarah away in defense as she moved in to hug her. Sarah let go of her sister and, with her hand on Mina's shoulder, guided Mina toward the door. Mina jerked away, and Ruth shot her a dirty look. Sam glanced up quickly and nodded, smiled at Mina, and looked back to the ground. Mina was pleased to see that her presence made him as uncomfortable as he made her. Sam tipped the driver and started toward the building.

"God help me," Mina muttered as she smoothed her shirt and followed them inside.

They led Mina through a small and equally ugly mauve lobby and suffered through what seemed to be the longest elevator ride ever, up to the fourth floor. They entered the condo's living area, and Ruth carried Noah down a hall and out of sight, never even looking back at Mina. She returned a moment later and signed something, forgetting that Mina didn't speak the language. The sudden urge to turn and run, beg the driver to take her back to the airport and away from these people struck her. The only thing that stopped her was the fact that the driver was a man, and she was inclined to never trust one again. She'd been betrayed and abandoned once again.

"We ordered takeout; it'll be here soon," Sam announced.

Mina nodded and asked if she could use the bathroom. Much to her disappointment, Ruth said she'd show her the way and told her she'd be leaving and would return tomorrow.

Ruth had planned on staying for dinner, but every time Mina flinched or jumped at innocent contact with another person, the severity of what Mina must have endured gnawed at her, and her guilt felt as though it might make her vomit. *Why didn't I fight as hard for Mina as I did for Sarah,* she wondered over and over until it became less of a question and more of a guilty verdict. Ruth couldn't accept that, short of kidnapping her in the night, there wasn't a thing she could have done but wait for Mina to be ready to leave.

"I'm going to give the three of you time to get to know each other," Ruth explained to Mina as she escorted her to the bathroom. "I'll be back in the morning."

Mina only looked at her aunt, hoping her face expressed something that would make her change her mind.

"Everything will be alright. I promise," Ruth told Mina and then gave her a tentative hug.

Damn you for doing this to me, Mina thought as Ruth walked out the condo door.

Mina saw two rectangular things in the bathroom, both vaguely resembling toilets, and she didn't know which to use. This simple fact was what made her finally begin to cry. She couldn't even use the bathroom as she was accustomed to. She made her best guess as to which rectangular thing to use and assumed she had guessed right when it flushed after she waved her hand all around, frantically searching for the lever. Curiosity got the best of her, and she opened the lid of the other thing. A stream of water shot up and hit her in the face when she hit a button on the side of it. *Of course Sarah has a bidet,* Mina thought, *probably one of the many things God continued to punish her for.*

She looked up into the mirror, sunglasses off, trying to steel herself. She touched her black eye, still sore, but focused on her other eye. The one she was missing and in its place was a prosthetic. She'd lost it a few months earlier after Thomas punched her, and his pinky ring had done irreparable damage. Letting her get a prosthetic was the kindest thing Thomas had ever done, though Mina knew it was only so people wouldn't talk.

She ran her hands through her hair, impressed that she hadn't butchered it earlier when she hastily chopped off her ponytail and traced her finger along the scar that ran the length of her hairline. She grew angry at Sarah for seeming like she didn't have a care in the world, not even any shame, about the state of her hair, while she had this constant reminder of the time Thomas threatened to shave off her hair and force her to walk around bareheaded for the rest of her life.

This was a common practice in Radiance as there was no better means to control a woman and keep her in her place than to force her to wear her humiliation for the entire community to see. Before Thomas arrived in Radiance, it was a rare occurrence, practiced by her father only as a last resort. He trusted women more than Thomas did, and it grew in frequency after Thomas was granted the slightest bit of power over the community.

Mina knew how uncomfortable she made people on the rare occasion she left the house without her prosthetic eye, and she considered removing it, just to spite Sarah and Sam. But angry shame came over her, and she left it in place. Mina told herself that she should take pity on Sarah and try to help her and that maybe if Sam turned out to be a man after all, being the size of a woman would make for a safer man. Perhaps Sarah was with Sam because, like Mina, she had the good sense to fear real men. Whatever their reasons were, whatever *they* were, Mina knew she was a guest here and that she had to get used to these things.

She wiped tears from her cheeks and dabbed concealer from her purse onto her bruised face. She couldn't hide it completely, though she didn't suppose she needed to. They knew why she was here. She put her sunglasses back on, though, for she was neither ready nor interested in having to explain her black eye to anyone, least of all them.

The three stood in uncomfortable silence for a moment until the arrival of the food saved them. Sarah set the table while Sam un-packed the food.

"We ordered falafel and kebabs," Sam looked over to Mina, "you like them?

She wanted to be agreeable, as she always was, but she also wanted to answer what felt like a sincere question honestly, and she re-sponded by moving her head in an awkward circle of both yes and no.

Mina was momentarily happy to be trying something she'd never tasted before. She loved food and sat at the table, feeling the slightest bit relieved.

"Did you have a nice flight? Comfortable? I bet you're exhausted. What's the time difference, one or two hours?" Sarah fired questions at Mina in sign language while Sam voiced them.

Mina was frustrated that Sarah wouldn't just speak. She wanted to hear her sister's voice and not hear Sam's because it didn't help deter-mine Sam's gender in the least.

"Can you just… talk? I don't know sign language, and Sam speaking for you is confusing," Mina said and was annoyed that Sam still signed what she'd said.

Sarah looked to Mina and simply shook her head, no, and then signed something which Sam didn't interpret this time.

"If you can't 'just sign' then no, she can't 'just speak.'" Sam told Mina. "We sign here. You'll have to learn."

"Oh, sorry." Mina returned her attention to her food and picked at it. "My flight was fine. Noah slept most of the way."

Sam signed to Sarah, his face perfectly conveying the short tone in which Mina spoke.

"Mina, can you take off your sunglasses? It'll be much easier for me to read your lips if I can see your whole face," Sarah asked.

Mina reached for her glasses but stopped herself. She wasn't ready to bare her bruised face. "No, I'm sorry. My head... I have a headache."

The three carried on eating in silence, all painfully aware that this was forced togetherness, and they all had some adjusting to do. Between bites of food—which Mina didn't care for, but she was starving—she took in the dining room. It didn't match the outside of the building. Like the bathroom, most everything was square and angular, ultra-modern. They ate on square plates, and their water glasses had square bottoms. The light hanging above the dining table had bulbs encased in square glass boxes. The inside of the condo looked like it was trying to apologize and compensate for the dated exterior.

Sarah caught Mina staring at her. Her gaze burned right through the dark glasses. Mina felt sorry for her that she didn't have any hair, which would have made her even prettier.

"I'm sorry, I don't mean to stare. You looked very different in my mind," Mina said, refusing to make eye contact with either of them.

Sarah laughed; the first audible thing Mina heard come from her.

"I look different in my mind too," Sarah joked, and she and Sam laughed as Sarah touched her head.

Mina didn't understand what was funny.

"I'm sorry God never gave you your hair back," Mina pointed to Sarah's head. "I bet you have nice wigs, or... do you wear that scarf thing?"

The sign for "wig" struck Mina as being quite simple as Sam signed for Sarah what she'd just said, and again, Sarah laughed.

"Wait, what? *God* gave her back her hair?" Sam stopped signing and appeared utterly confused.

"Our father said that was why she left. She lost her hair because she was not fit to be a part of Radiance," Mina explained, as plainly as she would any indisputable fact.

Sam signed for Sarah, and both of them roared with laughter. Mina flinched as Sam banged his hand atop the table in his laughing fit. The weak, raspy sound of Sarah's laugh surprised her, though she couldn't say what she expected Sarah's voice to sound like.

"Is that what he told you?" Still chuckling, Sarah patted Sam's hand. "I shave it. Well, Sam does. He's a barber. I probably wouldn't do a very good job myself. And no, I don't wear hijab."

"Oh, I... see. That must be so humiliating." Mina tried to imagine what in the world would cause a woman, especially one as attractive as Sarah, to want to be bald, and she didn't notice Sarah's smile become a look of contempt.

The loss of her hair was a litany of conflicting things all at once to Sarah—intimidating, surprisingly freeing, it had been terrifying but was no longer. It was so many things, but humiliating was not one of them and the assumption, Sarah felt, was an insult to her character.

If only Mina knew... Sarah thought, angrier at Mina for believing their father's lies than their father for telling them.

Maybe, Mina thought, her relationship with Sam wasn't so different from hers with Thomas. Maybe Sam made her do it. But she seemed far too happy about it for that to be true. Perhaps she'd been even more cut off from the rest of the world than she thought, and this had become a popular thing for women to do. Some weird feminist statement or something. Then Thomas's favorite Bible verse came to Mina's mind. *For if the woman be not covered, let her also be shorn: but if it be a shame for a woman to be shorn or shaven, let her be covered,* 1 Corinthians 11:6. She'd never seen it put to use for anything more than to shame a woman into submission, but Mina decided that she had never seen a Muslim woman without her head covered, so if they choose to not be covered, this must be what they have to do. She didn't feel any better, but at least this was rationale she could relate to. Mina didn't want to voice any of these thoughts, so she looked down at her plate and continued eating.

They finished their meal in silence, each glancing up when they thought no one else was. Mina paid no attention to her food; she didn't even taste it. She chewed and swallowed mechanically so she could go to her room and be alone. She didn't belong here, and she was angry at just how badly she wanted to go back home. At least there the silence was welcome, and she knew exactly where she fit.

After dinner, Mina excused herself and sat on the edge of her bed, willing herself not to cry. She spotted the TV hanging from the wall opposite her bed and turned it on. She'd never had a television in her bedroom before. Thomas was very controlling of the entertainment she consumed. She felt a little bit daring as she skimmed the channels—there were at least three hundred of them—and the sheer amount and variety shocked her. She wasn't accustomed to choices. Hers had always been to do what her father, and then Thomas, said, or face a fist/belt/whatever the tool of choice was that day. She felt a rush when she turned the volume up and tuned in to some show with a bunch of women wearing bikinis, but that quickly vanished when she heard footsteps nearby, and her survival reflexes automatically muted the sound.

She looked around her bedroom, at the four blank walls, save for the TV. It felt like a mirror. The room was empty, with no part of her displayed, as was her life. Mina didn't know how to do this, how to co-exist with people so drastically different. Her life, both with Thomas and Abraham, had always been strictly controlled. She was told what to do, where to go, what to think, and what to feel. And now what was she supposed to do?

It had been years, a decade at least, since Sarah sat in her bedroom crying because someone hurt her feelings. She liked to believe she was unaffected by the opinions of others. She'd worked so hard to just be okay with having this damned disease. She shouldn't have been surprised, though. One person, Sam, had made it bearable, preferable, even, so naturally, one person could reduce her to tears over it. She didn't know if she was more hurt or angered by what Mina said. Either way, it warranted tears. From the moment Sarah saw how similar they looked, every negative thought she'd had about her sister vanished. She was a taller, younger version of Sarah. Well, cult indoctrinated Sarah, anyway, she thought. Seeing so much of her own face in Mina's, it felt like she was a part of her, and Sarah wanted to know everything about her sister and tell her everything about herself. But one stupid comment killed that.

Sam came into the bedroom after he'd finished cleaning up from dinner. Sarah had left the table as soon as Mina shut herself in her room.

"You okay?" Sam sat down next to her on the bed.

"Yeah. I don't know. I don't know why that upset me so much."

"Well, we figured she wouldn't be super comfortable at first, so this isn't a complete surprise. Try to give her a break. Chicago probably feels like a different planet."

"Yeah, I guess. I figured she'd have a problem with us, or you, not my hair. Didn't think I'd be a goddamn leper."

"I'm gonna go try to talk to her, give her the stuff we picked up, maybe smooth things over." Sam didn't move from the bed until Sarah nodded.

She wanted to know what the hell Mina's problem was. She wasn't the one wearing sunglasses at the dinner table, for Christ's sake. But it was for the best that Sam was going to talk to her and not Sarah. She didn't exactly have a track record of being kind and forgiving after she'd been hurt, and for all his talk about Mina having to "deal with it," Sam was a peacemaker, always had been, and Sarah loved that about him. He never could leave things alone if they'd gone or ended badly.

Sarah reached for a sock from the pile of clean laundry on the bed and tossed it at Sam as he walked out of the room. "Tell her she's going to need to learn to sign if she's staying. Because this is *not* how it's going to work," Sarah signed, feeling calmer now.

A knock at Mina's door startled her. She put her sunglasses back on and opened it. Sam stood there, dangling two shopping bags from his fingers.

"We knew you wouldn't be bringing any clothes or anything, so we did some shopping. Got a few things for you and Noah." Sam handed her the bags and stared at her for a moment before continuing. "Some friends of ours own a clothing shop up on the north side. I asked if they could put together a few outfits for you. Didn't want to get it wrong. I hope they're okay until you can get your own stuff. Didn't think Sarah's clothes would be your style." Sam laughed at the image of Sarah wearing anything that wasn't revealing. "Oh, and we got you a new phone. It's all activated and stuff. We added you to our plan."

"Thank you, so much, that's… thank you." Mina again willed herself to not cry. She couldn't recall the last time anyone had done something so thoughtful for her. But this thoughtfulness confused her even more, making Mina wonder if Sam was actually a woman. Only a woman would think to do something like this, Mina reasoned.

Sam turned and began to leave Mina's room but paused.

"Mina, you're at home here. We want you both here." He turned back to Mina. "You don't have to hide anything. You can be comfortable."

Again, Sam turned to leave, but Mina stopped him. Something came over her, and she grabbed his shoulder. When Sam faced her again, Mina removed her glasses and rubbed away some of the concealer around her eye. She looked him right in the eye and began crying.

"I'm sorry, Mina, I didn't know." Very hesitantly, Sam reached for her face to wipe away her tears. She didn't recoil at his touch.

Mina cried harder, and Sam pulled her, slowly, into a hug. It had become automatic for her to pull away from physical contact, but once his arms were around her, she let the floodgates open, and she wept. She felt comfort, safety, and it was the first time she could recall ever allowing herself to cry about her life. Sam stood holding her, this rude woman he'd just met, and he stayed there until Mina's tears stopped. When Sam let go, Mina touched the cut under her eye and felt compelled to explain.

"My husband, he—"

"You don't have to do that. You don't have to explain."

Mina sat down on the edge of her bed, and Sam leaned against the wall, sliding all the way down it until he sat on the floor. They were silent for a moment.

"So, Sarah, she makes you uncomfortable?" Sam said. It was more of a statement than a question. "Because she's Deaf or her hair? And don't worry, most people don't know what to make of her. She's got that way about her."

"I knew she was Deaf. I guess I just expected she'd be different. She looked different when I pictured her. And Ruth didn't tell me about you."

"Is that a problem?" Sam questioned her but not with any hint of challenge in his voice.

"No. I don't know. I don't know what I'm supposed to feel about anything." Mina didn't want to admit to her jealousy that Sarah's life didn't resemble hers in the slightest.

"Well, I'll give you a tip to make things easier," Sam smiled at Mina. "Don't assume things about Sarah. Whatever you think about her, you're likely wrong. I hated her when we met. She was easily the rudest woman I'd ever met. You'll get to know her, though. It'll get easier."

"So, what are you? A man, or..." Mina finally blurted out the question that had been nagging at her.

Sam laughed, relieved by the question.

"I'm trans," Sam said, a grin pulled up the corners of his mouth.

That answer didn't help Mina at all, so she waited for more, one eyebrow raised, trying to figure out what that meant.

Sam realized his answer wouldn't suffice, so he continued, "I'm a man, but my body doesn't quite match that, so I'm fixing it."

Mina didn't know what "fixing it" meant, and she was still confused, but at least she had a definitive answer.

"It's getting late," Sam said, breaking a long moment of uncomfortable silence, "but we can keep talking if you want. I know you must have questions."

Mina considered her response. She knew she wouldn't likely sleep much that night anyway, and Sam was right. She had so many questions. "I would like that, thank you. But I need to check on Noah quickly."

"Not a problem, I need to say goodnight to Sarah," Sam said, and the two left Mina's bedroom and headed in different directions in the hallway.

Noah was still sound asleep. There was a puddle of drool beside his head on the pillow, and he slept sprawled out, unguarded. Thomas had never put a hand on him, but the atmosphere of violence, even though Noah never saw it, always made him sleep tightly curled up. Seeing him sleep so peacefully and freely for the first time was a relief and Mina thought that he was okay, finally, so she would be as well. She looked around the room and laughed to herself, noting what must have been a rushed attempt to provide a suitable place for a child, as she saw toys still in their boxes and instruction pamphlets littered around the floor from assembling the new furniture. Mina couldn't imagine anyone not wanting children of their own, but she appreciated the attempt to welcome Noah. They'd even gotten a little nightlight in the shape of Mars.

Mina returned to her bedroom to find Sam waiting for her.

"So, you and Sarah are getting married? That's... allowed?" Mina asked, desperate to end the uncomfortable silence and hoping her question wasn't offensive.

"Yep. Even if I wasn't going to change my gender on all my legal stuff, gay marriage has been legal here for a while."

Mina noticed that each time either of them spoke of Sarah, a smile unlike one she'd ever seen followed the mention of her name. She couldn't imagine feeling so full of love for someone, save for Noah, that you couldn't contain it and just speaking their name brought such joy.

"Have you been together for long?"

"Little over five years. I just proposed two days ago, though, and I think Sarah will be planning the wedding for the rest of our lives. That's okay though, I can wait. Already got what I wanted."

There was yet another awkward silence between them, as Mina tried to imagine Sarah being anything other than intimidating. She wanted to get to know this Sarah that made Sam so happy.

"You asked what made me uncomfortable about Sarah," Mina finally spoke. "I thought she would look more like me. I thought we would at least have that in common. On the plane, I had this stupid image of her letting me practice my hairstyling on her. And why does she want to have no hair? Who wants to be bald? Does she... is she a trans-person too?" Mina asked, desperate to understand Sarah and how on earth she could be comfortable walking around looking like she did and hoping there was an easy answer.

"Transgender. And no, she's a cis woman." Sam couldn't help but laugh at the idea of Sarah being trans. "She used to look like you. She did for a long time. She had long hair, but that's a story for her to tell you."

He could tell Mina still wanted more, and he could certainly understand the feeling. Sarah was something of a mystery to most everyone upon meeting her.

"Listen," Sam continued, "one good thing to know about your sister, it'll keep you two from butting heads, is the more you suggest she shouldn't do something, the harder she's going to try to do the opposite."

"Oh, I could never do that," Mina shivered at the very idea of being defiant. "I always try to do what I'm told. It's much easier that way."

"Yeah? Well, what's that?" Sam looked at her calmly, gently challenging her. "What are you supposed to do?"

"Here? I have no idea."

CHAPTER 7

S arah struggled to force from her mind that the reason she'd decided against getting a wig in the first place had been to catch
Mina off guard, make her uncomfortable. If Sarah's appearance was
the problem, it was her own doing. And perhaps it was a bit of both
her decision to forgo a wig plus Sam being trans and their engagement. That latter had briefly turned Sarah into someone she was
ashamed of, after all.

Whenever she thought of the day she met Sam, she still felt that
thing that brings crushing shame right back to you, years later, when
you've said something you sorely regret. The adrenaline of shame you
can taste, the shudder that overtakes your body at the cringe-worthy
memory. Sarah had never so much as thought about transgender
people outside of the fleeting thought once or twice that they exist,
and after Sam told her he was trans, well, Sarah was surprised he was
still willing to speak to her again.

Sarah had gone into the barbershop late one evening with Ryan,
the guy she'd been seeing at the time. They'd not been seeing each
other for long enough for that to seem like a regular activity to do
together, but Sarah was hungry and not in the mood to bargain, so
she accompanied him on the promise that they'd go to dinner next
door after. Sarah waited in the empty barber's chair across from Ryan
and mindlessly spun herself back and forth as she studied the photo-
graphs that hung around the shop. Not the usual photos of modern

and edgy hairstyles on gaunt women she'd grown accustomed to seeing at salons, but stunning black and white portraits of nude women. She liked them so much she was tempted to ask the barber working on Ryan where they'd come from. Sarah was so engrossed in the photos that she didn't notice when Sam appeared behind her until his hand was in her hair.

"What'll you have, crew cut? Nah, maybe a mohawk?" Sam said to her.

Sarah shot out of the chair so fast that she tripped over the footrest and hurriedly signed, "Deaf. Not here for a haircut. I'm just waiting," from where she'd landed along the wall.

"It might come as a surprise to know that I can cut Deaf folks' hair too," Sam signed in return.

Sarah was shocked that Sam had responded to her in sign language and not with the far-too-common look of pity mixed with disappointment. So stunned that she actually found herself imagining herself getting a haircut from a barber. From this barber. She shook the notion from her head as Sam held out his delicate hand to her and pulled her from the floor. Sarah couldn't take her eyes off of him as he pulled her from the floor. Sam had striking green eyes and impeccably styled red hair. She felt goosebumps form on her arms as she took in the sharp lines of his jaw and the way his neatly trimmed stubble framed his face, and she hoped he didn't notice. She'd never felt such a strong attraction to anyone before, and she couldn't put her finger on exactly what it was about Sam that caused such a reaction.

"Sorry, I'm just waiting for him," Sarah pointed to Ryan.

"Sit back down, it's alright. I'm just here to lock up."

Sarah wanted to sit. She'd worn the wrong shoes for all the walking she'd done with Ryan, who refused to pay for parking, so they'd ended up on a residential street twelve blocks away. But she was not about to risk this guy touching her hair again and finding the large bald spot her part was hiding.

"You like the photos?" Sam asked when he saw her staring at them again.

"There's stunning, you took them?"

"Yeah. I rent a studio once a month. Got another shooting day coming next week if you're interested," Sam told her as he wrote his number on a scrap of paper and handed it to Sarah. "Text me if you want. I'm Sam."

"Sarah," she responded, finger-spelling her name as she admired the boldness of this guy giving her his number right in front of Ryan, who was, not surprisingly, unaware and wrapped up in himself, as they both tended to be during their time together. Neither Sarah nor Ryan had said as much, but they'd both agreed to date the other solely because they were nice to look at.

After four days of being unable to stop thinking of Sam, Sarah texted him to ask what was involved in a photoshoot. She didn't care about having her photo taken. She just wanted an excuse to be near Sam again, to feel the electricity she had when he smiled at her as he pulled her from the floor of the barbershop. In the four days since they'd met, she thought she'd fallen in love, first with his eyes, what a cool and crisp green they were, like new grass in the spring, yet still somehow warm and welcoming, and then the innocent ways he had touched her. She'd been so intently focused on the memory of this barber she'd met that she barely noticed when Ryan dumped her, for precisely that reason.

"Come by on Saturday and find out," was all Sam said in his reply.

So, she did. Sarah walked into the warehouse-turned-studio and possessed by something entirely new that made her forward in ways she'd never been before, the moment she saw Sam, she reached for him and kissed him.

He kissed her back but paused. "Aren't you with that guy from the shop?"

"No, we broke up," Sarah said, reaching for him again, her fingers skimming his chest.

Sam darted out of her reach. He needed to tell her a few things before she touched him again. He always told women that he was transgender, long before any relationship could blossom. He hadn't on the first date he went on after he started transitioning, and the heartbreak of the woman's reaction wasn't something he'd allow himself to experience again. Easier to just get it out of the way and let the rejection happen before any feelings entered the equation.

He grabbed Sarah's wrist as she reached for him again. "I'm transgender."

Sarah's hand dropped to her side, and she felt her face change, to what she couldn't identify.

"I'm not gay..." Sarah told him after a moment, "I date men."

Sam gave one quick nod before he shook his head, disappointed but having experienced this too many times to be surprised. "Right. You take care then," Sam signed and motioned toward the door.

Sarah was repulsed by what she'd said. She hadn't meant it quite like that. What she wanted to say was something along the lines of "I've never dated a trans man before," or "Oh, okay, well, this would be entirely new to me, but I'm not put off by that." Instead, she said the worst thing possible and insulted him. Worse than that, she'd hurt him.

After two days of stewing in her guilt and no word from this man she still couldn't stop thinking about, she sent him a three-paragraph long text. Sarah explained what she'd meant to say and apologized profusely for coming off as such a terrible person and for being downright cruel. Sam was usually quick to write off anyone that thought of him as anything other than a man, plain and simple, but he was inclined to forgive Sarah, give her a second chance. He replied, "Let's try this again. Dinner? Thursday? Meet me at the shop at seven?"

Sarah smiled as she nodded her head in a vigorous "yes," as though Sam could see her, and her grin remained as she texted back her excited reply. She'd never been more grateful than she was for the second chance Sam gave her that day.

Sarah wanted to soften herself to Mina, put herself in her sister's position, and let her off the hook for hurting her, so she thought about her relationship with Sam and how they'd gotten to this perfect place after she'd so badly hurt Sam. Sarah knew it was only due to Sam being so forgiving and allowing Sarah that second chance, and she tried to imagine what Mina had endured. The most violence that had ever existed in Sarah's relationship with Sam had been all the times he'd moved to touch her hair before he knew about the alopecia, and Sarah would slap his hand away. Or the few times they'd been arguing about something stupid, and Sarah's vivid signing lead her to accidentally hitting Sam in the nose or poking his eye. Sam was fluent in sign language, but the concept of "signing space" was foreign to him, and he often stood too close to Sarah, making arguments a contact sport.

Sarah fell asleep to the wonderful and clumsy memories of how she and Sam had become an "us" and she woke annoyed by a subtle but insistent poking at her pillow. Surely there were better ways Sam could wake her up, she thought, as she slowly turned over and opened her eyes. Noah stood beside the bed, the top of his head barely as high as the mattress, his wide eyes waiting for acknowledgment. Sarah propped herself up on her elbow and noticed he had stripped himself down to nothing but his diaper, which sagged between his legs.

"Did you pee?" Sarah asked him, not quite awake enough to remember he wouldn't understand her signing. But he responded to her with a nod of his head, and he patted his diaper, seeming to naturally understand.

"Fine, come on."

Sarah dragged her tired limbs from the bed and pulled on a pair of pajama shorts. She walked to the bedroom door, but Noah stood, stock still, his arms raised above his head, fingers spread wide, and his eyes closed. Sarah thought the child looked like he was engaged in some kind of sun praising ritual, but she understood he wanted to be carried. This was precisely why she didn't want kids of her own. She liked sleeping uninterrupted and not having to cart around urine-soaked children. She picked the boy up, backwards, and carried him as she would a bag of groceries, his behind resting on her hip. They went into the bathroom next to his bedroom. Sarah pulled off his diaper, not quite sure how the things worked and stood him in the corner of the shower. When the water was warm enough, she sprayed off his bottom half. It only occurred to her after he was soaking wet that there was likely an easier way to clean him. Noah laughed each time the spray him, seeming to understand the absurdity of the situation, and he reached for the sprayer. Sarah considered him for a moment before joining him, fully dressed, in the oversized shower stall, and when the sliding glass door was closed, she gave the boy the sprayer.

"Go to town, kid," she signed and couldn't help but smile at him.

His laughter was contagious as he seemed to lose control of himself with joy each time he sprayed her, and she reacted. Noah carefully watched his aunt's hands when she spoke to him, often trying his best to mimic her movements, and when she pulled the second sprayer off the wall and sprayed him, his little body stiffened with excitement. This was not at all how she wanted to spend her time at two a.m., but she couldn't deny it was fun. When Noah grew tired of playing in the water, he dropped the sprayer and shifted his interest to Sarah's head. He patted it with his chubby little hand, and then patted his own, patted hers, and again, his own. He continued this until she shook her head no, to which he responded by more insistently patting his own head, growing irritated by her refusal. One last time, he pushed his hand to Sarah's head and then hit his own, with both hands this time. Sarah knew what he was asking, and after the way Mina had reacted to her lack of hair, she certainly would not be the one to touch her son's hair, no matter how much he begged. He began to cry, and Sarah was shocked by her natural inclination to console him.

The ease of communicating with a toddler surprised her. Noah didn't seem to have any interest in words and understood her language naturally. She toweled him off and then carried him back to her bedroom, so she could put on dry pajamas. Sarah put him down in the corner and told him to wait while she shut herself in the closet and quickly changed. He hadn't moved an inch when she opened the closet door, and Sarah appreciated his willingness to obey.

Noah and Sarah made their way to the living room where his new toys were, and they played, building a city of blocks and then destroying it, only to rebuild, over and over. When he finally became sleepy again, Sarah picked him up, and they lay on the couch, his head resting on her chest. He quickly fell asleep as Sarah marveled at having just had an enjoyable time with a toddler. She hoped this was a good sign for the mess of her and Mina.

Sarah picked up her phone to text her aunt, hoping it would wake her up. "Are you kidding me???" Sarah typed, limiting herself to only three question marks, though that didn't come close to matching her bewilderment and frustration. Her finger hovered over the send button, but instead, she deleted the text, then typed it again, and deleted it again. She had much to say to Ruth, about the way she'd just dropped Mina here and left, about the lies told to Mina by their father, about the state Mina was in, but Sarah's better judgment told her the middle of the night was not the time to pick a fight. So instead, she thought about Noah and worried about how Mina would react to her cleaning the boy instead of interrupting her and Sam so Mina could tend to her child. She wanted to let Sam do what he did best and clean up the emotional mess, and she fell asleep with Noah on top of her, hoping that they could try again in the morning.

CHAPTER 8

M ina and Sam talked until sunrise when he said he wanted to shower before Sarah got up and used all the hot water. He left Mina's bedroom but returned a moment later.

"Almost forgot, we got you this," he said, hobbling back through the door on his crutches holding a flat rectangular package. "It's one of Sarah's favorite prayers. Thought it was fitting."

Mina unwrapped the gift and didn't quite know what to make of it. It was a framed piece of paper with a long passage in Arabic calligraphy.

"It's beautiful, but what's it say?" Mina asked.

Sam didn't know Arabic, nor could he read it, but that prayer was one Sarah often referenced and even had hanging from the rear-view mirror in their car, so Sam knew it by heart.

"O Allah! Protect me and protect what is with me and deliver me and deliver what is with me. By Allah I commence my journey and by Allah I seek to accomplish the purpose of my journey and by Muhammad I have set out towards my destination. 'O' Allah make me overcome all my grief; and make easy for me all difficulties; and give me more goodness than I hope for; and keep away all evil of which I am apprehensive for my health. O the most Merciful."

Mina smiled at the translation, it was a perfect gift, and she thanked Sam with a hug, surprising herself with her display of affection and having touched a man without fear or reservation. Her first day in her new home had not gone anything like she imagined it would. She and Sam had talked about everything. Sarah, their relationship, Sam's job. They didn't speak of Thomas. Mina imagined it was with Sarah she would stay up all night talking. In her mind, they had everything in common and so many things to discuss. As it happened, though, not only did she and Sarah have nothing beyond appearances in common, but even the things they could have talked about were made difficult because Sarah wouldn't speak, and Mina couldn't sign. When Ruth reminded Mina of Sarah's deafness, she hadn't considered how differently they would communicate. Mina had never known a deaf person before, so she assumed Sarah would read her lips with ease and that it would be a minor difference.

With Sam, though, talking was easy. He didn't pry or judge with his questions but asked things in such a way that Mina could tell he truly wanted to know more about her. They had much in common too. Both artists—Sam, an amateur photographer, and Mina, a painter —talked easily about where they saw beauty in the world, and they shared an equal adoration of music. They both loved cooking and had equally strong beliefs and morals. While Sam maintained that he was an atheist, the moral code by which he lived placed value in what Mina believed true Christianity did. This fascinated her because she had always been taught that only Christians, only God-fearing people, could be of good morals. After all, only Christians had been given the path to piety. In a few short hours, Sam had caused Mina to question much of what she had been taught was right and wrong in the eyes of her faith.

After a long shower spent smelling all the soaps and various shampoos that lined the tub, Mina made her way out of her bedroom. She wondered how long it would take her to grow accustomed to living in a house that felt warm and inhabited. She entered the living room to find Sarah asleep with Noah draped over her body, her hand nestled in her hair, and she stood to watch them for a moment. Mina tried to cover the two with a blanket but woke Sarah, whom she greeted with the sign for "good morning," which she'd looked up on her new phone. Sarah responded with a quick twitch of her eyebrows, and Mina tried not to stare at her head, which had an odd pattern of stubble just beginning to appear.

Mina decided she would make breakfast for her new family. She went to the kitchen and searched the pantry for pancake ingredients. She was used to making pancakes from scratch and having bacon or sausage and was a little disappointed to only find a pancake mix made with flax seeds and some vegan bacon that Mina thought looked like a child's toy from a plastic play kitchen. Sam had told her both he and Sarah were vegan, so she made do with what she had, though she had no idea how to cook either item and was, by default, afraid of what might be in store for her should she ruin breakfast. Sarah entered the room, and the discomfort seemed to suck all the oxygen right out of the place. Mina clumsily signed "good morning" again, and when Sarah still didn't respond, she worried she'd gotten it wrong. She hadn't gotten it wrong; Sarah was just a champion at holding grudges. Thankfully, Sam soon arrived to ease the building tension.

Mina was uncomfortable with the way Sam held Sarah. He stood behind her, one hand resting below Sarah's naval, the other arm just under her chest, and his face buried in her neck, kissing her. Sarah held her hands over Sam's and craned her neck to return the kiss. As much as Mina had enjoyed talking with him, she still didn't understand Sam's gender. God made you what you were supposed to be. That wasn't something up for debate and certainly not something to question. In Mina's mind, Sam and Sarah were still two women who slept together and planned to marry, both of which also went against everything she'd ever been taught was okay. Sam let go of Sarah and suddenly draped his arm over Mina's shoulder in a loose hug, and she shot backward, out of his grasp, and broke eye contact. She tried to play it off as though he'd startled her, but it didn't fool him.

"I'm sorry, Mina, I didn't—" Sam backed away, his hands raised slightly, afraid to move again and frighten Mina more.

"What would you like to drink with breakfast?" Mina asked, desperate to not address it as she portioned breakfast out across four plates.

Sarah opened the fridge and took out a jug of orange juice, poured it for all four of them, whether Mina wanted it or not. She didn't. Orange juice hurt her teeth. Mina put her son in his new, brightly colored plastic highchair, and while he stared intently at his aunt, hoping for more fun with the shower sprayer, they sat down at the bar in the kitchen to eat, beginning another round of uncomfortable small talk.

"So, Mina trained to be a hairstylist," Sam said as he signed to Sarah. "Wouldn't it be cool if we could open a shop together?"

Sarah chewed her food deliberately. She swallowed, then very clearly and carefully said, "Yeah. Great. I'll be sure to keep my humiliating head far away."

She looked Mina dead in the eye, and her words cut her.

Sam signed to Sarah, without speaking it this time, and his hands moved quickly and forcefully. He shook his head and sneered. Sarah's hands moved faster yet, with more force, and Sam responded in kind. They were arguing, and Mina could tell it was about her. Their hands made slapping sounds as they fought, and Mina winced with every movement. Her heart was racing, and her throat tightened.

Sarah looked away, and Sam slammed his hand onto the counter, making the flatware jump. When Sarah got up to leave, Sam blocked her path, still gesticulating wildly. Mina's ears began ringing, and the room spun as she prepared for Sam to hit Sarah, and then likely her. Through her mind played one of the many memories of Thomas slamming his fist into the dining table before doing the same to her.

When Mina's mind returned to her, she was huddled in the corner of the dining area, her body smashed against the wall under the table. She sat in a warm puddle of urine. Mina shifted her jaw, trying to make the ringing in her ears stop, and slowly, she began to hear Noah crying a familiar cry. Mina looked up to see Sam holding him, standing across the room, and Mina didn't recognize the expression on Sam's face. He wasn't holding her son as a weapon, with a challenging look, daring her to try something, say something, and watch her son get hurt. Sam's eyes were soft and wet with tears, and he held Noah, pressing his head against his shoulder, and he bounced gently to calm the boy.

"Meeda. Meeda..." Sarah was repeating, and it took Mina a moment to realize Sarah was saying her name. She knelt in front of the table and held a hand out for her. When Mina didn't take it, Sarah crawled under the table, through the puddle, and sat beside her sister, reluctantly putting her arm around her shoulders, and she gently pulled

Mina to her.

"I'm sorry. I'm sorry, I'll clean it up. I'm sorry." Mina tried to pull away. She needed to get away from them both. She raised her hands over her head to keep Sam from dragging her out from under the table by her hair.

Sarah sniffed her nose, and when Mina looked at her, she saw tears running down her face. She looked to Sam, who was also crying and still holding Noah, and he took a step toward her. Mina pushed her body even harder into the wall, and Sam leaned on one crutch and inched forward a bit more when Sarah threw a hand up.

"Stop, dammit! She's afraid of you!" Sarah shouted.

Mina couldn't look at either of them.

"I'm sorry, it's my fault. I didn't mean to make Sam hit you," Mina said, her voice shaking. "I didn't mean to upset you. I'm sorry."

Sarah looked back at Sam, who signed for her what Mina had said.

"Mina look at me, please," Sarah said. She put two fingers under Mina's chin and gently lifted her head to meet her eyes. "Sam didn't hit me, see?" Sarah pointed to her face, which bore no bright red evidence a fist would leave behind. "You didn't do anything wrong, and I'm not angry. Sam would never hit me. Or you."

"But you argued, he hit the table…"

"I was being a bitch," Sarah told her, and when she saw her words had done nothing to convince Mina, she continued. "Banging on the table, stomping a foot on the floor, touching me. When I look away, that gets my attention."

Mina couldn't look either of them in the eye but was surprised to see that Noah had stopped crying and was contentedly resting his head on Sam's shoulder. Mina thought she needed to gather herself before she got into more trouble.

"I'm sorry, I need to clean this up."

She tried to pull away from Sarah. She was ashamed they'd seen this part of her. Sarah took her sister's hand, and wove their fingers together, held their fist close to her chest.

"Leave it, it's okay. Just sit here with me. Breathe."

"But I've ruined your clothes. I have to clean up."

"Nope, we're going to sit here, in the pee," Sarah insisted. "Just breathe. It's a spa treatment, you know. Urine therapy. Keep you young."

Sarah cracked a smile, and Mina couldn't help but laugh.

"I've never been to this kind of spa."

"Obviously, Mina, you aren't very hip. I mean, what's this?" Sarah ruffled Mina's hair. "You don't even have the family haircut."

"But I could never…" She ran her hand over her hair, clutching it for safety.

"I know, I'm just trying to get a laugh. Now come on, let's get you out of these spa clothes."

Sarah crawled out from under the table and reached out for Mina's hand. She took it. She wasn't accustomed to this part, the calm after the storm. Laughing after she'd been terrified. This was usually when she'd be cleaning up her own blood or hiding in her bedroom with ice on her face. Instead, someone else was cleaning up her mess without one cross word about it, and she had a sister asking to help her. It occurred to her that such an abrupt change, people living in such contrast to what she was used to, was precisely what she needed. Maybe there was no such thing as easing into a new life, into change. Perhaps it was better that Mina couldn't understand much about who her sister was or what she did because if she had understood her, wouldn't that mean she lived a similar life? Sarah had known, instinctively, how to calm Mina, and that was the most welcome unfamiliarity.

Mina's presence changed the very rhythm of life for Sarah and Sam in an instant. Sarah never imagined one man could break a woman so thoroughly. As bad as they'd assumed Mina's life with Thomas must have been, that didn't even come close to the reality of the hell she lived. Mina didn't understand that she could never do anything that would make Sam hit her, and she didn't understand that both Sam and Sarah knew that and believed it without question. Mina didn't know there was nothing she could do or say that would make either of them want to hurt her. The man—the thing—she'd married made her believe she was deserving of every beating. Mina believed she simply existed wrong, that it was an intrinsic flaw, and she had no sense of what safety felt like. Mina didn't know how to live in a home where pain, intentional pain at least, didn't exist.

Sarah had always been able to hold on to grudges for an unreasonably long time, but she felt her anger and hurt feelings seep out of her skin and dissipate into the air as she crawled under the table to Mina. Sarah wanted to shield her, pick her up, and hold her so she would know that she was okay now, that her big sister would protect her. Sarah forgot all about how much she had been hurt the day before as she sat there with Mina, and all she wanted to do was make her smile and forget how frightened she was. Sarah had the image of herself as a little girl in her mind when she looked at Mina, the way she used to hide under the covers from her father on the night she expected him to come in her room. She would protect Mina.

Mina trembled too much to even undressed, so as Sarah let the bath fill, she sat, helpless and shivering, as Sarah peeled off her urine-soaked clothes. Mina turned away and tried to hide the scars that covered her chest. Burn scars that left her chest looking like dark pink crinkled paper. Again, tears filled Sarah's eyes.

"I'm sorry, I didn't mean to upset you," Mina said. "I know it's ugly. I'm sorry."

"Mina, I just didn't know. Nothing to be sorry about."

Sarah pulled Mina's arms away from her chest and rested her hand on the scars, as though one kind of touch could heal them.

They stayed that way while the tub filled, looking into each other's eyes, and exchanging twenty years' worth of unspoken love that should have been shared long before now, through the simple touch of a sister's hand. Sarah felt how uncomfortable Mina was being naked in front of her, but the need for loving human contact took precedence over the embarrassment of her body.

They had rushed to take all the art off the walls of the spare bedroom on the morning of Mina's arrival. They wanted it to feel like her own canvas that she could express herself on. But sitting on the edge of the bed surrounded by empty slate gray walls, Mina appeared so small and fragile, as if the barren room could swallow her whole. Mina climbed into the tub when it had filled, and Sarah sat on its edge. The deep water that sat just above her chest only served to magnify her scars. Still shaking, Mina hugged her knees and cried softly as Sarah washed her back and shoulders.

"Am I hurting you?" Sarah asked, unsure if the scars still caused her pain.

Mina shook her head no. As Sarah went over her body with the washcloth, she took in all the scars Mina had collected over the last decade. Every one of them, save for her eye, had been given to her in a place easily hidden by clothing. A convenience that allowed her husband to get away with torture for so long. Mina looked away and cried harder into her hands when the washcloth neared her inner thighs, and Sarah didn't have to wonder why. She'd noticed when Mina climbed into the tub that what was supposed to be between her legs had been replaced by a crude and jagged scar. Sarah was sickened by the thought of the pain that must have caused her and wondered if that punishment was specific to Mina or if it was yet another way in which Radiance and her father found to brutalize all women. As she wet Mina's hair, she traced the scar that followed her hairline with her index finger and shuddered when she imagined what may have caused it. Mina looked like someone tried to scalp her. Sarah washed her sister's hair, and Mina continued crying until the tub was drained. Sarah held out a towel to wrap her in. When Mina stepped to her, she kept her arms around her. Sarah wanted to say something but was at a loss.

"That's not your life anymore. No one will ever hurt you again," Sarah told her, and Mina put her hand over hers.

As Sarah held her, the intricate details she noticed made her smile and get a bit choked up. They could have easily passed for twins if Sarah had been taller. Mina's hair was wavy, just as Sarah's had been. The red accent wall of the bathroom matched the lipstick that remained on her face, just as it did Sarah's, and the slate brown towel matched her eye color, just like Sarah's. Mina raised her hand, and patted Sarah's head, gave it a quick kiss. An apology, which Sarah readily accepted but no longer needed.

"Do you always wear red lipstick?" Mina asked, breaking the silence Sarah knew made her uncomfortable.

"Yep, have since I was fifteen. Only color that looks right. you know?"

"Me too," Mina said, still unsure about making eye contact. "Nobody else was allowed makeup, but Thomas… He wanted me to look pretty, so I always had to, to make him happy."

Sarah nodded and reached for her packet of makeup-removing wipes. She wiped the red from her lips and smiled. "Well fuck Thomas," she signed, and Mina needed no translation.

Sarah handed Mina a wipe, and they grinned at each other in the mirror as Mina wiped her lipstick away as well.

They struggled to have even the most trivial conversation, but at least now, both women were determined to keep trying until it felt natural.

That evening, after Mina had gone to bed, Sarah told Sam what she'd seen when Mina was in the tub. She told her not from a sensational urge to, but because he needed to know. He may be able to help Mina in some way Sarah couldn't. She said it was imperative that they keep it all in mind through every interaction with her. Sarah didn't think she could bear to cause another breakdown like they had that morning.

"Her burn scars, they're different than yours. They feel different. He did that to her, I know it," Sarah told Sam, who shook his head in sadness, or perhaps it was disgust. Disgust for Mina's husband, which would grow tremendously in both of them as they learned more about Mina's life.

After their first morning together, Sarah was positive things could only get better.

"One of us would have to actually hit Mina for things to get worse," Sarah told Sam that evening.

Sam was devastated to see that now, after that one incident in which Mina thought Sarah was going to be hurt, she flinched every time Sam moved, and he didn't want to be alone with Mina. He didn't want to scare her.

"How do I undo this?" Sam asked Sarah.

The hard truth was that they couldn't undo it. That fear was part of who Mina was, and Sarah figured it would take at least as long as her marriage had lasted to erase the fear if that was even possible. He had been grateful that Illinois required stylists to receive training in dealing with domestic violence, but now he was even more so, though, through all of it, Sam had never seen a person affected as profoundly as Mina had been. He didn't see any way in, nothing to cause that initial spark in her mind to change her belief that he would inevitably hurt her.

In all the time he had been with Sarah, Sam never asked questions about her father's cult. He figured that if she wanted to talk about it, she would. And he knew enough. Sarah told him what her father had done to her, and Sam didn't imagine Mina's experience had been any different. But still, he wanted to understand better who she was because of her life so that he could behave in whatever way would make her not fear him, so he turned to the internet. What he learned astonished him. Their father had been so masterfully calculating in the design of his cult that everything they did—everything people knew about—was perfectly legal. Everyone who came seeking admission into Radiance had to first divorce their spouses if they were married. That way, the woman swapping could never be called infidelity. And no woman in Radiance was touched until she was sixteen and perfectly legal. He found an article from the Sedona newspaper from two years ago about Mina and what the reporter called a sad case of untreated mental illness and self-harm. Of course, Sam knew better than to believe that Mina had burned her own chest with acid.

Even after he'd learned all he could, Sam felt no more prepared to help Mina than he did before. Sure, he had a better idea of what had been done to her, but he still understood her inclination to fear all men because, for Mina, all the men she'd ever come into contact with were dangerous and only wanted to hurt her. The only comfort Sam found was in the fact that Sarah would soon be working less. She only had two classes per week during the summer semester instead of her usual five, and with her home more, Sam could more easily avoid Mina. This wasn't the solution he'd hoped for, but it was what he had to make do with until Mina naturally came to trust him. He could only hope that she would.

CHAPTER 9

The second time a simple interaction between Sarah and Sam caused Mina to wet herself came just a day later. Sarah was rushing to get to the university to give an exam, but she needed Sam to get rid of the patchy stubble that was far too apparent after skipping the previous day. Sarah sat on the stool, annoyed, as Sam took his time.

"Oh, for Christ's sake, will you hurry up?" Sarah laughed through her irritation. "I can't wait until there's nothing left to shave so you can't act like you're molding some sculpture,"

"I'm gonna take my time and enjoy my topless wife-to-be until you learn to do this yourself."

"You won't see me topless for weeks if you make me late for work." Sarah continued to fidget and look at her watch.

"Woman, you better hold still if you don't want me to scalp you," Sam said as Mina entered the room.

"You want me to scalp you?" was what Mina heard and in Thomas's voice, not Sam's.

She didn't yet know Sam and Sarah well enough to appreciate that their bickering was part of their shtick, their charm. She stood frozen in the doorway, her eyes glued to Sam's straight razor held to Sarah's scalp, and they watched fear slowly take over her body as she stiffened, and pee soaked through her leggings.

Sarah had no choice but to leave Mina, terrified and broken, alone with razor-wielding Sam. She felt only slightly better, knowing that at least she had the summer to get to know her sister. She was beginning to understand the story her imam shared with her, of Muhammad and the cat, on the day before Mina's arrival when Sarah had sought his counsel. The story went that Muhammad was trying to get to the masjid for prayer, and a cat was asleep on his robe. Instead of disturbing the cat, Muhammad cut off the part of the robe on which the cat slept and left the cat in comfort and went to prayer with a cut-up robe. Sarah couldn't very well leave the part of herself behind that brought Mina comfort and take the rest to class, though.

Sam and Mina spent the day in an uncomfortable holding pattern, trying their best to avoid each other as they waited for Sarah to return home. Noah was drawn to Sam, they played together, and the little boy didn't share any of his mother's natural fear of him, of men, of the world as a whole. After a few hours of block city building and destruction—Noah's favorite thing to do—he fell asleep sitting on Sam's lap, his head resting on his shoulder. Mina carried the child to his bedroom for a proper nap, and as she walked back down the hall, she caught a glimpse of the burn scars covering Sam's torso as he changed out of his drool-soaked shirt. She didn't mean to stare, but she couldn't pry her eyes from the pink creased skin, and she instinctively reached for her own chest.

"Barn fire," Sam said when he saw her looking. "About fifteen years ago."

He carried on pulling his chest binder down, which Mina also had questions about but was far too afraid to ask them. She didn't understand why he wore it when his chest was already so small. She'd heard him talking on the phone about "top surgery" earlier in the day, and she wondered what that was and how changing one's body helped anything at all.

"Do they still hurt you?" Mina asked when she was finally able to break her stare.

"Only in the winter now when I let my skin get too dry. And this thing doesn't help," he said, touching the binder. "The things we do for beauty, right? Can't wait until I don't need this shit anymore."

Mina couldn't tell if he was making a joke or not, and if he was, if she was allowed to laugh at something she didn't understand, but Sam's openness let Mina feel more at ease, and she tried her best to joke back.

"Yes, I just hacked off my ponytail the other day. For beauty, as I'm sure you can tell from the lopsidedness." Mina smiled pensively.

This joking about a hasty decision and the easy conversation was new to her and so very welcome, but still, she didn't want to let herself trust it. She wanted to both know more about this fascinating and terrifying person and avoid him entirely because, what if? What if this was a lie, what if he was getting her to trust him so he could hurt her, what if she couldn't trust her own judgment anymore, what if...

"A barn fire?" Mina asked, surprising herself as the words left her mouth.

"Yep. You want the short version or the whole awful story?"

She shrugged her shoulders.

"Short version it is then," Sam said as he pulled on a clean t-shirt and sat on the bed.

"My parents got rid of me when I told them I was trans. I was only fifteen, so I went to the one other place that felt like home. I'd been riding at the same barn since I was a little kid, so the people at the farm were more like family than my own was anyway. An older gay couple owned the place, and they offered me the stable hand house. It was this tiny little thing, looked like a Hobbit house, but it was empty and somewhere to stay, so I accepted in exchange for working the farm. When I was twenty, on New Year's Eve, this group of neighbor kids thought it would be funny to scare the horses with fireworks..."

Mina reached her hand out for Sam's when she noticed he'd stopped the story, so he could compose himself. He wiped his face uncomfortably, sniffed his nose, and continued.

"Anyway, long story short, the fireworks caught the hayloft on fire, and I got trapped inside trying to get my Eddie out. He died with twelve other horses, and I've got this nice souvenir now so I can remember it every day."

Sam didn't look at Mina when he finished telling the story, and so she sat beside him, holding her hand over his, trying to force out of her mind how she'd gotten her own scars. She was grateful Sam wasn't looking to trade stories, as much as she appreciated his willingness to tell his. She wasn't there yet and didn't imagine she ever would be.

Following their first two turbulent days together, Sarah spent all of her free time with Mina. Sarah took her shopping for a new wardrobe, and Mina asked if she'd take her to get her nose pierced too. She wanted a tiny stud that matched the one Sarah wore. Sarah thought it an odd request, but what was the harm? Mina could easily remove it if she changed her mind, and she had to admit, she thought it was cute that Mina wanted to mimic her. When Friday came, the sisters were out shopping when it came time for Friday prayer, and Sarah had plans to go to her masjid.

"You can come in," Sarah said in the parking lot when she saw Mina looking toward the masjid as though it would eat her, "No one is going to try to convert you."

Mina shook her head quickly and continued to stare at the building. It didn't look like she imagined it would. In fact, it reminded Mina of the stories she'd been told about how her father had started his cult —in a house that looked as ordinary as any other. Mina had looked up mosques on her phone a few days before. While everything she found was grand and usually a tourist attraction in other countries with stunning tile art and minarets, Mina still expected something more than a house made into a mosque. She studied it as Sarah walked inside and made a mental note to ask her sister if her mosque made men and women go in separate doors and be in separate areas like she'd read they did.

The prayer service ended, and people poured out of the door. A distinct difference between their departure and that of the people in Radiance at the end of church service struck her. These people appeared to be one big family. The men shook each other's hands and patted each other warmly on the upper arm, while many of the women hugged. Some women took the scarves off their heads and stuffed them into their bags, while others left them on, and Mina admired all the different styles in which they wore their scarves. She thought it was almost like different women styling their hair differently and added yet another question for Sarah to her ever-growing list.

Sarah walked down the sidewalk toward the car with three other women, all of them smiling and signing, engrossed in conversation when a car slowed as it approached them. She watched the window roll down and then watched a man lean out and fling a fast food bag at them and spit in their direction. One woman ducked, and the bag of trash hit another woman. "Go back where you belong, terrorist!" the man shouted and then peeled out as he sped away. This shocked Mina, but what truly surprised her was their reaction to it. Two of the women waved and smiled, while another turned and shouted to the man, "Wa Alaikum salaam, brother!" Sarah bent down to pick up the trash that had spilled out of the bag as it hit the other woman's chest and jogged it back to the trash can that sat at the corner. The women parted ways after Sarah caught up with them, and she got back into the car, smiling.

"What?" Sarah signed when she noticed Mina staring at her. She knew what but wanted to get Mina to ask anyway.

"Are you okay? That man..." Mina asked, mildly concerned that they were in danger now.

"The guy with the McDonald's bag? He's harmless. Stupid, but harmless."
"What does *wa-lake-um salam* mean?"

"Peace be upon you. It's one of those handy greetings that can be used in any situation imaginable."

"But why were you friendly to him after he said that to you?"

"Because we're Muslims, Mina," Sarah said, as though it was the most obvious thing in the world.

"Why are you a Muslim? Why is the mosque a house? Are there separate woman doors? Why don't you cover your head like the others?" Mina asked her sister, her questions spilling out much faster than she intended them to.

Sarah laughed out loud, and the sound of her laughter, its genuine warmth made Mina feel safe and at home. The more she heard the sound of her sister's voice and her laugh, the more she appreciated it, and not only because she was becoming easier for her to understand when she spoke. Sam had told Mina that Sarah spoke only rarely, much preferring to sign and have someone interpret for her, so Mina felt that the fact that Sarah spoke readily and easily with her now was something special that only the two of them shared.

"Whoa, slow down, one thing at a time," Sarah grinned at her sister. "The masjid—not mosque—is a house because that was the best option we had when we formed the masjid here. You may have noticed, people aren't exactly doing cartwheels over our existence, so buying a house and making it a masjid was the easiest way to go."

Mina hung on Sarah saying "we," and she wondered if Sarah played a part in forming this particular congregation, or whatever the Muslim version of a congregation was.

"We don't have separate doors. I would never attend a masjid that did," Sarah continued, "and I don't cover my head because what am I going to cover?"

Worried she had upset her once again, Mina stumbled over her words. "Oh, I didn't...I mean...Those other women...They—"

Once again, Sarah laughed and put her hand on Mina's shoulder. "Jesus, Mina, lighten up. I'm messing with you."

"Oh," Mina said and hoped that soon, it would become more apparent when Sarah was joking and when she wasn't.

"I don't cover my head because it's just not my thing. I tried it in college when I first reverted, but it never felt right, and I didn't want to make my faith feel forced. I needed everything I did to have a reason that resonated with me."

"But how are you a Muslim when they hate everything you and Sam are?" Mina asked and immediately regretted it when Sarah took more than a second to answer her.

"How are you a Christian when all the religion has ever done is hurt you?" Sarah asked in response.

"Not all Christians are like that, though. You don't have to practice like our father does to be faithful."

"Exactly. You answered your own question. Islam isn't whatever the hell you've been told about it," Sarah began, and went on to explain exactly how she had become a Muslim and why. She explained to Mina that she had only intended to learn about the religion, that after 9/11, living in DC, she wanted to understand why it happened.

Mina listened as Sarah explained that Islam was the first faith to give women equal rights and how it promoted education and that charity was one of the five requirements. She had never seen someone look so happy when discussing what they believed. Sarah told her sister that it was okay for her to question what she'd been taught to believe. That it was something she should always do. She told her Muslims even had a specific term—ijtihad—for the act of questioning your faith, and that mystified Mina. If nothing else, she knew that questioning what their father and Thomas preached was dangerous at best.

"What I didn't expect," Sarah explained, "was to find that Islam taught everything I had long believed to be true. I never did find out why 9/11 happened or why there are terrorists, but I suspect it's the same reason our dad is the kind of man he is."

Sarah was surprised by how much she enjoyed spending time with Mina and how quickly it had gotten easier to talk to her. They had so little in common but so much to discuss. Sarah didn't want to bring up the painful subject of Mina's husband or their father, so instead, she asked Mina to tell her about Red Ranch, the town she left so long ago the image she had of it had all but faded from her memory. Mina's descriptions of its beauty allowed Sarah to remember it perfectly, and she couldn't say she was surprised to learn that it hadn't changed a bit aside from growing exponentially. Of course it hadn't.

Sarah asked how Mina had come to be a hairstylist, and Mina wanted to hear all about what Sarah taught at the university. Mina asked if she could learn to sign, and with that, Sarah could have sworn she felt her heart was actually swelling in her chest. After just one week, Mina was making more of an effort to get to know Sarah than their father ever had. It was after their last shopping trip that Mina asked the question she'd wanted to for days.

"Does it bother you?" Mina asked, pointing to Sarah's head.

"What, my hair?"

"The way people stare; they look at you with pity."

"If I had a dollar for everyone that offered me misplaced pity, well, I sure wouldn't be driving this Honda."

They both laughed at Sarah's bad joke. Every time she could get her to laugh, Sarah saw a bit more of who her sister was, or who she could be.

"Mina," Sarah began, sharply changing the tone of their conversation. "I'm sorry we didn't grow up together, that I abandoned you. I'm sorry that your life has been so hard, so different than mine. That I let myself forget about you. I want to make it up to you. I need to."

Sarah thought about how different their worlds were and how much she wished she'd been able to stop every horror from happening to her and her throat began to ache with the sting of impending tears.

"You don't have to be sorry for me, Sarah. You didn't forget about me —you didn't know me. Besides, if our lives had been the same, where would I be right now?"

Mina touched her shoulder as Sarah tried to gather the nerve to ask her next question.

"Mina, I have to ask you something, only because it worries me, and I want to help. In the tub the other day... I saw... How did you—"

"I know," Mina interrupted her, "You want to know who cut me."

"It's just, I saw how you jerked away when the washcloth brushed against you. It still hurts, doesn't it?"

"Yes, it does. All the time. Thomas. He caught me... I deserved it. That time, I deserved it." Mina told her, refusing to look Sarah in the eye.

Sarah knew that nothing she could say right then would make Mina believe she didn't deserve what he'd done to her, so instead, she focused on her being in pain.

"I'd like to take you to see my doctor, is that alright? You'll like her a lot, she's a good friend of ours. She'll be able to help with the pain."

"Will you go with me?" Mina asked, and in that moment, she looked like a scared little girl hoping for the safety of her mother.

"Of course."

"Okay, then I'll go."

After a long and uncomfortable silence—the only thing they all seemed to excel at—Sarah caught her sister staring at her head and chuckled at her preoccupation with the whole thing. Of all the things she could have obsessed over, that was what she'd stuck with.

"I'm sorry I hurt you the other day, Sarah. It's just, Ruth didn't tell me. She showed me an old picture and back home, hair, it's... it's complicated." Mina said, ashamed that she still couldn't bring herself to explain herself.

"It's okay, Mina, really. That was a hard day for all of us."

"But why? You're so pretty, and Sam said you used to wear your hair long. Why does he make you have no hair now?"

"Oh God, Mina, no wonder I make you so uncomfortable! You think Sam made me do this? Like what, a punishment or something?" She couldn't hold in her laughter at the thought of Sam making her do anything at all. "Sam did it for me, Mina. Do you know what alopecia is?"

Mina shook her head no.

"It's a condition, makes your hair fall out. Some people lose a little; some lose all of it. Mine started when I was about fifteen." She was relieved to see Mina looking less uncomfortable.

"But you don't wear wigs? You like it this way?"

Mina still didn't look convinced that Sarah wasn't suffering the loss of her hair, so she shared with her the story of how she arrived at the decision to cut it off. Mina seemed more at ease with each breath, and for that, Sarah was grateful. By the end of the story, Mina had tears in her eyes. Sarah told her how beautiful Sam made her feel and about the proposal that came after, and finally, Mina looked content, pleased with what she'd learned.

"I'm so glad you have Sam," Mina said as she mindlessly felt the scar that ran her hairline.

"Me too. This is taking some getting used to, but I don't regret it. Haven't felt the need for a wig so far."

"Well, if it means anything, you don't need hair. You're very pretty," Mina told her, afraid that she'd offend her again.

"Oh, now you say that!" Sarah playfully pushed her. "And Mina, we had the best sex that—"

"Sarah!" Mina was wide-eyed, her hands over her mouth.

"Hey, you wanted the story, there it is. You'll understand, one day. You'll meet a guy that loves you for all the things you think you shouldn't be." Mina fidgeted in her seat at the mention of meeting a man. "You know, if Sam had asked me the day before to marry him, I'd have said no. But there's just something about looking right at the thing you're most afraid of, with the person you're most afraid of seeing it and knowing they're not phased. That's when I knew he was the person I was meant to be with."

Mina didn't say anything. She only offered a weak smile and looked out the window.

"You know you never deserved to be hurt or punished for anything, right? Whatever Thomas did to you, everything he did to you, it's not your fault, okay?" Sarah couldn't bear the thought of Mina ever wondering if she or Sam would hurt her.

"We don't have to talk about that, Sarah," was all she said. They drove home in silence and didn't bring it up again for weeks.

CHAPTER 10

The one thing Abraham's community did not have was a good relationship with law enforcement. No, what they had, which kept dealings with the police to a minimum, was a bunch of fearful women, who, no matter what, knew better than to seek help from outside the gates of their community.

So, when Thomas called him over to the house he shared with his daughter to show him the dried blood in the sink and Mina's severed ponytail laying neatly beside it, Abraham was conflicted over whether he should contact the police or not. On the one hand, he was sure he had trained his daughter, his one obedient daughter, to stay. Like a good dog. You could kick it, starve it, keep it on a chain outside, and still, it would perform for you. That's what good training did.

Mina was a good dog.

On the other hand, Abraham was aware of the things Thomas did to his daughter, and while he believed what a man did with his wife in the privacy of his home was that man's business, he wondered how much a man could kick a dog before it bit back. The third and Abraham believed the most unlikely possibility was that an outsider had come into the community and had done something to Mina, perhaps taken her, to hurt him and Thomas. Radiance had made enemies of some of the residents of Red Ranch who, instead of learning Abraham's vision, made assumptions that a community kept separate by gates and a wall could only be up to nefarious things. They'd also made enemies out of those who had been exiled from Radiance. Former community members who refused to follow the rules or questioned Abraham too often.

He wouldn't risk the hit his image could take if it got around that his daughter had defied both him and Thomas if that was in fact what she'd done, so Abraham had no choice but to call the police, spin it as an abduction, which he was positive it wasn't.

The town of Red Ranch was expansive but barely a town at all. It had just over a thousand residents, and a two-thirds of them either lived within Abraham's community or, at the very least, they were a member of his church. The police force consisted of the chief, a sergeant, and his three deputies. Somehow, not one of them subscribed to Abraham's teachings. Abraham felt that the chief had it in for him, and he wasn't wrong.

Chief Miguel Edison had been a cop for thirty-five years and had developed a good sense about people, whether they were decent, running from their pasts, secretive, or living a lie. Chief Edison believed Abraham to be the latter two, and he just didn't like him, the way he always talked about his wife and his daughter, but Miguel had never met either woman.

Miguel knew Radiance to be an anomaly of a cult. The least of its oddities was the name. The community was named for the cult, The Children of Radiance, and Miguel had always believed the name was just plain stupid. He thought it sounded more like a chorus line of gay men or drag queens, and it never failed to make him chuckle. Shortly after Abraham founded Radiance as a church in Red Ranch, the FBI offered a four-day workshop on cults—their hierarchies, their psychology, the telltale signs they were breaking the law, and Miguel had gone to it. He understood that often times, cults practice polygamy or child marriage and that the hierarchy of most cults kept a strict separation of the leader and his family and that of his followers.

Radiance, however, had an odd hierarchy. There was no polygamy to speak of—in fact, there was no marriage, at least in the legal sense, at all—but it was common knowledge that the men all shared the women. The Sisters, they called them. Each man had a main Sister with whom he lived and was responsible for, along with the children that woman had given birth to. But upon joining the community, Miguel knew that each man was required to divorce his wife if they'd been married before joining Radiance to sever any ties that would cause the man to think he didn't have to share the woman. This practice also allowed Radiance the convenience of never having to worry about any existing—but rarely enforced—adultery laws.

The women were treated like community livestock, passed around the group, and impregnated as often as they could be. Miguel had tried to start conversations with them on the rare occasion he saw a member of Radiance outside of the community gates, but they never had anything but glowing things to say about their lives and Abraham. They all reminded him of the Stepford Wives. He'd seen more than a handful of the women walking around bald-headed—one day they'd had the telltale bun all the women wore, the next time he saw them, their hair was gone, and they looked defeated—and he couldn't begin to imagine what purpose that served, though he knew enough to assume the worst. But nobody so much as complained, so there wasn't a thing he could do for them. They were one big, sick family, as far as he could tell.

Miguel had gone to one of Abraham's church services—another odd feature of this cult was that their services were open to whoever wished to attend—and it never struck him as anything more than a regular Southern Baptist sermon, except for the few occasions Abraham had gone out of his way to stress the bits of his sermon about women existing for men. They all dressed modestly but seemed to wear what they wanted, clothing that Miguel assumed was in fashion. Save for the occasional bald woman, they all looked like ordinary people and not like one might imagine cult members would look. It had always struck him as odd, the parts of secular, modern life Abraham allowed his members to participate in. At the end of the day, though, Radiance and its residents never did anything illegal. At least nothing that was ever reported or blatant enough to justify Miguel spending the money and manpower of his tiny police force. How would he explain it to anyone that asked? He was investigating them because he just didn't like them? Because they gave him a funny feeling?

A couple of years ago, Miguel had done as much investigating as he could, with the help of the lone reporter for the Red Ranch Gazette. Mina, Abraham's daughter, had been hospitalized with what everyone said were self-inflicted burn wounds all over her torso. Miguel learned a great deal about the man, but nothing he could use to catch him in a crime or even a lie. Abraham had an older daughter, Miguel discovered, who left home when she was fifteen and had never been back, and he had an estranged twin sister as well.

Miguel made sure that if ever the police were summoned to Abraham's community, he would personally answer the call. They'd never gotten a call from within the gates, and they had certainly never gotten a call from Abraham himself. When dispatch requested police respond to a possible abduction, Chief Edison had all he could do to not be giddy. He finally had reason to go inside.

Abraham and Thomas met Miguel and one of his deputies at the gate of the community, Radiance, where both men lived in mansions next-door to each other, and for two men who'd just had their daughter and wife abducted, both were perfectly poised and calm. Abraham looked exactly as Miguel imagined a man named Abraham would. He had long, snow-white hair that he wore tied back in a low ponytail and an equally long beard that rested on his chest. Miguel wouldn't have been surprised to see the man wearing robes and sandals, being followed around by a goat or whatever sort of animal people kept in biblical times. The expensive suit he wore didn't match the rest of the picture. Thomas looked a bit skeletal, Miguel thought and had an inexplicable air about him that left the chief unsettled. Thomas might have been the palest man he had ever seen, and the ever-present five o'clock shadow ring around the sides of his shaved head only made him look even whiter.

"Dispatch said your daughter, Mina, is missing? And your grandson?" Miguel asked.

Thomas spoke before Abraham could.

"It appears that way, Chief Edison," he confirmed. "She's always home when I return from the church in the evening, and there's some blood in the sink."

"And you have no reason to believe she just took the boy and left?" Miguel couldn't resist asking.

"Mina knows better. She would never take Noah from his father like that," Abraham chimed in, making sure to set the scene exactly as he wanted the police to find it.

"Oh, you'd be amazed by some of the things women are prone to do if it gets in their heads that they're unhappy," the deputy said, trying to hide a smile. He'd caught on quickly to Miguel's angle here.

"Will you show us the bathroom?" Miguel asked.

Abraham and Thomas lead the way up the hill to the second biggest house at the end of the cul-de-sac. The biggest was Abraham's home. Thomas and Mina shared the second largest because the leader could not be outdone by his second in command.

The air of vacancy inside the house struck Miguel, and he felt a chill race up his spine. If not for the faint smell of chicken being cooked, the house would have appeared to be for sale and staged. The furniture seemed to be untouched, and not one photo or painting hung from the walls.

"You having company?" Miguel asked Thomas and motioned toward the food aroma. It struck him as rather odd that Thomas was carrying on with his dinner plans as usual when his wife and son were missing.

"Man's gotta eat, doesn't he?"

"If my wife went missing, dinner would be the last thing on my mind." Miguel failed to hide his contempt for the men.

"My routine keeps me calm. I've also been praying. Would you like to question the validity of that as well?"

"Just doing our job, Mr. Roth. We have to ask difficult questions," the deputy added, seeing that Chief Edison was at a loss.

The men made their way to the bathroom, Miguel and his deputy keeping a close eye on anything that could be a sign of a struggle, or, more likely, Thomas having hurt his wife along the way. There was nothing to see, no broken or disheveled belongings, no messes anywhere, which Miguel assumed was an advantage of having a full staff to clean up one's every mess.

The bathroom, at first glance, seemed to be equally absent of incriminating evidence.

"This is toothpaste. Some blood in it, sure, but it's toothpaste. No criminal is gonna hit a woman and then let her brush her teeth before he abducts her. And this hair? Look how nicely it's laid. Almost looks gift wrapped," Miguel said, concerned about the amount of blood in the toothpaste but confident he was right. The severed ponytail was among the strangest things he'd seen in his usually quiet career as a police officer, but it certainly wasn't something to warrant concern.

It was when Miguel turned around and saw the blood-soaked washcloth and the bloodied towel hanging from the towel bar that he began to worry this could be more than a simple case of a fed-up woman leaving her husband. He stepped to the bathroom doorway and looked across the hall to the bedroom, where he saw a white pillowcase and sheet also with dried areas of blood. He nodded for his deputy to stay put with Thomas and Abraham while he went into the bedroom to get a better look.

"This blood is dry. Old. Twelve hours at least," Miguel shouted from the other room.

"Something happen here last night, Mr. Roth? You two have a fight you want to tell us about?" The deputy asked.

"Mina is a turbulent woman. She had a small cut on her cheek. She fell. We had a disagreement. That's all. My wife would never leave me, and I've done nothing to her." Thomas answered and covered his right fist with his left hand, hiding the bruise on his pinky, left behind by his ring when he'd punched Mina.

Chief Edison shot into the bathroom, his fingers jamming into Thomas's chest hard enough that the man winced, and he pushed him against the wall, holding him there.

"Look, you son of a bitch," Miguel tried to calm himself before he said something, did something, that would hurt the chance of these men going to prison. "I know you did something to her. I know what you all are. Everybody knows what you are. I'm going to find out what you did here and when I do, you're gonna regret ever bringing this goddamn cult here. I promise you that."

Miguel knew he didn't have nearly enough evidence to arrest either man and make anything stick, so he called in the investigators from the state police in hopes they could find what Miguel and his deputies weren't equipped to. Miguel was relieved that whatever had happened to Mina appeared to be a minor injury, and there was no evidence of the little boy having been hurt. She'd either taken him and run, or Thomas had taken them both somewhere. His gut told him the latter wasn't the case.

"You'll have to stay somewhere else, Mr. Roth. This is a crime scene now. But don't go far." Miguel turned to Abraham, hoping to pick up on some kind of reaction from him. "We'll find your daughter and grandson, sir, I promise."

The old man revealed nothing.

"I see. I'll collect some things and make arrangements," Thomas said, his hands clasped calmly at his waist and his face vacant of any expression at all.

"No, you won't. You don't touch a thing, just get out. Your things are my evidence."

The deputy escorted Thomas and Abraham out of the house, and Miguel stayed behind to continue his search while he waited for the investigators. He'd handled domestic disturbances many times but never one like this, never one where the husband was able to remain so sickeningly calm, and never a possible murder.

Miguel made his way to the dining room that sat just off the entryway to wait for the investigators. He sat in a chair, and when it collapsed under his weight, he saw the tiny spatters of blood, old brown blood, around the floorboard, and he knew this was going to be anything but a simple investigation. As he rose to his feet, his phone vibrated with a message from another of his deputies.

Mina's phone had been found on the side of the road, just outside of town.

CHAPTER 11

The day of Sam's top surgery had come, at last. He felt as if he'd been waiting his whole life for this day and being able to go into surgery surrounded by family made the day that much more perfect. After his parents threw him out, for a long time, Sam gave up hoping he'd ever have people that supported him without question. Now surgery day had come, and he would wake to the smiling faces of Sarah, Mina, Noah, and even Ruth.

Sam had been feeling unsettled, desperate even, for the last several weeks. He'd cut his hair, which he'd always been rather fussy about, only for Sarah, to help her through losing her own. He hadn't anticipated the effect it would have on him, though. He saw more of a man when he looked at his reflection now until he glanced at his chest and saw the small but obvious-to-him breasts he bound daily.

Both Sam and Sarah appreciated the irony that the one thing most men feared—going bald—turned out to be what allowed Sam to feel like a *real* man, whatever that was.

Sam had never been particularly bothered by his chest. He didn't feel it belonged on his body, but it didn't repulse him. It had always been small enough to disguise without too many people noticing and with the right binder, even looked like pecs. Lately though, with what he thought of as his very manly—and very obvious—balding, the two parts of his body didn't match up, and Sam grew wildly uncomfortable in his skin. He felt as though he was walking around in a push-up bra, begging people to look at his chest.

Every step in the process leading up to this day felt like a new insult to Sam. First, there was the year of therapy he needed because while he believed everyone could benefit from therapy now and again, it still delayed his life becoming what he needed it to be. He had been taking hormones and out as Sam, the man, for several years already, so that particular requirement was never a problem. He'd been through the inevitable losses that come when someone begins transitioning. His family was the first and the least surprising, and he didn't particularly miss them. Not since they'd all but disowned him after he first told them he was gay two decades ago. The loss that hurt Sam was that of people he'd thought were close friends. Those who never quite articulated to him what their problem was or why—though he was sure he knew—they just slowly faded away like morning dew on the grass, its presence readily notable yet impossible to pin down the precise moment it evaporates as the sun rises. One day he had friends who invited him places and hung out at his apartment, and as he came out, slowly and methodically, there were fewer and fewer people around to celebrate with him when he first heard his voice changing, or the first time he needed to shave his face. Still, though, Sam thought of this as a necessary sacrifice. He was living exactly the life he wanted—that he needed—after all. And soon enough, Sarah was there to celebrate these seemingly small but life-affirming moments with him, and that, he knew, was all he needed.

The cruelest insult of all had occurred just two days before Sam's surgery day. He'd gone to see about changing the gender markers on all of his identification, and he learned that because he'd had the misfortune of being born in Michigan, he would forever remain legally female, simply because the Midwestern hillbillies, as he thought of everyone in the state, had more authority over his body, his identity than he did. To have his birth certificate be truthful and match who he was, Sam would need "medically appropriate" surgery—both top and bottom surgery—the latter of which he had no desire to put himself through.

When he'd returned home that day, it was the first time Sarah could recall seeing him in tears over what had otherwise been a fairly mundane but joyous process. He had come home from the Secretary of State's office and slammed the door of their condo so hard that Sarah felt it in her teeth.

"I can't change it," was all he said.

"Why? You checked off every box."

"Because fucking Michigan is why. Apparently, the governor needs to measure the size of my dick or something to decide for me whether or not I'm a man."

Sarah thought for a moment and chuckled to herself, recalling the time she had been pulled over by a cop for playing music too loudly —if she couldn't feel it, she couldn't enjoy it—and what any thinking person would have recognized as innocent sign language, a woman merely stating that she was Deaf, the officer took as her behaving threateningly and resisting, so he forced her from her car and pulled his gun on her. She was left shaking from the incident for days until Sam came home having stolen a large yellow "DEAF" street sign. He told her he would fashion a sandwich board type outfit for her with the sign. Then he put aside his jokes and got to work ensuring that Sarah would never again be so violated simply because of how she existed in the world and ordered for her a special "hearing impaired" license plate. Sarah wanted to do the same for Sam now.

"Maybe we can get a really realistic-looking dildo and glue it to the bumper, next to my fancy Deaf plate?" She asked, trying hard to suppress a smile.

"Only if we can get a miniature one for my license too."

Sam laughed and kissed her, grateful that she could appreciate the absurdity of all the rules imposed upon people just trying to live a good, private life as well. Grateful, too, that he had her to provide some levity to all the technical details of his transition that he felt would otherwise be overwhelming and daunting to him.

Sam woke from his surgery to Sarah's hand gently resting on his bandaged but flat chest. He couldn't name what he felt though it seemed as though he'd crossed some arbitrary finish line of manliness. He'd not even seen his body yet, but he didn't need to. He'd done it. He was whole now, and all the pieces fit. No longer would every day begin and end with the art of hiding and revealing any part of himself.

Mina kept her eyes on Sam, and the moment she noticed he appeared awake enough to talk, she began firing questions at him. So many she'd been holding in, and in this moment, she was compelled to ask them. Mina had questions about so many things, and while both Sam and Sarah usually hated being questioned, Mina did it in a way they didn't mind and even encouraged. She needed to learn about the world, and who better to frame it for her than them, they'd agreed.

"So," Mina hesitated, "do you get the next part now?"

"A penis? Nope. Don't want one."

"But how can you be a man without one?"

His mind still foggy from anesthesia, Sam began to speak the first thought he had. *How can you be a woman after what your husband did to you?*

Seeming to read his mind, Sarah interjected before Sam could get a word out. "He's got the body he envisioned, so he's content to stop now. Some guys want that surgery, but a lot don't. There isn't one defined path, Mina, not for anything."

Sam was released several hours later, his family armed with all the post-op care instructions one could ever need—they felt collectively ready for anything—and only Sam was a bit squeamish about the drainage bulbs that hung from his incisions. As prepared as Sarah and Mina believed they were, both were grateful that finally, Ruth had shown up.

She'd disappeared without a text or call to either of them after she'd dropped Mina and Noah off that first day. Sarah knew why. She knew Ruth well enough to assume guilt was crushing her because even though she'd had no idea what Mina had been enduring, Sarah was consumed with the guilt of not having gotten her away sooner too. Both Sara and Mina were angry with Ruth for disappearing, but she was a surgeon, and they wanted her there to ensure Sam's recovery went well.

The day after Sam's surgery, realizing they'd forgotten to grocery shop with all the excitement of the last couple of days, Sarah and

Mina took Noah and went shopping. Ruth was left to tend to Sam, who had always resisted being tended to at all.

Ruth expected Sam to sleep, so she'd brought her needlepoint to keep herself busy. A hobby she used to mock as something old ladies did that she would never resort to, which she had taken up during her chemotherapy to help with neuropathy in her fingers, and it stuck. She was currently working on a piece for Sarah and Sam that read, "Ask me about my feminist agenda." She was nearly done and very eager to give it to them.

Sam, however, had other plans.

"Where the hell have you been?" He asked Ruth when the door closed behind Mina and Sarah, his voice still raspy from surgery. "Do you have any idea what a mess she is? And you just leave her here and disappear? Sarah and I couldn't even sign near her for the first couple of weeks, for God's sake. She thought we were gonna hit her. What the hell, Ruth?"

Ruth feared this moment. She'd sensed both Mina and Sarah were angry with her, but she knew that if anyone brought her absence up, it would be Sam. He was fiercely protective of his family, and she had hurt them.

"I know. I'm sorry," Ruth said, her eyes closed so she didn't have to see Sam's disappointed face.

"Oh, well then, it's no problem if you're *sorry*." Sam hadn't planned on tearing into Ruth like he was, it was not usually his nature, but six weeks of the stress of tiptoeing around Mina in his own house had taken a more significant toll than he expected. "I can't believe you thought we'd know how to help her. And do you have any idea how endlessly frustrating it is to live with someone who has no concept of cleaning up after themselves? And God forbid I say something to her about it, and she pisses herself in the corner."

"She's always had maids…"

"Yeah, no shit, Ruth, that's not the point. We've had to change everything about how we live while you've been off, what, feeling your feelings? You need to stay here. We need your goddamn help."

"Are you finished?" Ruth was growing annoyed, though she

wouldn't argue that Sam didn't have reason to be so angry.

"I don't know, you gonna come out of hiding?"

Honesty, Ruth knew, was the only thing Sam would accept at this point.

Sam tried to sit upright but couldn't move his arms to the point of lifting himself. Ruth came to his side to help him, and as he tried to shoo her away, his hand hit one of his drainage bulbs, and he yelped in pain. Without a word, Ruth put her arm around his back and gently lifted him before taking a seat atop the coffee table in front of Sam.

"I can't look at her, Sam. I can't look at her scars and the way she cowers every time you move. I knew what a narcissistic, awful bastard my brother was. Of course he'd make Mina marry a man just like him. I knew... but I never knew. I didn't know it was that bad, and I never even bothered to ask her. I should have known, Sam. We talked every month. I should have known."

"You should talk to Sarah about that. She's feeling the same irrational guilt." Sam said, slowly forgiving her as he felt the sadness and tension pouring from Ruth.

"I took care of Sarah like she was my own child. Why didn't I care enough about Mina to do the same? Was I really so stupid to believe she'd hold her own?" Ruth looked away and wiped tears from her face. "I should have taken her away a long time ago before she got married. I disappeared because I can't look at her, Sam."

"We need you here. Mina needs you here. And Noah, a few minutes with him and everything bad disappears. Stay. Please."

Ruth knew she wouldn't be able to cope with any added guilt coming from Sam and Sarah. She understood the only thing she could do was stay and face Mina, and what she'd let happen to her.

"Okay." Ruth agreed though she wasn't confident in her conviction.

Ruth stood from the coffee table to give Sam a hug. She remembered just in time as she reached for him that hugs would probably be horribly painful right now, so instead, she awkwardly hugged his head.

"Wow, kiddo, you've really got quite the bald spot here!" She joked, her mind eased that Sam wasn't actually mad at her. He'd just needed to vent his frustration. If anything, he understood because Sarah felt the same way.

"Right? And Sarah never even mentioned it. She just let me go on sporting a comb-over."

"Well, I was just going to say that I think you look good. Handsome. I don't know why you men all worry that women don't find balding men attractive. That is not the case, my dear, not the case at all." Ruth smiled as she patted the crown of his head.

"Baldness is virility! We have so much testosterone coursing through our veins that our hair is overwhelmed by its sheer strength, and it has to fall out in awe." Sam couldn't help but laugh, even though it hurt his healing chest.

"Yes. That's exactly how it works. You keep telling yourself that," Ruth shook her head, smiling, as she returned to her chair to do her needlepoint.

CHAPTER 12

A braham believed that it was his personal failing that Mina had run. He had failed to give his daughter God, the fear of God, in some tremendous but unnamable way, and he no longer believed he was capable of righting his wrongs. He couldn't recover his community from this. After forty years, Abraham's perfect vision was failing, and he was powerless to see it back to glory. Abraham had hoped to soften Thomas's approach with his people before passing the role of Father on to him, but perhaps they needed the firmer hand of Thomas after all.

In grieving his failure, Abraham had taken his yearly sabbatical early. Every year, for two weeks, the old man would go away, to where no one knew, to study the Bible, to pray on how he would continue to lead and grow Radiance. He had been gone for three weeks now, and his absence was beginning to be questioned by members of the community.

Thomas was certain Abraham would soon step down as the Father.

Radiance was coming undone before Thomas's eyes, and he was desperate to stop it, to keep the only place that had ever been home intact. The community was purging families as it never had before and those who stayed were left broken by the nightly disappearances of some of the children they'd had a hand in raising. Nine families, most of them newer members of Radiance, had vanished during the night in the weeks since Mina left. Nine pairs of men and women had decided to go and take with them the children each of the women had given birth to, and Thomas was left to reassure his community that all would be well, that this was nothing more than a minor blip in the radar, a test of their faith, and that Radiance would continue as it always had. But he needed to do something to solidify the connection, the role played by those who had remained. Anything to keep more women from taking a cue from Mina and somehow convincing their man to leave with them.

Thomas believed that eventually, Mina would have no choice but to return to him, to Radiance. He knew what the children meant to her and refused to believe she'd be able to stay away from them forever. What woman could be happy with only one child? When she did come back to him, she would see what her defiance had brought to all the woman she'd abandoned.

The Ceremony of Sacrifice, Thomas named it. He started with the few women he counted as his wife's friends. He called them, one by one instead of the usual public display, to the church. He wasn't out to shame them into submission. This, he believed, would serve as a re-baptism. A sacrifice the women would have to make, recommitting themselves to the men and to Radiance. Mina had poisoned their minds with her willful disregard for the community's hierarchy and laws when she left. Thomas knew people had been talking. He could feel it every time he led service, every time he walked down the street.

Thomas believed this was his one and only chance to steer his people in the right direction, the path of righteousness, submission to men, the chosen leaders. Submission to him. Radiance was being re-born, in *his* image, and this was but the first of many changes to come in his mission to repair the harm Abraham's weakness had brought upon them. Step one: remind the women of their place. He had no step two yet and hoped he wouldn't need one.

"Sister Mina has left *you* to atone for her sins," Thomas told the first women he summoned to the church. "Will you obey, or will you leave the community and your children?"

"I will, Brother," the woman said, unsure of what she was agreeing to obey.

How dare this woman call him "brother," Thomas thought. He would soon be the Father, and he would be given the respect he was due.

Thomas ordered the woman to her knees and, razor in hand, he felt his power, his position, growing each time he heard the woman struggle to muffle her sobbing as her hair so easily gave way to his blade. He regretted never doing this to Mina when he had the chance, for he could think of no better way to tell a woman that she belonged to him. Perhaps she would have been a better woman if he had reminded her of her position in the world more than once. Sure, Abraham preached to the men that collectively, the wives were theirs, to share, to join with in growing their community, but Thomas knew they were his to manage. They would do what he wished, look how he wished, fear as he wished. By the time he was through, not one of the wives would have the audacity to even look up from the ground in front of her without permission. Mina had caused this, and when she returned, she too would have to pay the price. His breath grew heavy, and his chest pounded, high on power as he felt his victim crumble as he worked.

Thomas tended to thirteen women himself before he summoned all of the community to the church. The thirteen women all sat in the front pew, heads down, avoiding the prying eyes of their husbands and sisters.

"Family," Thomas began, speaking into the small microphone, "Sister Mina has left us rattled. This woman, whom so many of us saw as our matriarch, has abandoned us, and in doing so, she has shaken our faith. She has gone to live among the sinners outside these gates, and we must set ourselves apart, my brothers and sisters. We must recommit to reviling all that is outside these Godly walls. The temptation of the secular world was too great for her, and her vanity, a demon we all knew she struggled with, was stronger than her faith."

The residents of Radiance whispered in murmurs of shock. For weeks now, they had been living under the impression that an outsider had come and taken Mina and Noah. For Thomas to tell them the truth now, they felt Mina's betrayal viscerally. She had run away and left Thomas to grow ever more despicable.

"Brothers, these thirteen devoted sisters have begun the sacrifice that must be made. They sacrificed that which may lead them to the path Mina chose, and the rest of our sisters will make this sacrifice. We cannot leave our women untended as we have. We cannot allow them to wonder, even for a moment, if there is something for them out there. They must feel their essential role in Radiance. A role of submission and humility, the role of mother, bearer of our future. Our sisters are vital to Radiance, and God calls on them to acknowledge this sacrifice. If a woman be not covered, let her be shorn! Covered in humility, bathed in reverence and obedience. Sisters of Radiance, this is what must be done until the day Sister Mina returns to us. Let her feel your sacrifice, allow it to pull her back to the Radiant path. Will you submit, or will you abandon us, abandon our future, our children, as Mina did?"

Thomas asked the men of the community for volunteers, and at least thirty of them did, eagerly. Thomas had a way of speaking that allowed the men to aspire to the position he held. No one told them that all they would ever be were pawns to feed his maniacal ego. The men stood at the front of the church, and one by one, each of the women was shorn. They all knew they would remain this way unless Mina returned. No one dared speak it, not before and certainly not now, but every woman knew why she had left. And Thomas only proved this now. He was a monster. An egotistical and violent man, and each woman felt this deeply as they saw him smirk as the men worked. When the sisters were through, it fell on them to do the same to their daughters, all the unpaired girls over twelve years old.

Thomas was pleased with the uniformity of the sisters when his ceremony was through. Uniformity, he believed, created equality, and if each woman looked identical to every other woman, none of them would feel that tinge of jealousy that might make them act out of line. These women needed to be broken, forced back into submission until they understood how fortunate they were to be chosen to carry the seeds of Radiance. The sisters would be bound to each other and to Radiance, and the men by their shame, and Thomas had never been more pleased with himself than he was when he stood at the pulpit and saw every one of the wives wearing Mina's shame.

Thomas asked the men to carry armfuls of the shorn hair out to the courtyard in front of the church and leave it in a heap. When it had all been gathered and swept into a neat pile, Thomas led the community in prayer.

"We submit to you, Father God. We sacrifice the glory of our wives to honor you and beg of you to bring Sister Mina back to us. We will recommit to this sacrifice each day until you see us as worthy once again. We pray that you ease the burden of our wives as they bear the responsibility of our future. Take away all temptation and allow our wives to find their beauty in your purpose. Lead them from the temptations that took Sister Mina away from us and lessen the shame she has left on her sisters." Thomas preached and then tossed a match into the mountain of hair.

When the pile was nearly burned out, Thomas dismissed the women and brought the men back into the church. He explained to them that this would be a daily ritual each man observed with whichever wife he was with at the time until Mina returned. He explained that this was the only way to strengthen the bond the wives had to the community and to each other, as it was the only way to keep them from straying. He told them that any woman who refused was to be brought to him and that any pair who did not observe the ritual would be given one chance and then would be cast out, to be replaced by a pair more dedicated to the survival of Radiance.

When Thomas dismissed the men, he took a slow stroll through the streets of Radiance, pleased to see so many of the women in tears, mourning their loss and comforting each other. He couldn't believe that any woman would be willful enough to leave now. What woman could walk among people outside these walls while carrying this shame? They'd been stripped of their beauty, their God-given glory, and because of this, they were bound to him and to Radiance.

Abraham returned after five weeks away, disturbed when he walked through the gates to find every one of the wives bareheaded. He believed in what the Bible taught, that there was nothing more shameful than to force a woman to be bare and uncovered. He had resorted to this as the most severe punishment for women who strayed from the teachings of Radiance, but he simply couldn't believe that every single woman had committed a sin so grave as to be deserving of this. He knew immediately that it had been Thomas's doing, and the young man would answer for it.

CHAPTER 13

S arah hadn't seen her father in over twenty-five years. Most days, she could get by without ever thinking of him, although she did more now since her sister's arrival. But her thoughts of him no longer controlled her or dictated her behavior as they had for so long. She no longer thrived on spite. The day Sam cut off what remained of her hair, her last shred of bitterness went with it.

When the light for the doorbell flashed, and Sarah opened the door to her father, she nearly didn't recognize him. She stood frozen and unsure of what to do, whether she should worry about Mina's safety, her safety, or not. Sam wasn't at home; he'd taken Noah to the park to play with his little plastic bat and ball. She and Mina were alone to deal with this man who had hurt her so many times and who had allowed Mina to be tortured by her husband. Sarah didn't know if she could protect Mina if it came to that.

When she didn't hear the door close, Mina went to see who was at the door and if Sarah needed any help. Her signing was progressing quite quickly, being so immersed in it, and she was proud that she could act as an interpreter for simple exchanges. Mina appeared behind Sarah at the door and stood, equally frozen.

Abraham looked at Sarah and then at Mina, and he reached for her and barely grazed her cheek with his fingers when Sarah batted his hand away. He reached out to touch Sarah, and Mina grabbed him by the wrist and pushed him away. The sisters felt the unspoken shared history of the things he'd done to both of them.

"What do you want?" Mina asked him, her boldness taking Sarah by surprise. "Why are you here?"

"I wanted to see you, make sure you and my grandson were okay. May I say hello to him?"

"No," was all Mina said.

Abraham ignored Mina's refusal and turned his attention to Sarah.

"Sarah, my beautiful girl, what happened to you? What have you done to yourself?"

Sarah couldn't read his lips. It had been too long, and his beard obscured his mouth. But the look on his face, the pity mixed with disgust, gave him away. Sarah shrank into herself as he reached for her again, and when his fingers touched her head, she couldn't hold back her tears. She felt Mina's eyes on her, as though she was searching to understand why Sarah had suddenly become a different person, a weak person who couldn't keep herself composed in front of a man she despised. Mina was familiar with shame, and she didn't need an explanation to know it had just consumed her sister.

"I did it. It's my fault," Mina lied to their father. "I was practicing my hairstyling, and I made a mistake. I like it, though. She looks beautiful. I think I may try it myself, actually."

The three stood for a moment longer, Mina's hand tightly gripping Sarah's, and when neither of them showed any sign they were going to let Abraham into the house, he sighed and turned away, and he left.

"Mina, you have to believe me when I tell you, I didn't know what Thomas was doing to you. I never knew. I believe you now. I've seen what kind of man he is, what he did to all of our women last week... You have to believe me, Mina," Abraham said as he neared the elevator.

Mina didn't believe him, she refused to and didn't say a word, and she watched him board the elevator looking defeated for the first time in his life. Mina closed the door, and Sarah clenched her jaw waiting for her sister's questions that she prayed would never come.

"I didn't want him to think you were sick, or crazy or something," Mina said. Sarah smiled and opened her mouth to speak when, as if Mina read her mind, she continued, "and we're not shaving my head."

"Come on. Just a little?"

"No."

"Please?"

"No."

"But... I'm beautiful! You said so!"

"No."

◆ ◆ ◆

Feeling the air in the condo had been tainted by their father's presence, Sarah and Mina went out to ride the bus. The bus had quickly become Mina's favorite part of living in the city. There was no public transit anywhere near Radiance, and even if there had been, she wouldn't have been allowed to use it, and she certainly wouldn't have had any reason to enjoy it.

It was hard for her to articulate exactly why she liked it, and Sarah loved that Mina was so entranced with something as simple as a bus system. But for Mina, it was a reminder that the world was full of people all on various levels of happiness and pain, comfort and misery, and every day that she rode it, she had new conversations, and she rarely saw the same people twice. She liked being able to get on the bus and greet the driver, and always get a smile in return. Most people got on silently and never once made eye contact with the driver, as though they were being chauffeured around by a robot and not a human being deserving of pleasantries. This was an existence Mina understood too well. In Radiance, of course everyone knew who she was, but everyone, aside from the few close friends she'd made, refused to look at her. Some women despised her, believing that she had it easier than the rest of them, being paired with Thomas. Others knew what he did to her and were ashamed they were powerless to help. Mina had always been astounded by the willful oblivion of the former of the two. How anyone could not see how much she suffered was simply beyond her.

After lunch, Sarah asked Mina to go to her masjid with her for the second time. This time, curiosity won out over her quickly fading fear of Sarah's religion, and she agreed to go. She had been watching Sarah pray several times a day, and it amazed Mina how refreshed, how peaceful, Sarah appeared to be each time she got up from the little rug she knelt on as she went through the physical motions of each recitation. This was not something Mina ever imagined religion or faith could do. She believed in God, and she believed in the Bible, but for her, it was more something she did because that's simply what one does, not because it filled any need in her. It was the same way she'd come to think of gender now that she knew Sam. Mina behaved like a woman and dressed like one because that's what she knew, what she had always felt she was supposed to do because it was the only thing she'd ever learned how to do. If she felt anything about faith, it was resentment that something completely out of her control had allowed her to live in the situation she had. She knew if she'd been born male, she'd have been in her father's position, one of power over women. Though she couldn't fathom viewing women the way he did, so she believed that between the two choices, womanhood was, for her, the lesser of two evils. Though now, thanks to Sarah and Sam, she was able to understand what it was to be a woman and feel her femininity in a way that made it feel like her own, like something she could dictate and define and not something put upon her. Mina longed to have a similar shift in how she thought of faith and God, though she still had much she wanted to understand about Islam before she so much as brought up her curiosity with Sarah.

CHAPTER 14

On the surface, Mina appeared to be adjusting to life away from Thomas. She even seemed happy to anyone looking on. She had a routine, she played an important role in her new family, she'd even stopped flinching and bracing for pain anytime Sarah or Sam would sign vividly. She'd been seeing a therapist, Mary, an older woman with a low and soothing voice, at Sam's urging. During each session, she spoke of wanting to be someone else, needing to, so she could forget her past because every inch of her body reminded her of him. She felt like she would come undone, lose all of herself and all the progress she had made if she couldn't find some relief. That relief began with Noah. "Mama, no hair" had become the boy's favorite phrase, and he begged Mina every time he saw Sarah. She adored how much Noah loved his aunt and that he wanted to look just like her. She'd never allowed him to become close to anyone before, and seeing that Sarah, Sam, and Ruth all loved him as much as she did made everything else so much easier. He was well-loved and happy, which allowed Mina to try and accept the same for herself.

On this morning, when he made his daily "mama, no hair" request, Mina finally indulged her son. She stood him in the tub on top of a trash bag she'd spread out and mowed off his dark curls with the clippers she'd taken from Sarah and Sam's bathroom that morning while they were out on their daily run. Noah was in dire need of a haircut anyway. It was summer in Chicago, and the humidity was comparable to what Mina imagined a rain forest would be. The weather made both Noah and Mina look like they wore clown wigs.

Mina was careful with the hair clippers. So many times, she'd been forced to use them on an unwilling victim, and she needed them to stop being an inanimate object that she feared. Noah made this easy as he laughed, and his body shuddered with joy while he played with bunches of hair that fell into his open hands. More than that, Mina didn't know how to properly use clippers like the ones Sam had, and she laughed when she saw the result of her ineptitude. In Radiance, the only ones she'd ever used were from those cheap drugstore sets that come with the multicolored plastic combs. Sam's set had none of those, only several different metal blades that needed tools to change, so Mina used them as they were, which left her little boy nearly as bald as Sarah. She knew this would thrill Noah even more, though, so she didn't care much that this was not her intent.

When Mina finished with him, she rinsed him and dried him off, and sent him on his way. He ran out of the room shouting for Sarah, and when he found her, his squeals of joy nearly brought Mina to tears. She never thought he'd be able to be this happy. Mina didn't follow Noah out of the bathroom. Now it was her turn.

She was being healed. Each conversation she had with Sarah or Sam gave her a little more trust in people. Each breath she took of the air far from Radiance mended her from the inside out. Yet still, every morning, as she looked in the mirror to comb her hair after showering, she felt the ever-present ache of her hair being a weapon. She still saw Thomas behind her. Her body still braced to be beaten, and she was desperate to be someone else or at least see someone else in her reflection. She told Mary of her plans. She told her of the role hair played in Radiance, and she told her of her jealousy of Sarah and how she seemed so strong and comfortable. Mina told Mary she needed to never again feel the sensation of Thomas's hand dragging her around by her hair. Mary told her it could be a beautiful symbolic gesture. An acknowledgment of her rebirth into a life that was her own to design and live. Mina had always liked symbolism.

Mina stared herself down in the mirror. *He's not here. He can't hurt you*, she told herself. She flipped the switch on the hair clippers and smiled and cried and laughed all in one confusing wave as, for the first time in her life, she felt tension giving way instead of hurting her as the clippers effortlessly cut through her hair. The warm blades against her scalp gave her goosebumps. It hadn't felt like this on the night of her pairing ceremony. Perhaps she imagined it differently than it had actually happened, but Mina remembered those clippers causing her pain. With each pass she made over her head, emotion built up inside her. An emotion she couldn't name, and both reveled in and needed to be free of. She couldn't move fast enough; the feeling of becoming increasingly lighter and free of pain was intoxicating, and she was eager to show her family the new Mina she was creating.

Finally, she was through, and when she looked back at herself in the mirror, she saw exactly who she'd hoped. Not herself, not Thomas, but Sarah. Mina was sure that if she could just see Sarah in her reflection, just for a little while, she could also become the things Sarah was, which Mina desperately needed to be. Strong, happy, in control, and unashamed. Pleased with her decision, she brushed the loose hair off her shoulders and made her way out of her bedroom to rejoin her family in proud strides.

"I cut my hair," Mina said to Sarah and Sam as she entered the living room.

They looked at her in unison, eyes wide and mouths agape.

"You sure did," Sarah said. "You okay, Mina?"

Sam was speechless and somewhat unsettled by how strongly Mina now resembled Sarah.

"I want to tell you how I got this scar," Mina said, trying to force herself to look each of them in the eye as she touched the long scar. Sarah and Sam sat on the couch. Sam pulled his legs underneath him like he was settling in to watch a movie. Mina sat across from them and tried to calm her somersaulting stomach. What she was about to tell them, she believed, would either solidify her place in their family, make her one of them, or get her kicked out for having spent the last few months lying to them. Mina couldn't say which she believed would be more likely.

"I met Reina eight years ago. She was a doctor from San Francisco, but she went to university in Arizona, and she moved into the rental house behind us, just outside the walls. Thomas spent a lot of time away, traveling for our father, evangelizing, and one day, after Reina had watched him leave with a suitcase, she came over to introduce herself.

We spent six hours talking on the day we met. We both had so much to say that we even forgot to eat lunch. I knew when I first met her that I had feelings for her that I had never felt for my Thomas, that I'd never felt for any man. I didn't speak of what Thomas did to me, but I think she knew. She had to have known.

Over time, we fell in love. We would talk about leaving and being with each other forever, even though we both knew that could never happen. Eventually, I couldn't hide the things my Thomas did. Reina wanted to help, but I never let her. What could she do for me anyway? I couldn't divorce him, and the times I had tried to tell our father or the police about his beatings, they believed him, that I'd done it to myself out of jealousy and spite, and then I would get beaten even worse. There was nowhere I could have gone to get away, and there was just nothing in my mind that I could do except exactly what I'd been doing.

Reina eventually learned that there wasn't much she could do to help, so she just took care of me while Thomas was away. She would put wound cream on my head where he had torn out a fistful of hair and put arnica gel on my bruised face. I lost count of how many times she had to set my broken nose and put a stitch or two in cuts. I survived his beatings so I could feel her hands on me. She never touched me as she would if we were a couple, but just the light touch of her hands when she mended me was enough. I didn't need anything more to know she loved me. We spent time together nearly every day while Thomas was at the church, and on the days we couldn't, we shared glances through our windows. I knew it was wrong to want to be with her or even think of her as I did, but she loved me, and I needed someone to love me.

We spent six years being in love and just being happy to be in each other's company. She knew I could never take home gifts from her, so instead, she just wrote me love letters that she would read to me and then tear up and toss them into the wind. I always liked to think about how far her love notes traveled in the breeze. Maybe they would make it all the way to a place she and I could have been together.

Then finally, after so many years, Reina and I had a chance to spend a whole weekend together. Thomas was going away for the weekend. He left on Thursday after morning church service and wouldn't return until Sunday evening. For almost three whole days, I got to forget who I was, what my life was like, and just feel loved. We didn't do anything, not really, even though I knew we both wanted to. I was happy to just fall asleep for two nights in her arms. By Sunday morning, I had pushed out of my mind my whole life with Thomas. I was Reina's, and she was mine.

We went to our favorite cafe to have breakfast, and Reina must have forgotten about my real life too because she leaned over the table and kissed me. I was so happy; I had never been kissed before. It was like a knife to my heart, knowing that I had to go back home, back to belonging to Thomas after breakfast, but I did because I knew what would happen if I made any other choice. But I was so happy still, so I thought it would be good if I tried to look nice for him and make him a special dinner.

I was in the bathroom trying to get my hair to curl when he came home a little early. I heard him come in, and I shouted, "Hello my love, I'm so glad you're home." He didn't say anything back, I just heard his suitcase hit the floor, and he came storming into the bathroom. He grabbed the back of my hair, twisted his fingers around to get a firm grip, and forced the hot curling iron onto my neck, and I cried out. He started screaming at me, "You think you can keep things from me, Mina? I know what you did! I know what you did!"

I didn't know what he was screaming about because I never imagined he could have found about Reina and me. He yanked on my hair and threw me into the wall. When I fell, he grabbed my hair again and lifted me to my knees. I saw both of us in the mirror. He had never looked like that before, and I could tell that this time he intended to kill me. He picked his straight razor up off the vanity and pushed it so hard into my scalp. "Always in the mirror, primping your hair, you think you fool me? I know what you are!"

I heard myself begging him not to do it, but in my mind, I was hoping he would do it because at least then if I had no hair for him to grab, he couldn't hurt me. He pulled the razor all the way across my hairline. It cut me so deep, and so much blood ran into my eyes. It burned. He dropped the razor and tightened his grip on my hair. Next thing I knew, my face was smashing into the marble counter, and then nothing, it went black.

I woke up, I don't know how much later, in a puddle of my blood with him standing over me. He was holding a bottle of something in one hand and his razor again in the other. He didn't look mad anymore. He seemed so calm like everything was just fine. That worried me, but I didn't try to get away from him. I thought he was just going to cut off my hair or something, and I wasn't going to fight him over that. He could have my hair if he wanted it.

He started talking again, almost in a kind tone, "You want to be with women, Mina? Eat pussy? That's a disease I can cure you of."

He ripped off my panties and forced my legs apart so hard I felt something tear in my hip, and then he grabbed me between my legs and pulled on me. I let out a sound I'd never heard before, that delicate part of me being pinched so hard between his fingers, it made my ears ring. Then he started laughing, and he had this look on his face. I started saying what I thought would be my final prayers in my head. I tried to pull away from him, but that just made him squeeze harder with his fingers, and then he took the razor and just cut it off. Just one slice and that was that, like I was his livestock being castrated without a care about the fact that I was a human being, I was his wife. I was bleeding so much I couldn't tell if I was peeing myself or not. I started to black out, but he held me up by my hair and propped me against the wall. I couldn't look away from all the blood. It was all over the bathroom floor, pools of it, and it was still flowing out of me. The room was spinning, but he had his hand in my hair to make me stay upright. I couldn't move, everything hurt so much, but I think I must have been out of my own body because when he dumped the bottle, I didn't feel it burning through my clothes and eating away my skin. I just smelled it, and it was the most awful stench.

I don't know who called the ambulance, if it was Thomas, I don't know why he didn't just leave me to die there on the floor, but I woke up, I don't know how much later, in the hospital. I looked down at my chest and saw that where my breasts used to be was just mangled raw skin. Both of the things that made me a woman, Thomas had stolen from me, and for what? Because I kissed a woman? I stayed in the hospital for four months, and I never let myself think of Reina. I had made myself believe that all of this was her fault. She kissed me at the cafe. I had to believe that because letting myself miss her was just one more thing that hurt, and I couldn't bear any more pain. I made myself hate her, and I wondered about my son, whom I had just given birth to a month before Thomas attacked me. Hating Reina and getting home to Noah were the only two things I thought about in the hospital.

I got home and learned that not only had he stolen parts of me that weren't his to take, but the community had also decided to punish me for what I'd done to Thomas. They'd decided I was to be publicly shamed in the usual way—my hair. To be honest, though, the whole spectacle Thomas made of it didn't bother me at all. His first failure as a man, I guess. I stayed there at the front of the church on my knees as he cut off my hair, and all I could think was, *I can't feel any of this.* I didn't feel anything anymore except the fury I had that would protect Noah. Was I supposed to after what he'd already done to me?

But I had been violated twice, once by Thomas and once by my community, both of which are supposed to feel like home to a woman. That was when I stopped thinking of myself as a human being. I took care of my son, and I survived Thomas's fists. I never spoke to Reina again. She came through the back gate and knocked on the window at least a dozen times before she gave up because I didn't answer. Sometimes I would look out my bedroom window, and I'd see her. She'd look at me and wave. I didn't know what she was waving at. It couldn't have been me because I didn't exist anymore.

I stopped taking Aunt Ruth's calls too, I was too ashamed of what I'd done to myself to talk to a woman like her. I didn't believe she would ever be able to understand my life. Then one day, I don't know what changed, but I picked up the phone and called her. "Please help me," I said to her."

Mina looked up at her sister and Sam and took a breath, surprised by how empty she felt after telling them her story. Her once passionate feelings for Reina had faded to an emotionless retelling of a story that barely felt like her own. Reina had gone away, the memory of her and the electricity she'd once felt by just knowing she was near her, forced from Mina's mind, and she prayed she'd be able to do the same with Thomas.

She offered a weak and fearful smile to Sarah and Sam and simply said, "That's why I did this to myself. I need to be someone else, to be free of Thomas."

"Well, Sarah 2.0 is coming along nicely, huh?" Sarah said to Sam as they got ready for bed that evening.

"What do you mean? Mina? Be nice. She's finding herself."

"No, she's not. She's finding *me*. I don't even know if she realizes it. Hell, I didn't until today."

"Imitation is flattery or however that goes," Sam joked though he'd have been lying if he said he didn't find Mina's choice a little odd after the story she'd told them.

"I can't even imagine surviving what she had to, but Jesus Christ, Sam, what is she doing?"

"She's lost, Sarah. You can't tell me you weren't when you left that place for school. And why does it bother you anyway? She's not calling your bald head humiliating anymore, at least, right? Just let her be."

"Okay, but when I vanish, and we end up with a Body Snatchers situation here, I told you so," Sarah smirked.

Sam wrapped his arms around his fiancée, and she turned into him, resting her face on his chest, and breathing him in. When they were close like this, Sarah was intoxicated by his scent. He always smelled of a blend of spice and woodsy notes but not in the too-common *I'm a man and bathed in cologne to prove it* way many of the men Sarah had dated in the past did but in a subtle, *come hither and breathe me in, allow me to melt away your self-control* way. Sarah's hands found their way under his t-shirt, and she traced the outline of his abs from his naval to his chest. Her fingers skated around his pecs, and it was then that she realized she'd not even seen Sam's new body since his top surgery because Mina was there every time she turned around.

"I miss you," Sarah told him before she began slowly lifting his shirt. She raised it over his head and tossed it to the floor. "I miss this. We need us back."

Sam kissed her, and they stumbled their way backward to the bed. Sarah laid back, her body feeling nearly ready to explode in anticipation, and she closed her eyes as Sam crawled up the bed over top of her. Sam's lips grazed her ribs when she felt the air in the room shift as it always did when the door had been opened. Her eyes shot open, and over to the doorway where she saw her sister standing, pajama-clad, ready for bed.

"Case in fucking point," Sarah signed slyly to Sam, and they exchanged looks that told Sarah he suddenly understood exactly what she meant. Mina had taken over their life together entirely, and they had no idea how to change course.

CHAPTER 15

"Why do you think we hold on to our bad memories?" Mina asked her sister. "Why are they always right there, waiting to hurt us?"

They arrived at the hospital early in the morning for Mina's reconstructive surgery. Sarah sat beside her sister in an uncomfortable gray chair while they waited for the surgeon and anesthesiologist to come in. Mina looked helpless and fragile wearing the thin gown, which amplified the frightened look on her face, framed by the blue surgical bonnet that covered her head. Mina had come to trust her sister, and that was the only reason she agreed to this.

Sarah knew that Mina was only there for her. She had taken advantage of her sister's need for approval and convinced her to have the surgery. Mina would have been content to just carry on as she had been, as if what Sarah had seen that day in the bathtub had never happened, as if she wasn't in pain with every step she took. Sarah wondered if she was projecting, but she didn't believe Mina would ever be able to heal and move on if every second of her waking life reminded her of her husband, so she'd asked Sam to call the gynecologist they both saw. Sarah knew their doctor had done extensive reconstructive work on victims of female genital mutilation, and she believed she'd be able to help Mina.

Sarah tried to hide the guilt that consumed her as she waited with Mina for the doctor to come wheel her away. Her stomach churned, and she couldn't tell if it was because she knew she'd manipulated Mina and was afraid Mina knew, or if the sickly sterile scent that filled the area they occupied—a tiny space, room only for a bed and the small chair beside it, surrounded by an ugly pastel patterned curtain —was overwhelming her.

There were two absolute truths Sarah had learned about Mina in the weeks she'd been living with her and Sam. She was too afraid to do anything that required independent thought, and she would do whatever Sarah or Sam asked her to do. Sarah sat knowing she'd done exactly what Mina's husband had spent years doing to her, exploiting a weakness she'd spotted to get her to do what she wanted. What Mina needed. Sarah told herself it was all to help Mina, but she'd taken advantage of her nonetheless. She wanted to believe that when all was said and done, Mina would see that it was a good thing. When she told her sister about the surgery, Mina didn't look excited, or even relieved, by the prospect of having functional anatomy and not being in constant pain. Instead, she wrote down on a scrap of paper—her version of whispering to Sarah—*I don't want to be raped again.*

Sarah wondered how she would be able to convince her sister that she would never be raped again when she knew no other reality. She couldn't tell her that if she did this, sex would be nice again. That was inconceivable to Mina. So instead, Sarah explained that this surgery was necessary because leaving "down there" as it was may make her sick. Sarah despised having to say things as though her sister was an unintelligent child, but in a lot of ways, she was still a child. Mina was learning how to live and who she was by watching and mimicking, the way a child does, and Sarah and Sam were her role models now. And so, Mina lay in the hospital bed waiting to be wheeled away to the operating room and put to sleep while someone did to her yet another thing she didn't necessarily want. Sarah couldn't let herself consider whether or not her forcing this on her was a violation of Mina too.

"Maybe we keep them because if we hold them for long enough, they'll give us something, they won't just be bad memories, they'll have a purpose," Sarah finally answered Mina's question and prayed it would one day be true for both of them.

The two didn't talk while nurses came in and out, and the anesthesiologist came in to give her a sedative and begin the process of readying her for surgery. Instead, they exchanged glances every couple of minutes. Mina appeared as a little girl longing for reassurance that the world wasn't about to end, and Sarah offered her most reassuring smile. Sarah recited to herself a prayer for those setting off on a journey, her favorite and the same one they'd given Mina to hang in her bedroom. She wished the comfort of prayer was something she could share with her sister.

Sarah told Ruth about Mina's surgery and was incensed that she'd not offered to come with them to the hospital or even show her face to wish Mina well before they left the house that morning. Neither had spoken at length to Ruth since she'd come to stay in Chicago. Sarah knew she was saddled with painful guilt and couldn't blame her for avoiding Mina while she tried to figure out what to do with it. But this Ruth wasn't the one Sarah knew. There had never been a time Sarah could recall where Ruth hadn't shown up for her. She'd rarely ever even had to ask. Ruth just knew. But the more she learned about Mina and her past, the heavier that guilt became, and Sarah could see it slowly consuming her aunt more now that she was in closer proximity to Mina and harder to put out of her mind.

When the nurses came to wheel Mina's bed to the operating room, she grabbed Sarah's hand.

"This is what you want for me?" Mina asked.

Sarah didn't respond. She just held onto her hand, kissed her knuckles, and nodded. When Mina was out of sight, Sarah cried. Mina had been with them for months now, and she'd watched her change in some surprising ways, yet she still wondered who her sister was. She wondered how one goes about making a woman whole when she had hollowed herself out just to survive each day. Would they ever be able to tell what was Mina versus what she did simply to please Sarah and Sam? It was clear that Mina felt safety in being similar to her sister, but Sarah wondered how much of that was normal for a younger sister to want to be like her older sister and how much was an effort to make sure she never disappointed them?

Sarah was at a loss. She didn't know how to shape a woman into her own person, not without imparting some of herself onto her. She wondered how in the hell she was supposed to help Mina find herself, create herself when her only response to "What do you like?" was "What do you like?" Sometimes it felt like a depressing game of "Who's on first?"

Sarah left the hospital as soon as Mina was rolled out of sight.

She felt such a connection to Mina and so protective of her, but she couldn't shake the notion that she was very slowly being consumed by her sister. Mina was always with either her or Sam. When Sarah was at work, Mina was with Sam. When Sam was working, she was with Sarah. She was always there, always watching, learning. And the more sign language Mina learned—though Sarah was grateful her sister wanted to learn—the more similar Mina became to her. It seemed as though Mina was trying to become her, if for no reason other than she didn't know who else to be. Mina was crippled by fear and by her past. Both Sarah and Sam understood this, so they let her cling to them because they were safe. But they had not been alone together—not even to sleep—since Mina's arrival.

Mina had been suffering nightmares since she arrived, and she was afraid to sleep alone. She'd not admitted as much, but it showed in the way she would always try to keep Sam and Sarah up talking into the early hours of the morning, even though she struggled to stay awake herself. After a few nights of this, Sarah and Sam worked out a system. One of them went into her room every evening, under the guise of just wanting to chat, while she prepared for bed. With one of them beside her in bed, Mina would fall asleep quickly, and if she woke afraid, someone was right there to remind her that nobody could hurt her. It didn't take Mina long to figure out what they were doing, and while she was too embarrassed to acknowledge it, a couple nights per week, she would go into Sam and Sarah's bedroom and lay between them in their king-size bed. On those nights, with someone safe on either side of her, she never woke soaked in sweat from a nightmare. With the protection of both Sam and Sarah, Mina finally slept deeply.

Sarah hated feeling the way she did, she knew Mina needed her, but God did she need a break. She needed to feel her life like it was before it got all complicated by her family mess. She needed Sam. To reconnect with him. To touch him without Mina watching. She needed to take back her bed, her life, her fiancé. She needed to have sex with him. As she drove away from the hospital, it occurred to her that they'd never gotten to have a celebratory night for their engagement. Somehow, she had been proposed to, said yes, and then stopped sleeping with the man who would soon become her husband.

When she entered the condo after her drive home, during which she grew increasingly resentful of Mina and mad at Ruth for causing this sudden shift in her life, she found Sam and told him everything that had been on her mind as she drove.

"We need to plan our wedding. And this? All of whatever this is with Mina, it's got to change. She is going to sleep in her own bed, she's going to get her own life and—"

"Did something happen?" Sam interrupted her.

"Have you not been living here? You don't think it's a little much? She's trying to become me, Sam. It's weird, and it's too much, and it needs to stop."

"Okay, we'll get things back on track. Starting with a wedding," Sam paused, a smirk turning up one corner of his mouth, "Oh God, you're gonna make me dance, aren't you?"

Sam tried to diffuse Sarah's seemingly spontaneous anger. He understood her frustration. Mina's arrival and constant presence had been something like a flash flood that they'd not been prepared for and had been so overwhelmed trying with to fix that neither seemed to notice that they'd been swallowed whole by her, by the situation. But what could they do? They'd agreed to take her and Noah in, and now they had, and she needed far more help than either of them realized. They certainly couldn't abandon her now, after she'd made progress. The one thing Sam could agree with Sarah on without question was that it was unsettling how much Mina seemed to be trying to become her sister. But how much of that, he wondered, was the simple matter of Sarah having such a strong influence because she was there and because having spent her entire life not allowed to be her own person at all, Mina could only take from others what she needed to form her own person. Sam didn't have the answers they needed. All he could hope to do was slowly usher in change to get him and Sarah back to their life as planned and Mina into her own life independent of them.

That night Sarah slept with Sam alone for the first time in more weeks than she could recall, and for one night, she felt whole and like herself again and not like she was serving as an unsettling vessel through Mina would become a meek and quiet version of the woman Sarah used to be. In the morning, she would confront Ruth and demand that she step up, shoulder some of everything Mina had brought upon them.

Sarah was fed up with having to carry the weight of this between herself and Sam alone and was going to let Ruth have it, whether she deserved it or not. She stood pounding at the door of the apartment Ruth had been renting since after Sam's top surgery, thinking of all the words she had for her aunt. The least of them being how pissed she was that Ruth didn't even bother to show up to accompany them to the hospital for Mina's surgery.

After a couple minutes passed with no answer, Sarah used the key Ruth gave her and let herself into the small apartment. Sarah walked the few rooms slowly, shouting for her aunt occasionally. When she reached the bedroom, she knocked, much more softly than she had on the front door, and opened it slowly. She found her aunt lying on her side in bed, and her heartfelt as though it had dropped out of her chest the closer she got to Ruth. She reached her hand for her aunt, and when she felt no warmth radiating from her body, she choked back a sob and sat beside Ruth, suddenly numb. Sarah knew Ruth wouldn't answer, yet she repeated her aunt's name because that was the only thing she could utter. Sarah rocked back and forth on the edge of the bed, trying desperately not to cry, though she knew she had no good reason to hold back her tears. Nobody was there to see a moment of weakness.

Forcing her mind to stay focused and not lost to emotion, Sarah texted Sam. He'd know what to do.

"Ruth's dead," was all she typed. She hit send and put her phone back in her purse, not waiting for a reply.

They were told it was a stroke, but Sarah believed it had been her guilt that killed her. Ruth simply couldn't bear knowing what Mina had survived and what she hadn't let herself see.

Sarah hadn't had to put into practice her ability to shut down her emotions for two decades, largely due to the love Ruth had given her, though now she found herself doing it again, numbing herself so she didn't have to cope with losing the only person that had ever loved her enough to take care of her before she met Sam. Sarah couldn't bear the thought of Ruth having died alone and, even worse, died believing that Sarah was angry with her and blaming herself for what happened to Mina, so she didn't allow herself to think about it at all.

Sarah planned a memorial service for Ruth while Mina recovered. After Ruth's husband passed away, the only family she had left was Sarah and Sam, and now Mina, with her having severed ties with her brother Abraham long ago.

When Sarah shared the final details of the service with Mina, she shot her the subtlest of glares.

"So, I get no say in this? She was my aunt too, you know," Mina said.

Sarah was at a loss. In the months that Mina had been living with them, she'd bent over backward to avoid disagreeing with Sam and Sarah, and now she not only disagreed but did it with an attitude too.

"Is there something you'd like to change? You don't like what I've planned for her?"

"She deserves a Christian service, Sarah. She was a Christian."

"No, she wasn't. She stopped practicing decades ago, and I've never seen her touch a Bible in my life. I don't think she'd appreciate a religious service," surprised by how appalled she still was by the very idea of Christianity, especially when it came to Ruth, who had always been the antithesis of everything their father's faith preached.

"Her name is Ruth. It's in the Bible. She needs a Christian service," Mina said and began to walk away but turned back for the last word. "The memorial service isn't for the dead, is it? It's for the rest of us, still here without her."

Sarah wasn't convinced, but Mina cared enough about this to fight for it, something she was utterly terrified to do under any other circumstances, so Sarah conceded.

Ruth had been like a mother to Sarah for all her adult life, and she wasn't sure she was finished needing a mother. Among other things, Ruth had always given Sarah a window through which she could see her family's bullshit for what it was; narcissism, manipulation, evil, and Sarah loved her for affirming what Sarah had always believed was true about them.

The size of the crowd at Ruth's memorial service shocked Sarah. Each day she'd been dead, it seemed that Sarah learned something new about her aunt. She had no idea she was such a social, popular woman. Sarah always liked to imagine she got her penchant for being a hermit from her. At least a hundred people she'd never seen before came to the church and shook Sarah's hand or hugged her. After about the fiftieth hug, Sarah had to excuse herself and hide in the bathroom. She felt she would lose it, and the dam holding back her tears would break the next time someone touched her. She'd thought it hilarious in the past when every time someone would give Sam a strong hug—the kind that really means it—and Sam would cry. The deeper the hug, the harder he'd cry, like he was allergic to human contact. But now Sarah understood it. She could feel the sorrow these people felt for her, and the thought that Ruth must have spoken about her often to them was overwhelming.

Get a grip. These people do not need to see you sobbing like a little girl, Sarah thought, as she stared herself down in the mirror until the urge to start bawling was forced out of her mind.

When she returned from the bathroom, the religious part of the service had started, and Sarah had never been more grateful that Mina had forgotten she was Deaf and failed to get an interpreter. The preacher spoke, and Sarah couldn't read his lips, so Sarah sat relieved that she'd be able to keep her emotions under control for a bit longer.

When the service ended, Sarah snuck out before anyone else could talk to her, and when Sam and Mina finally arrived at the car, they rode home in silence. Once in the garage, both Sam, Mina, and Noah went into the building to take off their funeral garb and go about the rest of the day. Sam walked away with the little boy on his hip, and only Noah looked back at Sarah, still in the car, like he knew her secret and wouldn't tell anyone.

Mina came back to the garage when Sarah didn't come inside and found her sitting in the back seat of the SUV, crying. She'd let it all out when she was finally alone and couldn't simply shut her tears off now that Mina had appeared. Mina climbed in and sat next to her sister. She said nothing, only tugged on Sarah's arm until she gave in and rested her head on her thigh while Mina rubbed her back. After a while, she began drumming her fingers on Sarah's head until she sat up.

"You have so much snot. And it's getting all over my skirt," Mina grinned, looking proud that they'd swapped roles. She was making bad jokes to make Sarah feel better now. "You look like you're melting, Sarah. Half of your eyebrow is smeared."

Sarah wiped off what remained of her brows with her palms and laughed. "Fell out a couple weeks ago. Hair's all gone too. You wouldn't believe how much I'm saving on shave oil." Sarah smiled at Mina, but she didn't smile back.

"And you're okay? I know you've been anticipating this, but still, you're alright?" Mina asked, looking far more concerned than Sarah thought she should.

"I'm good, yeah. Would have been a lot worse if I hadn't done the preemptive bald thing, you know?"

Sarah could tell Mina had more on her mind than just her baldness, no longer being by choice, and she couldn't bear the weird tension anymore. "That's not what you wanted to talk about, is it? What's up, Mina?"

"Our father, he hurt you, and Ruth tried to help, didn't she?" Mina asked.

Ruth and Sam were the only people Sarah had ever admitted that to. How the hell did Mina know, Sarah wondered.

"What makes you think that?" Sarah didn't know why, but she felt defensive and pulled away from her sister.

"It's okay, Sarah. I didn't mean it to sound like an accusation. I just… I saw the way he looked at you when he came here, and I lived with him for sixteen years. I know what kind of man he is. I'm sorry if I'm wrong."

"You're not wrong," Sarah felt her face become flushed, "God. You're going to think I'm crazy."

"I won't. You can say anything to me. What is it?"

"He started when I was eleven. He'd come into my room, and the whole time, he'd be stroking my hair, saying things I couldn't understand. It went on for four years." Sarah took a breath. "It stopped when… Shit. I can't believe I'm saying this." Sarah covered her face with her hands and shook her head. She'd never admitted this part to anyone, not even Ruth.

"Sarah, it's okay. I understand. It stopped when your hair started falling out, right?"

"The very day. He had his hand in my hair, like usual, and this huge clump came right out in his fingers. He jumped off me like I'd hurt him, and a week later, I was gone. As much as I've always hated having to watch it fall out, I can't help but think that maybe this was how God answered my prayers. If He does that sort of thing, divine intervention, anyway. I know it's ridiculous. It's a disease, not God. It's stupid."

"Sarah... If you want to know stupid, I've been here thinking maybe God gave you that condition to help me feel better about how I had to deal with what Thomas did to me. You make it seem so much less frightening and terrible." Mina laughed.

"Well, maybe we're both right. Or we're both stupid."

CHAPTER 16

Weeks had passed since Thomas held his dreadful ceremony, and even the most loyal men and obedient women had grown weary. It was clear Thomas's demands served no purpose other than to be a show of force, control, by a man who was growing more disturbed by the day. Fifteen more families had left in the night without a word since Thomas had lit the mountain of hair ablaze, and Abraham couldn't blame them. In a fit of rage and a show of his ever-dwindling power, Thomas branded three women atop their heads with a sizeable "R." He brought them to Abraham, nearly giddy, explaining that he'd found a way to stop people from leaving, and Abraham knew the young man would need to be sent away.

He wondered how he could have been so wrong about what he'd seen in Thomas when the young man arrived in Radiance. Thomas had caused an upset with speculation as to just what he'd done to Mina, which in turn, caused people to begin questioning what Abraham preached. And now this—maiming women who had done nothing wrong—could easily get Thomas arrested should anyone outside the community find out. Until now, no one knew the cruelty Thomas was truly capable of. No one but Abraham, who was disgusted by the things the young man had done to his daughter, but he was steadfast in believing what he preached. Only God had a place in a relationship between a man and a woman. Not the government, not other men, not even the woman's family. Each of Radiance's Brothers were more or less free to treat their woman how they wished, so long as it didn't taint her for the other Brothers. Thomas had broken this rule several times over with Mina, to the point of her being removed entirely from the monthly rotation of Sisters. Still, Abraham told himself that what had been done to Mina was not what he would do, but he was not Thomas. He could not know how God guided him.

Abraham warned Thomas after he'd burned Mina and left both men scrambling for a story to tell their people that one more misstep like that would have consequences. Abraham believed that an unfaithful woman needed to face dire consequences, but Thomas had lost control of himself, and losing control was simply not allowed. Control was the pinnacle of Radiance. Control your mind and its natural inclination to sin. Control your body and its perversions. Control what you allow in from outside the community. Control your women so that they are never left wondering what their place is.

Thomas had nearly killed Mina with his loss of control before, and now he'd done it again, and there was no recovering from it this time.

For weeks after Mina and Noah disappeared, there had been police officers searching their community, digging through Thomas's house, talking to other residents about Mina, prying, trying to learn something about her and where she could have gone. Abraham wrestled with whether he should tell Chief Edison that he now knew where Mina had gone; she was with Sarah and Ruth. But admitting that would also end everything he had spent forty years building, as he had no doubt that Sarah would tell the police what he had done to her when she was just a girl.

Abraham never did anything illegal that people knew of. In no uncertain terms, he told each man upon his arrival in Radiance that no woman under sixteen was to be touched, not for any reason. When a woman turned sixteen, she would be paired with a suitable man and join the rotation of women to be shared, but never before she was sixteen years old. Breaking this rule would result in immediate exile, without question. Abraham had broken this rule—and the law —with Sarah, though he trusted that she would keep to herself his indiscretions from her childhood unless she was given a reason not to, until now. He realized the error of his ways back then and was a changed man. God called him to grow his following, groom new leadership so Radiance could continue to thrive long after he was gone. Abraham realized he had simply been wrong in understanding how he was to go about ensuring his community continued without him.

He had believed only his blood could carry on what he'd created, and so he'd taken to laying with his daughter because he needed a son. After Sarah left the community, Abraham took a new understanding of what God called on him to do, and he would choose a new leader when the time was right.

Thomas arrived in the community at the perfect time. Mina was fifteen and would soon be able to be paired. He'd come alone and eager to learn from Abraham how to be a man of God. Thomas had the same fire inside him, the same drive to build a community that gave men their rightful place in God's kingdom, the same understanding of the Bible's teachings, and the same charisma that had allowed Abraham to found and grow Radiance. Thomas was the one that would bring their faith to the new generations of young men searching for their place in the world and their place beside God. Now all his work, all of his mentoring was to go to waste.

Abraham called on the most trusted men within his community, those who had been with him since the beginning. He met with them to explain what he believed happened with Mina, and of course, to lay all the blame on Thomas, and he sought their input as to what each of them felt was the best way to handle Thomas. He told them that he had only recently become aware of the sins Thomas had committed against his daughter, and his feigned shock and disgust was shared by the men, who didn't know that Abraham had long known what Thomas did. He told them about the women he'd branded as well. They all agreed; Thomas had to go. If he left quietly, they would not share any information with the police. No need to draw even more unwanted attention from outsiders, they said. If he fought, well, that was a risk Abraham had to take even though it may mean exposing some of his wrongdoings, but he believed he'd easily be able to paint anything Thomas said as the rantings of a guilty man.

Abraham called Thomas to meet with him at his home. He took most meetings in his office inside the church, preferring to keep his private life private, but this meeting called for extra caution as Abraham didn't know how Thomas would react to his exile. He'd grown increasingly agitated and short-tempered as weeks passed and community members whispered their suspicions about him. For the first time, Abraham was grateful that Mina was not here to bear the brunt of his anger. He hadn't forgiven Mina for ignoring everything she'd been taught about being an example to the women of Radiance when she was unfaithful, and he would never forgive her for who she committed this sin with, but this disappearance, Abraham knew, was Thomas's fault alone. He had ravaged his daughter's body, and Abraham imagined that her survival instinct had taken over her mind, and she left so she could survive.

"You know why you're here," Abraham said to Thomas, who, sitting in the oversized leather reading chair, looked like a little boy.

"Yes, Father, and I apologize for what I've brought into the community."

Thomas's eyes and the dark circles under them reminded Abraham of the way a puppy would look at its master after it had soiled the carpet or destroyed a shoe.

"No, son," Abraham cleared his throat, suddenly struggling to say what he had been practicing. "It's time for you to go. You need to leave Radiance."

"Father, I—"

"No, Thomas. I warned you. I told you the last time you brought this kind of attention to us would be the last time. I meant it. Whatever happened between you and Mina is between you and Mina and God, but this suspicion of all of us, this brutality against these women who have done nothing to deserve it, we cannot have it. I will not have it. You need to go so the rest of us can return to peace."

"Father, I'm sorry. However you'd like me to repent, I will, gladly. Do you not care about finding Mina? Or Noah? He's my son."

"Mina made her choice. We both know where she's gone to, and we both know who is to blame. And I've made my choice. It's time for you to go, Thomas. It's decided. I'm sorry."

Abraham turned his head away, suddenly choked up that he'd been forced to banish his heir, the son he'd never been blessed enough to have. He feared that watching the young man leave would overwhelm him, and he could not afford to show any weakness. Not to Thomas and not to anyone in his community. He needed to remain firm in his decision and his enforcement of the rules everyone knew.

In an instant, Abraham was on his back looking up at Thomas, who wielded the old man's cane above his head and began swinging it, hitting Abraham about the head and face, and Abraham died without fighting, without making a sound more than a death rattle. The way he looked at Thomas in the seconds before the first blow, he appeared to have accepted that this would be his end. He welcomed it, spent from weeks of trying to save face, explain away Thomas's erratic and ungodly behavior and his rantings during church services.

Death was easier than saving Radiance from Thomas.

Thomas regained control of himself, and before sneaking out the side door of Abraham's study that led into the back yard of the house, he cleaned out the safe and took Abraham's small address book from his desk drawer. He stayed in the shadows as he made his way back home to change out of his blood-soaked clothes. In the temporary safety of his locked home, Thomas searched the address book for Abraham's sister's address. He knew this must have been what he meant when the old man said, "We both know where she's gone." Thomas changed his clothes and put the money from the safe into a small bag. He packed just one suitcase and made his way to the Cadillac SUV Abraham kept parked between their houses but paused when he realized he'd forgotten something.

Oscar and Jed were the only loyal beings in Thomas's world now. He wouldn't leave them in the care of these ungrateful and betraying people. His mind slowed as he searched the closet for their travel carrier. The cats had never gone anywhere, but still, they had a carrier. Slowly and calmly, Thomas prepared the black and white polkadotted carrier, lining it with two small blankets on one side and the matching travel litter box on the other. The cats came trotting to him when they heard him rustling their bag of food, and he picked them up, nestling his face in the fur of their necks before placing them gently in their carrier. He had the thought that if he had known animals would have been a better alternative to people before all of this ever began, that he would have chosen their company instead of people. Then he had the thought that if he'd studied harder in school and had gone to college, he could have become a veterinarian, and there would always be a steady stream of people coming to him, needing him and what he offered. This thought hurt, though, so he stopped thinking and returned to the methodical packing of his cats and their necessities. With the cats sitting safely in the back of the Cadillac, Thomas got into the car. He started the engine, suddenly nervous again about the noise it made as it ran as if simply starting a car would be what gave him away as having just killed Abraham.

He drove away from Radiance, the only place that had ever been home, with the only man who had ever felt like a father now dead and deserving of it. Thomas followed the voice of the car's GPS as it led him to the freeway, and then to the next freeway, and the next, which would take him to Ruth's condo in New York City. There, he would find Mina and his son and bring them back to Radiance to show her what she'd caused.

CHAPTER 17

M ina watched her son color in his spaceship coloring book, and she recalled being a child, the moment she realized she could peel the paper off a crayon and it became an entirely new instrument. With one simple change in appearance, the admission of who she really was, the only part of herself she felt she truly knew, she felt like that crayon, capable of so many new things all because she'd peeled away her wrapper.

She told her family about Reina, whom she hadn't stopped thinking about, longing for since she spoke her name. She'd thought she'd gotten over her, she'd forced herself to, but now it seemed that merely telling the story of how they'd met and who they had been to each other had started to rekindle long-dead feelings, slowly over the last couple of weeks. Now, when she looked at herself, she didn't see a woman who had let her husband reduce her to nothing. She saw Sarah, who was everything she wanted to be. She felt strong and, at times, she felt unafraid, which was a novel emotion for her. Instead of a scared woman running from something, she was running toward something, welcoming so many new experiences, beginning again, confidently. She was no longer Sister Mina, Abraham's daughter, and Thomas's prisoner. She was Mina. Telling the story of Reina, admitting her love for her, and cutting off her hair, felt like revenge even though it would never be served.

More profound changes were happening as well, changes in the core of who Mina was. She'd made this one admission, and it had a ripple effect. She asked for permission far less often now, and she'd started to question people when they did or said things she disagreed with or didn't understand. Faith felt different as well. For months now, Mina had been watching Sarah perform her daily prayers, and she longed to feel what Sarah seemed to. She'd asked Sarah about the prayers, what they did for her, and their deeper purpose. Mina imagined she would feel so smothered if she had to stop everything and drop to her knees in prayer at five set times a day.

"It's refreshing. Liberating, actually," Sarah told her. "I start my day with gratitude, I end it with gratitude, and three more times, I get to hit the reset button where everything but gratitude shuts off for a few minutes. I look forward to it."

The deciding factor for Mina was the hijab. Sarah had introduced her to a group of women, all hijabis, at the masjid, and each one of them welcomed her questions. She asked about the headscarf, and each woman gave a similar yet distinctly different answer. One told her she chose to wear it because it was a constant reminder of God and that she was lucky enough to be a Muslim. Another said she wore it because she appreciated the modesty it allowed her. The last woman she asked told her that one of the reasons she wore it was that it forced people to get to know her as a person, to understand who she was and value what was inside her instead of judging her solely based on what she looked like. They all told Mina should they ever decide hijab was no longer for them, the choice to stop wearing it was solely theirs, between them, God, and no one else. This notion stunned her. Choice and religion had never been two things that could coexist in her life.

Mina thought that "hijab" was simply an article of clothing, the scarf that Muslim women wore to cover their hair. Now though, she delighted in knowing it was a whole concept, a set of behaviors, beliefs, that embraced modesty. Hijab was a way of living with God and among people according to what she believed was the best reflection of God. Hijab was something for her alone to interpret and choose, and not something for anyone to force on her. The one thing she took pride and comfort in from her father's teaching—that a woman should honor herself with modesty—was hijab.

Hijab, Mina discovered, was *her*.

Mina's decision to convert and don the headscarf was an easy one but not a hasty one. First, she learned about Islam as Sarah understood and practiced it. Then came learning even more from the women she'd met at the masjid. The very fact that there were so many different interpretations of how one could practice one faith made it that much more appealing to Mina. She was fascinated when the imam told her of ijtihad. It was, he told her, one's God-given ability of independent reasoning, creative and adaptive thinking about God and Islam, and what it meant to be a Muslim. He told her that she should be continually questioning her beliefs, asking herself if how she believed and how she practiced her faith was the best way to live and serve people according to God's teachings. The act of questioning God and how Christianity was to be practiced had been strictly forbidden for all of her life, not just within her father's community but throughout the faith as a whole. There was no tradition of progress and reexamination of holy teachings in Christianity. You believed and practiced what the head of your church told you to. The notion that Islam had no religious leaders, at least not as Christianity did, made it all so much more appealing to Mina. Her faith, her interpretation of the Quran, was for her alone. It was her obligation to interpret its teachings according to her best understanding of them, and this was such a welcome relief after a life of religious enforcement and restriction, all because of one man's view of Christianity.

Mina said Shahada on a Friday after the midday prayer service.

"We have a new sister joining us today," the imam said to those gathered in the masjid. "Mina is Sarah's sister, and we welcome her as she begins her journey as a new Muslim. Please, gather around Mina."

The small crowd gathered around Mina, and she recited the words she'd been practicing, "Ash-hadu an laa ilaaha illaallaah, wa ash-hadu anna Muhammadan-ar-rasool ullaah."

As she said these words, it occurred to Mina that praying with her sister for the first time was also the first time her prayers were not simply begging God to either save her life or end it. She no longer needed to do this. She no longer questioned why she was alive. Living was a gift, not a burden. And every time she thanked God now, she meant it.

Mina and Sarah did still have their differences, however. Part of the draw to Islam had been its practice of modesty, as Mina was and always had been a modest woman. Her beliefs in how a woman should present herself to the world had not changed, despite Sarah's efforts. Instead, they had been reaffirmed by her new friends at the masjid. Sarah had hoped Mina would leave that behind with her broken view of Christianity. She wanted to blame the religion, Mina's faith, for giving her a life she was forced to run from. Sarah viewed her sister's modest dressing the way many women did, something Mina could and should choose to be rid of now. Sarah despised their father so much that she refused to see there were aspects of her former life that Mina wanted to hold on to.

Mina saw Sarah as a beautiful woman, ideal, like a Renaissance sculpture with soft curves, feminine hips, and strong features. She drew the stares of both male and female admirers, and Sarah liked that very much. She told Mina that if God hadn't wanted her to use her body to her benefit, He wouldn't have given her a body that drew so much attention. Mina admired her confidence; she just couldn't agree with her view of modesty. They disagreed and argued about this often.

"Just try it, Mina! Show a little elbow. It's freeing!" Sarah would mock her.

It always stung Mina a little, knowing she thought of the beliefs she'd held for so long as trivial, and Mina prayed that eventually Sarah would understand or even appreciate it. She never told Sarah that, though. She would have been offended. She'd told Mina once before that the idea of praying for other people, for them to change, was the most offensive thing she could imagine. She told Mina to try praying as she did—never for other people to change, only for herself, to be better able to understand and help them.

It was after one of these arguments about Mina's modesty that Sarah asked her sister something Mina had hoped she never would. Sarah was curious to know if perhaps this part of Mina was something she'd gotten from her mother; the mother Sarah never knew.

"Mina," Sarah began cautiously, "What's our mother like? I never got to know who she was."

"She was… sad. A very sad woman," was all Mina could think to say. "I'm not the right person to ask. I don't have any good things to say about her."

Mina had been aware of who her mother was for as long as she could remember but never saw the woman as a mother, but just another unfortunate victim of her father's. Unlike the child-raising practices everyone else had to abide by in Radiance in which the birth mother raises every child she bears, the two daughters Abraham had fathered were taken from the woman that had given birth to them and were raised by Abraham alone, as he had not ever paired himself with a woman in the community. He hadn't wanted any woman to feel that she was of higher stature than any other, as his mate. The girls' birth mother was kept in a nice house, and Abraham had arranged her pairing to one of the wealthier men of Radiance, thinking this would make up for having her two daughters stolen away from her. Mina had never spoken to the woman, only exchanged glances on the occasions they passed by each other, and Mina often wondered if the woman even wanted to know her daughter. Mina wasn't sure if she wanted to know her. She didn't know what to make of a woman who could give birth to two children and never have contact with them, even though she lived only a few houses away. Mina knew this was a rule enforced and therefore never to be broken by her father, but she imagined she would have found a way if she was in that position. Nothing would ever be strong enough to keep her from her child.

"You don't have to say good things, just tell me honestly," Sarah said.

Mina hesitated, weighing how much Sarah really wanted to know the truth and if it would only serve to hurt her. She decided that if nothing else, Sarah deserved her honesty.

"I lived six houses away from her for all my life, and we never spoke. She looked at me when we passed each other by but not in the way I looked at her. She didn't see me; I don't think she wanted to. I only ever wanted to say hello to her and ask her why she had no interest in us, but I never could. I think she made herself hate me."

Sarah considered what her sister told her for a moment. She'd never felt the pull to get to know her mother or to have her as a mother. Perhaps because she'd gotten everything she needed from Ruth, or maybe it was because she had never had the time to grow to resent her as Mina had.

"Mina, I'm sorry, I don't know what to say. But I'm sorry you never got to know her."

Sarah pulled her sister toward her and kissed her temple, leaving behind her bright red lipstick.

"You look so much like her, though. Your eyes, your lips, even your hands," Mina tried to satisfy Sarah's curiosity.

"And here I was thinking I'm unique. Damn."

"Oh, you are definitely unique. I've never known anyone like you." Mina smiled at Sarah and rested her hand on her forearm.

Mina trusted Sarah before she arranged the surgery to repair the damage done to Mina by her husband. She'd trusted her from the moment Sarah crawled under the table and held her on her second day living with them. She had nothing to base her trust on, it was something foreign to her, being able to trust, but when she was with Sarah, Mina felt things she'd never experienced. Safety, warmth, unconditional love, and Mina imagined these were components of trust, so when her sister told her something would be good for her, Mina believed her. Sarah knew she'd been afraid to see a doctor, so she went with her and held her hand through the entire painful examination, reassuring her every time Mina looked at her.

After the surgery, Mina trusted her completely. Sarah was right. Having the operation allowed Mina to have moments where she didn't have to relive what Thomas had done to her. Before, Mina had to remember every time she sat down, every time she used the bathroom, every time she put on her underwear. Every step brought her pain, and every pain brought back to her the memory of Thomas standing over her with scissors. The way she was free to exist after the surgery reminded Mina of a poem she had read from a book Sarah had given her, shortly after she and Noah moved in.

To me every hour of the light and dark is a miracle,

Every cubic inch of space is a miracle,

Every square yard of the surface of the earth is spread with the same, Every foot of the interior swarms with the same.

To me the sea is a continual miracle,

*The fishes that swim—the rocks—the motion of the waves—
the ships with men in them,*

What stranger miracles are there?

Everything, without pain, felt novel, and as though it were a miracle—even the simplest things as having a conversation over a boring breakfast of yogurt with Sarah. Mina was experiencing life unobstructed by torment, and that in itself was a miracle to her. She was again becoming a human being, being tamed by kindness, losing the wild creature focused only on survival she had become at the hand of her husband. She was being seen and considered and loved, and for her, this was as miraculous as God's creation of Man. Wild things maintain strong focus. That is how they survive. But human beings, they can forgive. They can let go. That is how they survive, and to Mina, surviving was a miracle.

Mina was finally healing, with the help of two people who wanted nothing from her but for her to be happy. She had grown into this life, just as Ruth promised she would, without ever realizing it, and for that, she was both thankful and angry with herself for letting it happen without cherishing each new moment.

CHAPTER 18

The barbarity of the attack that killed Abraham was unlike anything Chief Edison had ever seen. Even in case studies from the many seminars he'd attended, he'd never seen quite so much overkill. If not for the long white hair tied back into a loose ponytail and the white beard, Miguel wouldn't have been able to recognize the dead man as Abraham. His face had been beaten into oblivion, his limbs broken, his teeth missing and scattered around the floor. Miguel wondered what in the world he could have done to cause Thomas—he knew Thomas was responsible for this—to kill the man he referred to as Father. Granted, all the residents of Radiance called Abraham "Father," but in the weeks they'd been investigating Mina and Noah's disappearance, Miguel had heard Thomas refer to the man as "Father" in a way that felt different. It felt as though Thomas truly believed Abraham to be his father.

Miguel hadn't needed any of the residents of Radiance to confirm his suspicion that it was Thomas, but several had approached him, now that they were free to do so, and told him stories of Thomas and all he had done recently. He spoke with the women who had been branded atop their heads and convinced them to see a doctor at the small hospital a few towns over. He instructed the men to be vigilant and protective of the women and children. He told them that Thomas may return, and they all understood that if he did, it would likely be to cause further harm to the people he believed had betrayed him. Miguel wished he could tell everyone to leave Radiance

—he wanted nothing more than to see it become a ghost town—but he knew none of the residents had any money, nor did they have anywhere else to go. He would call a humanitarian organization of some sort, he told himself, and they would come to help these poor people adapt to life outside of the walls of Radiance. He was sure there had to be such an organization.

The oldest member of the community, the man who had unofficially taken over as community leader since Abraham's death, told Chief Edison that Thomas had likely gone off to find Mina. He told Miguel that while he had no idea where she might be, he was sure that she would die if Thomas found her. Maybe not immediately, the man warned, but eventually.

Miguel had the little information he'd dug up on Sarah and Ruth from a couple years ago when Mina was hospitalized, so he started there. The state police, who had sent a team of investigators to Red Ranch to investigate the murder, had already sent out a BOLO, so Miguel contacted both the Chicago police and the NYPD to tell them directly what happened and that it was very likely Thomas was on his way to either city. Neither department could do much more than be on the lookout, Miguel knew the information didn't warrant a protection detail, but he felt better having done something to protect Mina and her child.

Thomas drove each day until he felt his eyes grow heavy, and he stopped in the smallest town he was near every night. He assumed that the police would be looking for him by now, and he wouldn't risk showing his face in a city until he arrived in New York at Ruth's door. He'd taken interstate twenty to interstate thirty and would soon be on interstate forty, the route that took him through the fewest major metropolitan areas. He'd also swapped out the license plate on his Cadillac in the middle of the night at the first motel he stayed at and stopped shaving both his face and head and was pleased with how drastically different such a simple change made him look. Nothing would stop him from reaching Mina.

He finally arrived in New York City in the early afternoon of his fifth day on the road. He went to Ruth's door eager to surprise Mina—he bet she never expected he'd come looking for her, and she clearly didn't know him at all—and he waited with his fists clenched behind his back after he rang the buzzer for Ruth's unit. The voice on the intercom wasn't one he recognized.

"I'm sorry, Ruth moved a few weeks ago," the voice of a young woman said through the intercom, though he knew it wasn't Mina's.

"I'm sorry to disturb you, ma'am," Thomas said, playing up the Southern accent he knew made him sound polite and innocent, "I'm an old friend, come to tell her that her brother has passed away suddenly. I was hoping to break the news in person. Nobody should hear that over the phone, ya know?"

"Well, I have an address to send mail to. Would that help?" The naive woman asked.

"Oh, that would be just great, thank you, ma'am."

Thomas typed the address into his phone as the women recited it over the intercom, and he returned to his car, already planning his route to Chicago. At least New York to Chicago was a shorter drive, Thomas told himself, trying not to lose his temper at no one in particular. There would be plenty of time, and certainly good reason, to take his anger out on Mina when he finally got to her.

CHAPTER 19

Sarah exited the cab and stood at the closed and guarded gates of Radiance. Ruth's death had been utterly devastating. Both personally because Ruth was, for all intents and purposes, Sarah's mother, after all, and regarding her plan to force a little distance between herself and Sam and Mina. Sarah had brought Clarke, her friend and interpreter at the university, with her. She would have preferred Sam's company, but he needed to stay with Mina in Chicago, and Sarah didn't want to ruin the surprise she'd planned for her sister. Sarah gave Clarke the short version of everything she felt he needed to know about Sarah's family and the cult on the plane to Arizona. She was sure he had very many questions, considering that they'd worked together for the last ten years and she'd never admitted any of this to him, but he was kind enough to not ask them.

She peered through the wrought iron bars at the children outside playing. They played at the small park Sarah remembered enjoying during her childhood while the mothers all sat looking on from benches in the shade. Every single woman she could see was either bald-headed or had barely a swath of stubble covering their scalp. Three of the women sat with their heads wrapped in bandaging, looking like they'd just had brain surgery. For a moment, Sarah feared what had happened in Radiance after Mina's escape, and she wondered if she should turn around and go back home.

The man in the gatehouse, a cult member, of course, came out to greet them, "Can I help you? What's your business here?"

Clarke tapped Sarah's shoulder and signed for her the guard's greeting when he had her attention.

"I'm Sarah…uhh… Roth," she signed, stumbling over her last name. She'd changed hers to Mead, Ruth's married name, when she turned eighteen but realized the name Roth would more likely gain her entry into her old hell. "This is my interpreter, Clarke."

The man stared at her. She couldn't tell if he was confused about how one of the bald, shamed women had gotten out or if he thought he recognized her. It had been twenty-five years; she didn't imagine the latter was possible anymore. Whatever the man thought, it got him to open the gate, and Sarah started up the street toward her father's house. She stopped, though, and instead turned to go to the park. She took a seat on one of the sun-drenched benches, between two of the bald women.

"Hello," Sarah offered the women with a smile. She watched for one of them to say something in return, and neither did.

Sarah felt the eyes of every woman around on her, and she struggled to contain a chuckle as she felt them reeling, trying to figure out who she was, when they'd had to watch her public humiliation, and she could tell they just couldn't place her. She'd often wondered if anyone there would remember her or if they hated her for leaving and therefore forced the memory of Abraham's first daughter out of their minds. She sat on the bench until the sun began to burn her head, and as she walked away, she turned back and recognized one of the bald women to be Anna, the one girl that had befriended her when she was a child. Sarah didn't acknowledge her though, what would either of them possibly have to say now? *How you been? Hey, like your haircut!*

She continued up the path toward Abraham's house, Clarke following closely behind.

Radiance looked quite different than she remembered. There were a hundred more houses at least, all so close together, on various side streets branching off the main street that led directly to Abraham's house. The house Mina lived in was easy enough to spot. When Sarah lived in Radiance, "The Father's" mansion sat alone at the top of the hill, the closest neighboring house over two hundred yards away. Radiance was smaller then, and Sarah was astonished by how this terrible little community had managed to grow continually, and by so much. Now the house Abraham had built for Thomas stood next to his and was the only one that was nearly equal in size.

Sarah had come to Red Ranch for Reina. Ever a romantic, she had hopes of going to Reina, telling her all that had happened with Mina, telling her that Mina was still in love with her—which may or may not have been true—and bringing Reina back to Chicago so Mina could live her fairytale alongside her sister. Visiting Radiance hadn't been part of Sarah's plan, yet it felt unavoidable. She wanted to see her mother, if not to meet her and speak to her, then at least to know what she looked like now. Compare the woman she was to that which Sarah had built her up to be over the years.

Sarah stopped in her tracks, overwhelmed by an uneasy feeling which she couldn't place. She was inclined to ignore it, as she knew nothing about Radiance anymore, so the whole idea of it made her uneasy, but this feeling was one she couldn't shake. There was something wrong here. Was it wise of her to push her luck in a place that had allowed such evils to happen to her sister? No, she told herself, she should follow her instinct. Besides, what would she say to her father or anyone at this point? What would she do, give him a look of disappointment, and shake her head? Tell him his sister was dead and that finally, she was over the things he'd done to her? She doubted either would bother the man in the least. And what could she say to her mother that wouldn't make her hate her life even more than she imagined the woman already did? As for Thomas, she wasn't afraid of him, but recalling Mina's scars and how she'd gotten them, angering the bastard wasn't something she wanted to chance.

"Never mind," Sarah told Clarke. "Let's do what we came to do."

Mina had described Reina's house so perfectly that Sarah didn't even need to look for it. She knew exactly where it would be, and just as Mina told her, it had a door painted turquoise. Suddenly regretting her lack of planning, Sarah held her breath as she knocked on the door, hoping that Reina would be home, that she even still lived there.

The moment Reina opened the door, she knew who Sarah was. Even if Mina hadn't told her she had a sister, the resemblance was uncanny.

"Reina? I'm—" Sarah began.

"Mina's sister, I know," Reina looked at her and then offered a friendly but quick smile to Clarke, not needing an explanation that he was there only to interpret.

The two stood staring at each other for a moment, Reina marveling over just how strongly Sarah resembled Mina, before Reina finally said, "Tell me she's not dead. Tell me she's gotten the hell away from here, and she's happy, please."

"She's not dead. She got away from here. She and Noah live with me now. As for happy, well, that's why I'm here."

"Thank God. I've been sick worrying. I used to see her every day. I mean, she quit speaking to me years ago, but I saw her every day, at least. And now, with this shit about the old bastard being beaten to death...I just...thank God she's away from here and not dead too." Reina told Sarah, it escaping her that "the old bastard" was Sarah's father until the words had left her mouth.

Sarah didn't know what she was supposed to do or feel about Reina's admission. Part of her wanted to cheer that he'd finally gotten what he had coming, part of her wanted to instantly appear back home to keep Mina safe. She knew Thomas had gone looking for her and Noah. That was the only logical part of all of this. The evil—and apparently crazy—man wanted his wife back.

"Abraham is dead?"

"I'm sorry, I didn't mean—"

"No, it's just...It was Thomas, right?"

"He disappeared with Abraham's car a few days ago. Cops think it was him, and yeah, of course it was. Look at what he did to Mina. Look at what he did to all those women." Reina gestured toward all of Radiance.

"Yeah, I noticed the hair and the bandaged women. Thomas too?"

"Dude came unhinged after Mina and Noah disappeared. I heard he rounded up all the women, shaved their goddamn heads, and then set the hair on fire. Made my curtains reek. When that didn't do whatever it was supposed to, he branded some of them on top of their heads. It's the Scarlet Handmaid's Tale over there."

Sarah didn't bother trying to hold back her laughter, however inappropriate it was. She appreciated too much that Reina shared her dark sarcasm about the cult. Immediately, she could see why Mina had fallen for this woman. Just as Sam was for Sarah, Reina seemed to be Mina's perfect balance.

Once the awkward introduction was through, Reina invited Sarah and Clarke to join her at a cafe in Red Ranch so they could discuss why Sarah had come. Sarah explained that Mina had told her and Sam all about the two of them, and though she wasn't sure it was for her to tell, she told Reina why Mina stopped so much as acknowledging her. Sarah was thrilled to learn that not only did Reina understand and didn't blame Mina for disappearing the way she had, but that her love for Mina hadn't faded at all. After all this time, Reina told her that she still thought about her every day, still caught herself looking to the gate in hopes of catching a glimpse, a smile, from the woman she'd been in love with.

"Come back to Chicago with me," Sarah suddenly said.

"She doesn't want me anymore," Reina resisted even though she could have said yes without even giving it a thought. "I can't just up and go to Chicago on the hope that Mina will be happy to see me."

"I don't mean forever, just, for now. Come back with me and see what happens. Figure out the rest later. Mina still loves you. She needs you, Reina."

Reina had long wished to get the hell away from Red Ranch, away from being Radiance's neighbor, away from the desert. She hadn't left yet because of Mina. First, because the little time she could spend with her left her needing more, and after Mina disappeared, she stayed, hoping Mina would come back, not to Radiance, but to her door. Instead, Sarah had appeared at her door and wanted to give Reina everything she'd been hoping for. She couldn't refuse, she had to take the chance that finally, she and Mina could be together.

"Alright. I'll take a couple weeks of leave from the hospital and, I guess, see where things go from there," Reina couldn't hide her smile.

"How did you end up there? Living right behind that awful place?"

Sarah asked Reina aboard the plane that took them back to Chicago.

"That story," Reina began and shook her head still in disbelief so many years later, "should have won my Realtor an Oscar. That son of a bitch called it a 'gated community.'"

Sarah laughed, at the lie but more so at the wild things people will do and say to make a buck. "Well, technically..."

"He wasn't wrong. It *is* a gated community," Reina joined in Sarah's laughter, both feeling it inappropriate but also knowing so many things nobody else did, like they shared an inside joke about the insidious place.

"Gated community with a touch of religious extremism."

Sarah felt at ease with Reina, like she could finally breathe after months of suffocating under Mina's presence because this woman she'd known for all of four hours had agreed to her crazy plan. Sarah was all too aware that her sister had fallen for her fiancé—and who could blame her, considering how fast she had fallen for him herself —and she still was conflicted over the feeling that Mina was trying to become her instead of just being who she was, away from Thomas and Radiance. But Sarah was confident in her plan to bring Reina into the mix. Sarah and Sam agreed that Mina needed someone to cling to in order to feel safe and continue healing from her past, and they both agreed that it could not be either of them for much longer. Her plan wasn't entirely selfish, though. Mina's feelings for Reina were practically palpable all of the times she'd come up in conversation after Mina told them of her existence. If Sarah believed any two people were meant to be, it was these two.

CHAPTER 20

S arah lay dying in the entryway of their condo, bleeding and alone.

 Blood poured from her head but soon slowed to a gradual seeping as the pool surrounding her made its way down the hall and under the door. Soon, neighbors would be able to see it. Soon, what happened to Sarah in the safety of the condo building would be all anyone could speak of. The blood would remain, ruining both the hallway carpet and the flooring, as they would eventually sell the condo instead of having to be in the place where this happened to Sarah.

The day was meant to be a birthday Mina would cherish for the rest of her life. Her thirty-first and the first she'd celebrated free from Thomas and Radiance. Sarah returned with Reina from Red Ranch two days before and could barely contain the two surprises she and Sam had in store for Mina.

While Sam recovered from his surgeries, the barbershop was put up for sale. Sam told Sarah that he was fed up with working for other people and felt it was time for him to take a chance at building his own business and that he wanted to do it with Mina. And so, she and Sam leased the space and had spent the last several weeks having it renovated and turned into Sam's perfect vision of his own barbershop. Mina would finally have the chance to make something for herself, her own life.

Reina would be at the new shop to surprise her when Sarah and Sam took her there under the guise of celebrating her birthday with lunch at her favorite restaurant. Reina had the keys and waited at her hotel. She would be in the shop at one p.m. when Sarah and Sam arrived with Mina.

The pungent stench of fallen ginkgo berries filled the air with its sour odor, the sign that autumn was nearing its end, and the sky was a pure, bold blue. Sarah ran the twelve blocks home from the new shop, intent on enjoying what may be the last day of nice weather for months. Sam had taken Mina grocery shopping so Sarah could tend to some last-minute things before the big reveal, and Noah was at his preschool for the day. When Sarah rounded the corner on their block, she slowed her pace to a jog and smiled at a man who appeared to be sight-seeing, as so many tourists did in that part of the city full of old Victorian mansions and historic row houses. The man didn't smile back.

"Good morning," Sarah offered the rude man a quick greeting and wave and continued on her way home, annoyed by how rude some of the tourists could be. Asshole, Sarah thought, as she slowed her pace and climbed the front steps of the building. She checked the mail and jogged up four flights of stairs, and the moment she put the mail down on the table, the light for the door buzzer flashed. Sarah knew it was Sam and Mina with their arms full of bags, as Sam often rang the bell to be buzzed in, so he didn't need to put his load down. She buzzed them in and left the condo door ajar as she went about looking through the mail.

A sharp blow to the back of her head threw Sarah forward and as she collapsed to her knees. She knocked the framed photo of her and Sam to the floor as she clawed for something to catch herself. Another blow to the head and a kick in her side knocked her over. She managed to crawl a few feet away, scooting on her back as the room spun and her vision blurred, and just as she reached the corner of the hallway, she recognized the person attacking her as the man she'd just smiled at outside moments before. He was bald and thin, had pale skin with hatred in his eyes that she'd not noticed when she'd first seen him. He pushed the door closed behind him and stepped to Sarah and kicked her over and over, putting the full force of his body behind each kick. Sarah searched for something she could use to defend herself but found nothing. All she could do was lay in the corner and let whatever this man planned to do to her happen.

Sarah looked up just as the man raised a softball-sized rock over her head. He hit her over and over until everything around her faded to nothing. She struggled against the weight of her eyes closing as a realization came to her.

Thomas was killing her.

Thomas shook off his rage just as easily as it had come over him. Content that Mina was dead, he turned to the door and locked it, making sure no nosy neighbors came to see what the commotion had been. His irritation at the uneven floor made evident by the way the blood was running toward the door pricked at the accomplishment he felt for what he'd done. He picked the gray towel that hung from a nearby coat rack and put it on the floor in front of the door—something to keep the blood inside and give him a little time.

He stepped over Mina and began to make his way into the condo, curious to see how she had been living, what new things she had collected in the months away from him, but he paused. Something was not quite right about Mina when he looked at her, and he couldn't quite place what. What was it? Had he never noticed her body before? Were her breasts always so large? Had he shaved her hair before she left him, and it remained a permanent reminder of him? He felt anger rising again at his inability to recall these simple details, and he forced it out of his mind with a frustrated huff of breath and made his way into the condo. He stopped in a nearby bathroom and washed his hands, mesmerized by all the blood-stained soap foam flowing down the drain. He then made his way down into a bedroom where he found an opened closet full of men's clothing that looked as though it had been put there just for him. Everything was his exact size when he looked through it, even the shoes—an invitation to get away with his crime more easily. Thomas changed into a clean button-up shirt and a pair of jeans, leaving his blood-stained clothing in a pile in the closet.

He turned to leave the room and immediately realized his mistake. Hanging next to the door was a picture of a man no bigger than him with his arms around the shoulders of a woman. The woman he had just killed. A woman who was not Mina but her sister. It never would have occurred to him that sisters nearly ten years apart in age could be so strikingly similar. His mind suddenly clouded by a million thoughts and the shame of his tremendous mistake, Thomas ran back to the door he'd come in, leaping over the pool of blood that was growing larger still and out the door. How can a man not recognize a woman that belonged to him, Thomas wondered as he frantically made his way back to his car at the end of the block. He climbed into the back seat and opened the cat carrier and held one of them in each arm as though they could absolve him of the stupid error he'd made. Thomas's eyes burned, but he refused to allow himself any tears. He was not a weak man, and it was not his fault that Mina so strongly resembled her sister. He reminded himself of the disgrace Sarah had brought upon Radiance when she left, the secrecy she'd caused Abraham, and he told himself that while she was not who he had come here for, she was no less deserving of what he'd done than Mina. She had taken Mina from him after all.

Calmer now, Thomas put his cats back in their carrier and resolved to return for Mina and Noah. He would decide whether she would live or die when he saw her. Perhaps she wouldn't need to. Perhaps knowing what he had so easily done to her sister would be all the cause she needed to return home with him. He would return, maybe that evening, maybe tomorrow, and he would have his family again. As he drove the car away, he felt strangely comforted that he had not killed Mina after all.

Grocery shopping with Sam had become one of Mina's favorite things to do. Any time she was able to spend time alone with him left her feeling refreshed and gave her renewed confidence and a sense of safety, but in the grocery store, Mina took the lead in deciding what meals would be made that week, a novel thing for her, her family being happy with whatever she chose to make for them. Sam found dumb ways to make Mina laugh, like when he played shopping cart basketball and just tossed in any odd thing he saw. They'd made a game of it. Whatever Sam did manage to land in the shopping cart, Mina had to include in that night's dinner. This trip resulted in Mina having to make dinner with one carrot, a six-pack of now very bruised kiwis, tofu, a packet of mixed nuts, and one mandarin orange.

An awkward silence filled their ride home from the store, with Sam trying not to spoil the birthday secret and Mina wondering what he was hiding. Sam would look over at Mina, and when she caught him, he just smiled and shifted his grip on the steering wheel. He and Sarah had been finalizing their wedding plans, which was to take place in a month, so Mina assumed he was preoccupied with that.

"Nervous about the wedding?" Mina finally asked, unable to continue to endure the odd looks he shot her.

"Yeah. No. I dunno," Sam told her and laughed at his own indecision. "I'm not nervous about the getting married part. Been ready to do that since our second date. It's the rest. I don't know what to do with myself when I'm supposed to be fancy."

"Fancy?"

"Yeah, the whole formal part of the show. Gotta put on a suit and dance and use the right goddamn fork for the salad course. I don't know about any of that stuff."

"Well, let Sarah see you call it a show, and you won't have to worry about any of it because she'll kill you."

They both laughed because Sam knew Mina was right. Both believed no one had ever been more excited about a wedding than Sarah was, and Sam was dreading every part Sarah had been looking forward to since she was a little girl. He was not interested in the spectacle in the least while Sarah reveled in it.

"Oh, I know. That's why I'm just doing what I'm told. Sarah lives her dream for a few hours, and all I need to do is not fuck it up. Then happily ever after, right?"

"Exactly. And I assume someone will tell me which of you I'm the maid of honor for one of these days," Mina said. Both Sarah and Sam had asked her, and she'd said yes to both because being wanted for something of such significance by two people was overwhelming.

They pulled into the garage at the back of the condo building, and Sam unloaded all the groceries, three canvas bags hanging from each arm, and Mina followed him into the building and then the elevator. Sam was always grateful for the 1970's law that all condos over a specific size had to have two access doors on grocery day. Their second door opened into the kitchen, so he didn't have to walk through three other rooms to put down the bags. He put down the bags and reached around the corner to flicker the lights in the hall, as he always did to tell Sarah that they'd returned home. Sarah didn't respond, which was not entirely out of the ordinary, but something gave Sam pause, and he held his hand up to stop Mina, motioned for her to wait in the kitchen as he cautiously made his way out of the kitchen and around the corner. Mina did as he said.

Sam moved slowly through the condo, his hand automatically reaching for his messenger bag, which held his gun, but he wasn't wearing it. He'd put it down in the kitchen with the groceries, and he was suddenly thinking of the gun safe they'd bought prior to Mina's arrival, grateful his other guns remained locked away. He looked into each room of the condo, inside the bedrooms and bathrooms. Something was wrong. His heart and the tingling goosebumps on his arms told him as much. What though, he didn't know. His search completed, Sam was back in the living room, still unsettled. Only one area of the condo remained, so Sam walked toward the entryway, not expecting to find anything.

Mina heard Sam's keys drop to the wood floor, and he shouted for her. The urgency in Sam's voice made Mina want to run, but soon she smelled a tinny odor with which she was all too familiar, and it slowed her steps. She smelled blood, as she'd smelled her own a thousand times before. She smelled Thomas as well, and she fought her mind to stay in the present.

Mina found Sam on his knees in the entryway, his hands coated in blood, a pool of it surrounding a lifeless body. Mina didn't recognize the body as her sister until she looked at its feet and saw Sarah's ugly barefoot running shoes with individual spaces for each toe. Sam touched Sarah all over, frantically, and unsure what to do next, so he tried doing everything all at once. Mina's mind was quickly retreating into survival mode, and as she mindlessly backed away from the blood covering the entryway, all she could say was "Oh my God," over and over.

"Mina, call 911!" Sam screamed at her.

The ambulance and police took just minutes to arrive, but it felt like hours as Sam waited, kneeling in the blood of his soon-to-be-wife. The paramedics worked quickly, and the police searched the rest of the condo. Soon Sarah was loaded into the back of the ambulance on a stretcher, and the paramedics closed the doors in Sam's face. He shook himself out of his terrified haze and took off at a sprint to the hospital, which was only two blocks away. Mina followed behind, with clarity and fear. Sam may not have pieced together what had happened, but she had. Mina knew from the brutality of it, the path of destruction that lined the entryway, that Thomas had done this. He'd come for her and found Sarah instead.

The hospital staff wouldn't give any information to Sam. They kept insisting that they could only share details with family, which Sam responded to by pounding his fist against the counter and shouting, "I'm her husband! We're getting married in a month, fucking talk to me!"

If Sam didn't count as Sarah's family, Mina couldn't imagine who would, but it occurred to her, slowly, as all her thoughts seemed to be happening now, that she was her family, maybe they would talk to her. And so, Mina told the woman at the reception desk that she was Sarah's sister and wanted all information shared with Sam. And just like that, the woman agreed. Mina couldn't believe it had been that easy.

Mina and Sam waited for hours as Sarah was operated on, and as they sat in the uncomfortable maroon chairs, police officers came to speak to them, asking if they knew what happened, if they knew who could have done this. Sam, sounding barely conscious, answered every question with "no."

Finally, Mina gathered the nerve to tell them what she was sure of.

"It was my husband," she said, not daring to look the officers or Sam in the eye. "He came for me and my son."

The officers looked at Mina as though she was crazy before they asked for more information. Mina told them everything they wanted to know, and when they were satisfied that what she'd said seemed plausible, they said they would be in touch and prepared to leave.

"Wait. We have a camera in that hallway," Sam spoke softly and wiped his eyes with his bloody hands. "It's set to record for sixty seconds every time the front door opens. It'll be recorded in the app."

Sam took out his phone, unlocked it, opened the camera app, and handed his phone to the police. Mina watched the officers' faces change as they watched the attack happen on the small screen, taking turns wincing every few seconds. When the video stopped, an officer dragged his finger over the screen to rewind the video. He showed the phone to Mina, an image of the attacker entering the condo on the screen. "Is this your husband?" He asked. She said yes, and the officers handed Sam a pen and small pad of paper. "We'll need the password to your account to access the video again."

Sam nodded and scribbled down the username and password before returning to holding his head in his hands. When Mina looked at him, she saw two bloody handprints on the back of his neck. He had a habit of lacing his fingers together and hanging his hands behind his neck when he was stressed, and now his skin bore bloody prints in that shape.

"I'll be right back," Mina told Sam when the officers had left. She needed to do something for him, so she got up, pulled her spare headscarf from her purse, and went to the restroom. She wadded it into a ball and ran it under the slow-streaming faucet, and then rang out the excess water. When she returned to Sam, she took his hands in hers and slowly wiped the blood from them. His hands trembled as she held them. She bent his head forward to reach the back of his neck, and as she did, Sam's head fell onto her shoulder, and he cried. She'd seen Sam with tears in his eyes a few times before, usually on the occasions he saw her reacting in fear to something he'd done, but she had never seen him cry like this. These were tears of terror and love and loneliness. These tears left his body with the force of floodwaters, and Mina had to steady herself to keep her balance as Sam sobbed into her shoulder.

Sam and Mina waited as new people, frightened and crying people, came in after them and left before them, and each time someone new left, a little more hope that Sarah would survive left with them. Several times, Mina got up to pace the gray tiles that covered the waiting room floor, trying her best to avoid eye contact with the other waiting people. Mina felt bad for feeling as she did, but she wanted whatever was going to happen with whoever they waited for to hurry up and happen, so she and Sam might have the room to themselves. As she paced, she called Mrs. Kostas and asked if she could get Noah from preschool and watch him. The woman already knew what had happened. News travels fast when you live in such close quarters.

There was a clock that hung on the far wall, a large and simple one with black numbers, and after ten hours of listening to it tick, Mina took it off the wall and took out its batteries when no one was looking. Her act of rebellion against the hospital for keeping them waiting for so long.

Seventeen hours after Sarah was brought into the emergency room, the surgeon finally appeared to update them. She told them that it was not likely that Sarah would ever regain consciousness and that they should call whoever they would like to be able to say goodbye to her. She told them the bleeding in her brain had been severe and her skull had been fractured in numerous places and that on the off chance she did wake up, she would have significant deficits and would not be the same person she once was. The doctor explained that brain swelling leads to brain death and that Sarah suffered substantial swelling. She informed them that the decision of whether or not Sarah should be kept alive by machines would have to be made.

Mina was furious that it was to her that the doctor explained these things to and not Sam. How could they not understand that yes, she was Sarah's sister, but Sam was Sarah's life, her partner? How could they see this man who was the protector of their small family and just ignore his presence like he didn't even exist? Mina knew she could never make the decision the doctor had put on her. It was not her place, and certainly not something she was willing to consider.

The doctor told them they would be able to see Sarah in an hour or so, and she walked back through the doors she'd just come out of.

"The doctor, she's wrong," Mina told Sam, who looked up at her like she was crazy. "I'm supposed to be dead too, you know. I was supposed to die from the things Thomas did to me that day."

Sam looked at Mina, quite puzzled as to what Mina was getting at.

"I know you don't believe," she continued, "but God isn't finished with her yet. You think it's stupid, I know, but I believe God let me live after what Thomas did so that we could come here and have a life with you and Sarah. And that life, it's barely even started yet, so she can't die. The plan isn't finished yet. She won't die from this."

That admission was the first time Mina had ever had the nerve to share that much of her renewed faith with Sam. Mina didn't understand how Sam could be an atheist, but she respected his beliefs just as he respected hers, and Mina worried she might offend him or damage the wonderful friendship they'd built if Mina forced the issue of God. Mina prepared for Sam to walk away from her, or ask her to leave, or, at the very least, roll his eyes at her insistence. He didn't do any of those things, though. Instead, he put his hand over hers on the wooden armrest and offered her the sincerest smile he could muster as they sat and waited to be called back to see Sarah.

CHAPTER 21

M ina left the hospital alone. Sam wouldn't leave Sarah's side, and she couldn't stand to be near the horror she had caused, so she was returning home to put together a bag for him, so he could stay with Sarah. Mina couldn't allow herself to think about Sarah lying there in the hospital dying because of her. If she had never come, this never would have happened. Sarah wasn't supposed to be dead; she was. She was afraid to enter the condo, assuming Thomas would probably be there waiting for her—Mina knew he wouldn't leave without her and Noah. So, to make sure Noah stayed away from him and remained safe, Mina called the neighbor she'd asked to pick Noah up from preschool while they waited for Sarah to come out of surgery and told her what happened. Noah would be staying in the safety of Mrs. Kostas' home, somewhere Thomas would never learn about.

As Mina walked down the block toward the condo building, she saw a dark silhouette sitting on the front steps, barely illuminated by the streetlight. She accepted that now it was her turn to die. Thomas found her, and she knew better than to hope anyone would save her from him. Mina held her breath, prayed for a quick and painless death as she approached the person sitting on the steps. She forgot to keep breathing when she discovered that the person waiting for her was not Thomas, but Reina.

Mina rushed to her without saying a word and ran into her arms with a force that nearly knocked Reina off her feet. Reina should have felt like a stranger after all this time, Mina thought, but in the safe familiarity of her arms, Mina let out the last day's worth of tears. Tears she'd denied herself so she could let Sam cry.

"Mina, what's wrong? Where have you all been? I've been waiting, and nobody ever showed up. What happened?"

"He's here, Reina. Thomas found me. He hurt Sarah. She's going to die. Because of me," Mina explained through her sobs on Reina's shoulder.

Reina had no words she could offer Mina, the shocking contrast between what she'd imagined and what had actually caused them to forget all about her stole from her anything she could have said. Reina thought the whole plan had turned into some cruel joke and had finally come to the condo to confront the three of them for setting her up as they clearly had. She'd never imagined Thomas would be able to find Sarah. Even Mina hadn't known where her sister lived before she left Radiance, how could Thomas have found them? Reina held onto Mina tightly, and eventually, the two made their way inside. The police had finished with their very brief investigation at the condo, and the pool of blood, now with various bits of trash from the paramedics working on Sarah littered throughout it, was still not dry.

Reina searched the kitchen cupboards for tea. When she found it, she couldn't help but smile that Mina had clearly made herself a home here with an entire cupboard devoted to her tea collection. Reina always kept one of hers stocked to the brim with tea for Mina, even after she'd quit speaking to her. She found the variety she was looking for—mint oolong, Mina's favorite—and she put away the groceries, those still salvageable after having been left on the floor for a whole day, as Mina sat sipping from the steaming cup.

Finally, Mina spoke. "What are you doing here? How did you find me?"

"I guess there's no harm in telling you now," Reina hesitated. "Sarah and Sam bought a barbershop. They've been having it remodeled into a salon you and Sam could run. They were going to surprise you with it for your birthday. And I was supposed to be there sitting in the chair at your new styling station when they brought you there."

"You came just for me? You don't hate me?"

"I don't hate you. I could never hate you, Mina. Sarah told me everything. She came to Red Ranch to find me. And I can't blame you. I should have known better. Mina, I'm so sorry that happened to you. If I'd known, I never would have—"

"I'm sorry I left without telling you."

The two waited in silence. There was nothing left to say, not with Sarah barely alive in the hospital.

Finally, after Mina finished her tea, Reina spoke again. "You shouldn't sleep here, not until the police find Thomas anyway. Let me take you to my hotel. It'll be safe there. Thomas doesn't know I'm here."

"I can't be with you, Reina."

"Mina, I just want you to get some sleep, be somewhere safe. I'm not even thinking about us. We can worry about us later after all this is passed and Sarah's back home, okay?"

Mina wanted to disagree with Reina. How would Sarah ever come back home? She was as good as dead. The doctor said they might as well just kill her now because there's no hope. Mina believed what she told Sam, that Sarah wasn't done on this earth yet, but she still had her moments of questioning whether God really cared about people even a little bit. But Reina said those words so easily like they were a matter of fact. *And Sarah's back home.* Reina didn't know how bad it was. She hadn't seen Sarah's body. She'd never had to endure Thomas. But just as Mina told Sam that Sarah would survive this, she needed someone to tell her. Say the words so she could believe it was true, drown out the guilt telling her otherwise.

Mina let Reina take her to the hotel. They walked slowly, all Mina could manage, and all the way there, Mina's thoughts tore between thinking of Sam, Sarah, and how all of this was her fault, and Thomas, the fear of what he'd do when he found her. And he would find her, she was sure. Everything good and warm and welcoming that she'd allowed in since arriving in Chicago was tearing apart. Her family, torn. Her sense of safety, torn. Her home, torn by the pool of Sarah's blood.

Once in the security of Reina's hotel room, Mina stood and waited to be told what to do next. Part of her wanted to just go and offer herself up to Thomas now. It would be easier that way, instead of waiting and wondering when he'd appear again. Reina slid her hand beneath Mina's headscarf and held it to Mina's cheek.

"You converted," Reina said with a soft smile. "Islam. Huh. That's actually...perfect for you."

Mina didn't respond, instead choosing to study Reina. It had been nearly three years now since she'd allowed herself to look at Reina, though for two of those years, they had remained neighbors. She'd changed, but not so much Mina thought it new or unsafe. Reina had always let Mina do her hair. She'd been the only woman Mina could use more than a blow dryer or curling iron on. Reina let her do anything she wished, so Mina had always let her imagination run wild, and Reina ended up with progressively shorter styles over the years because Mina craved the power that came with changing someone, molding them into something else. Now Reina's thick black hair looked like she'd not allowed anyone else to touch it since Mina had for the last time. It felt as though Reina had been waiting for her, and Mina studied this face she'd not realized she was starving for. Her bronze skin, the small chicken pox scar on her cheekbone, and dark lashes lining her eyes, leaving her in permanent natural eyeliner.

As Mina studied Reina and let her face that felt like home—a different home—fill her mind, she again felt the nagging sense that she was doing something wrong. Though this time, she didn't also fear being caught. She simply felt wrong. Before, each time she was with Reina, Mina knew she was tempting fate taking such a risk when Thomas could easily find out, but she longed to be touched by someone who loved her. Now though, all she could think about was Sam and wanting to touch and be touched by him. She wanted to lie next to him, form her body to his, and be broken with him, beside him. She knew this desire was wrong as well but for entirely different reasons.

In both instances, though, Mina allowed herself to be with Reina because she needed love, and Reina offered it. Reina kissed her, and she half-heartedly kissed her back, all the while thinking of Sam and then scolding herself. Reina felt Mina's distance but chalked it up to everything that had happened in the last thirty-odd hours. When Reina was done kissing Mina, she asked if she could use the shower. She wanted to steam her cheating thoughts of Sam out of her body because she hated herself for realizing how she felt about him only after he might lose the woman he loved, which wasn't her. Mina wondered what, specifically, was wrong with her for always being drawn to people she couldn't have. First Reina when she belonged to Thomas, and now Sam when he belonged to Sarah.

Mina stayed in the shower until her fingers and toes pruned, and once in bed, she lay close to the edge, with her back to Reina. Reina didn't try to touch her again, and the two fell asleep beside each other though they might as well have been worlds apart.

Thomas spent hours driving aimlessly, his mind wrestling with what he should do—return now for Mina and Noah or wait until they no longer expected him. It wasn't until the sun had set that Thomas realized how hungry he was. He hadn't eaten all day. He decided he would stop at the McDonald's that caught his attention when he'd entered Chicago. The one that sat oddly in the middle of the tollway.

Thomas ordered Chicken McNuggets with BBQ sauce, fries, and an orange Hi-C. His favorite meal from his childhood, which incidentally, was the last time he'd been to McDonald's. As he waited for his meal, he noticed that he'd not cleaned his hands thoroughly enough. Some of Sarah's blood was still under his fingernails. Killing hadn't been his intention any more than it had been when he killed Abraham, but he was going where God led him, doing what God guided him to do and, in the moment, both deserved God's wrath. His wrath. That was the story he would tell should the police ever catch up with him and one he was coming to believe himself. Something had to be guiding him, for these things he'd done simply weren't things he was capable of.

Thomas sat down in a booth along the wall and smiled as he bit off the tips of the little boot-shaped nuggets. With each bite, he had the crystal-clear image of each woman he had forced to submit in Radiance. Each of them a vessel for the rage he couldn't contain. Rage, Thomas believed, Mina would finally feel herself when she returned to the condo and found her sister's body. With his meal clearing his head, Thomas decided he would wait a few days for the search for him to die down, and he would find Mina and his son, and they would return to Radiance where he would take the throne. The keys to Abraham's mansion. He would return to his people and begin leading them in the way they should have been all this time. The stupid old man and his leniency. Had he not understood that it was because of him that Mina had been willful enough to run away? Did he not know that all of this was his fault, and all of this could have been avoided had he only known when to step down?

He ate his French fries and wondered if Oscar and Jed would like fries. He'd never given them anything more than their kibble before, though he recalled Mina often slipped each of them bites of whatever she had made for dinner. He was mildly irritated that he couldn't remember if Mina had ever shared potatoes with them. Was he forgetting her so quickly? He shook his cup of Hi-C to separate the last sip from the ice and wrapped two fries in a napkin, and walked out of the restaurant, leaving his trash behind on the table.

He was mere feet from the Cadillac when he saw the flashing lights. Half a dozen of them at least. The police cruisers screeched to a stop, and the officers jumped from their cars, guns all trained on him, and they slowly came toward him.

"Thomas Roth?" One of the officers shouted.

Thomas said nothing. He dropped the napkin that held the fries he'd saved for Jed and Oscar and held his arms out as though he was about to be crucified. One officer put his gun back in its belt holster while the other two kept theirs aimed. The officer said things to Thomas as he secured his hands behind his back, but Thomas didn't hear a thing.

"My cats are in the back of my car. Tend to them, will you?"

Without another word, Thomas was frisked and put into the back of the police cruiser.

Mina jolted awake at the vibration of her phone beneath her pillow.

"Hello?" She mumbled into her phone.

"Ms. Roth? Good morning, this is Sergeant Tim Raines from the Chicago police."

Until that moment, Mina had forgotten all that had happened in the last forty-odd hours, and instantly, every detail rushed back to her making her head pound and heartache. She remembered Sarah's lifeless and pale body lying in stark contrast to the blood surrounding her. She remembered being at the hospital and waiting with Sam while her sister was having surgery that might save her life. She remembered Sam, and she reached over to the presence she felt beside her in bed and was again taken aback when her hand found Reina's soft shoulder instead of Sam lying beside her.

"Ms. Roth?" The voice on the phone repeated.

"Yes? I'm sorry, yes?"

"Ma'am, I wanted to let you know that your husband, Thomas Roth, he's been arrested. He was taken into custody late last night. You're safe, ma'am."

"Oh," Mina replied, unsure of how exactly she was supposed to respond to this news.

"And ma'am, there's another matter. Your husband had a carrier of cats in the back of his car at the time of his arrest," Sergeant Raines explained. "He stated they were yours, and we have them here at the precinct if you'd like to come collect them. Otherwise, we can take them to animal control today."

Oscar and Jed, Mina wondered, *he didn't kill them?*

"No, I'll come get them, sergeant, thank you."

Mina tapped the screen of her phone to end the call and dropped it back to the bed.

"Will you come with me to get my cats?" Mina asked Reina without looking back at her.

She couldn't look at Reina because she couldn't remember the night they'd obviously spent together or what had happened between them. Though she'd never had so much as a sip of alcohol in her life, Mina imagined this was what being hungover was like. A dull pounding filled her head, her eyelids felt heavy, and her body ached, and she couldn't recall what, if anything, she'd done with Reina.

"Oscar and Jed?" Reina asked, sounding shocked. "He didn't...you know...kill them?"

"No," Mina responded, equally dumbfounded.

Mina felt Reina's hand in her hair, and it took all her effort to not pull away from her touch. All the things she'd felt for Reina before, she felt again, but she also felt them for Sam, and she didn't know what to do with that. She certainly couldn't tell Reina that she loved her and was so happy she'd come all the way from Arizona for her but that she wasn't interested in only her, so thanks but no thanks. So, she did what she had for the last fifteen years of her life and lay still to let whatever was going to happen happen. Before everything had been torn apart by Thomas, Mina had been working on asserting herself, stating and claiming what she wanted instead of agreeing with what seemed like the safest option. Her therapist was pleased with the progress she was making, and now what? Now she was lying in bed half-naked, allowing herself to be touched by a woman she didn't want to touch her because she wanted to be touching someone else whom she couldn't touch. Nothing and everything had changed.

"I like your hair short. Looks good on you," Reina told her, and Mina could almost feel Reina's smile radiating through her fingertips. "Why the change?"

Mina felt offended by the question and couldn't understand why. It was an innocent question and certainly a valid one. The last time Reina had seen Mina, she wore her hair to her waist, and now it was a shaggy pixie style. Such a drastic change warranted questions; Mina just didn't want to answer them. She didn't want to be questioned. She didn't want to have to defend herself or her decisions anymore. Sam never asked her to justify herself. So instead of answering Reina's question, Mina took her hand and held it as she lay back on the bed, hoping that holding it would keep Reina's hand from wandering places Mina didn't want it to go.

Finally, Mina stood from the bed, and Reina followed her. They walked down the neighborhood's main thoroughfare, its bustling noise a welcome break in their silence. Reina didn't know what to say to Mina, and Mina had nothing to say to Reina that wouldn't hurt her. Reina continued to follow Mina, and she was surprised when they arrived in front of the hospital instead of the police station, but Reina didn't question it.

Reina continued following Mina through the maze of hallways to Sarah's room, and the moment Mina was by Sam's side, Reina knew. Now was not the time for her and Mina to be together either. For such a long time, Mina had been the one needing to be taken care of, and when she was with Sam, Reina saw Mina finally being the one to do the caring for someone else. Reina couldn't imagine the loss Sam was suffering. She'd lost Mina, twice, but never like this. They'd started their relationship with Reina knowing she couldn't protect Mina from Thomas, and when Mina had vanished, Reina made herself believe that she had run away, and it turned out she'd been right. She imagined the feeling of failing to keep safe the woman you were supposed to marry when you believed that was your job was crushing, and Mina eased that, lifted some of the burden for him.

Reina exited Sarah's room, the hospital, and then Chicago as quietly as she had come. She resolved that she would continue to wait for Mina because no matter how much it hurt to leave her again, she had somehow always believed that eventually, they would be together when the time was right.

CHAPTER 22

S am didn't mean to love Mina. No one sets out to love someone. That's not how it works. It always seemed to simply happen and take people pleasantly by surprise when it did. And Sam didn't mean for it to happen with Mina. It had been coming, he guessed, slowly growing alongside Mina as she grew into the woman she was becoming, but still, he wasn't ready for it when it came, but at the same time, he needed to love her because it didn't hurt. He wondered if it was reasonable to love two people at once—if it was love, if that was possible. Could he let himself continue to love Sarah as he had for so long, with all of himself, in ways he couldn't even fathom when he was sure the love he had for her now would surely kill him?

Sam lost hope three days after Sarah's attack. She'd been rushed back into surgery to deal with yet more swelling on her brain, and the last bit of hope Sam could muster fizzled when, hours after she was brought out of surgery, Sarah remained unconscious. Hope and optimism had never been things Sam was good at, for he'd learned years ago that having hope for a situation to go your way was the best way to set yourself up for disappointment. So, when Sarah's doctor told him there was very little hope for Sarah, of course he believed her. He sat at her bedside, devoutly, waiting as machines puffed and beeped life into her.

After ten more days of waiting and five more surgeries—none of which yielded results—he understood that even if Sarah ever did wake up, she wouldn't be the same, they wouldn't be the same, and he left the hospital at morning shift change before the kind nurse could tell him he should go home and eat.

He opened the door to their condo and sank to his knees just feet from the entryway, where he and Mina had found Sarah's body. He saw the remnants of her blood still filling the tiny crevices of the wood flooring, and he curled up on the floor on his side and mindlessly scraped at the blood with his fingernail. He fell asleep there, hoping that perhaps if the God Sarah and Mina believed in was real after all, maybe God blamed him for this too and would decide it best to kill Sam right there where he let Sarah suffer alone. Sam lay with his index finger still resting on the blood and didn't wake until that evening when Mina came home with dinner for one. She'd not planned on Sam being home, and Noah was with the neighbor.

Mina put her food down on the mail table and forgot about how hungry she was. She lay down on the floor opposite Sam and reached her hands out for his. He let her take them, and she studied the puddles of tears and snot on the floor beneath his face. After a few moments, Mina stood and pulled Sam off the floor. He didn't know where she was leading him to, though he didn't much care. In his bedroom, Mina pulled his shirt over his head, struggling against the weight of his arms, which he would not lift, as though he were a huge, petulant child. She pulled back the covers of the bed she'd made for him days before, and he dutifully crawled in without a thought in his head. Mina climbed into bed, still wearing her shoes, and pulled Sam near her.

For the first time in thirteen days, Sam allowed himself more than a brief nap, and he fell asleep with his head resting on Mina's shoulder, his arm draped over her stomach, and he slept, long and deeply.

The two woke the next morning to Mrs. Kostas, the elderly neighbor caring for their place and for Noah while they sat vigil for Sarah. Mrs. Kostas was vacuuming the area rug in the living room, and Sam knew it was guilt causing his suspicion, but it seemed like the old woman was only doing it with the intent of getting him and Mina up and out of bed, away from each other. The thought that he'd been unfaithful to Sarah weighed on him, but Mina was who he needed at that time. Sarah reminded him of what he'd let happen to the one person he was supposed to protect. Mina reminded him of what a person could become when given the love and protection they all desperately needed. The difference was winter and summer, unrelenting sadness and a sliver of hope and forgiveness. Soon, every interaction he had with Mina felt like it was cheating on Sarah.

While Mina performed wudu and prayed, Sam went to the living room where he heard Noah playing. The boy ran to him, holding his favorite toys—a dinosaur and a Barbie dressed as a veterinarian.

"Bapa Sam!" Noah joyfully squealed, and this brought a smile to Sam's face. They were Mama, Mama Sarah, and Bapa Sam to him. "Where Mama Sarah?"

"She's sick, little man," Sam told him, doing his best to not start crying. "We'll take you to see her soon, okay?"

The happy child nodded and returned to his toys.

Sam knew he was a despicable person when, on the fifteenth day of Sarah being unconscious in the hospital, he watched Mina unravel her headscarf after they'd returned home from the hospital that evening, and they exchanged the look Sam had once reserved only for Sarah. He kissed her, and she let him. Independent of his mind and morals, Sam's hands found their way under her shirt and slowly lifted it. She'd once been so cautious in hiding her scars, keeping her body from being visible, but now, the moment Sam tossed her shirt aside, she pulled his over his head and allowed him to lead her to her bed.

Sam wished he could say it had just been sex. Just two broken people fucking for the sake of clearing their heads, for relief, release, but he knew better than that. He and Sarah hadn't touched each other in months, save for a kiss here and a hug there, the obligatory things that become automatic in a relationship. They'd let their relationship take a back seat to caring for their family. Mina had become precisely what Sarah feared she would—a wedge between them. It seemed to have happened both slowly and instantly, though not in the specific way Sarah feared it would. They never argued about Mina or her presence in their lives but helping her heal and caring for her had become an all-consuming, albeit wonderful and fulfilling, task. Sure, there had been times both Sarah and Sam had resented Mina's presence, such as on those nights she slept in their bed between the two of them seeking safety. It was simple. Sarah and Sam had grown apart, and Sam and Mina had grown together, just as Mina and Sarah had. And now? Now the woman to whom Sam once turned to mend him when he was afraid or angry had become the constant source of his deepest fear, and Mina was there to be the antidote. Sam knew he would never be able to turn Sarah's machines off, but he understood that he would have to let go if he was to survive.

Sam and Mina woke unsurprised that they were naked and holding each other. Sam thought about how making love to Mina the first few times had been so different than it had been with Sarah. Where Sarah had been uncomfortable with the notion of being with a trans man and sex took some getting used to, Mina welcomed Sam's masculine body that lacked the one thing she still despised and needed no guidance in pleasuring Sam. Sam was appalled by what he'd done, what he knew he'd do again, but it was exactly what he needed and more than that, it felt good when everything else felt as though it was killing him.

Sam had been going to the hospital each day Sarah remained unconscious, and each day he waited became more painful. It had been just over two weeks since Sarah's attack, and the thought that he was ready to give up so soon sickened him. She was beginning to become recognizable again as the swelling and bruises that covered her face faded, and each day Sam saw more of Sarah in the body that lay beeping in the bed, the less he could stand to look at himself. Sarah had three long fault lines spanning her head held together with staples, and for each one of them, Sam could name a reason this was all his fault. It was because of this that Sam felt somewhat justified in sleeping with Mina. Emotion forced him to spend his days in anguish, sitting at Sarah's bedside, so in the evening, he let logic dictate his actions, and he went home and got into bed with Mina. A salve for his wounds that were reopened daily.

Sam took his time in the steamy bathroom after Mina had finished showering. He wiped the fog off the mirror and noticed how unkempt he looked for the first time in two weeks. He'd always been so vain about keeping his hair and beard neat, and now he had weeks of grown-out stubble, and his beard had grown down his neck. Sarah had always liked his beard, so he'd kept it for her, and he was flooded with emotion as he rubbed shave oil onto his face and head and rid himself of it all, trying to get the vision of Sarah telling him he looked sexy out of his mind. Clean-shaven, he looked again at his reflection and chuckled at the memory of Sarah insisting she had balls that he didn't because even after he'd cut his hair the day she decided to shave hers, he never could find the nerve to follow her lead, despite hating his ever-growing bald spot. She was right, he thought, and I still don't. And then, as it happened every time he allowed himself a memory of Sarah, the sadness of what he'd let happen to her overwhelmed him, and he hunched over onto the bathroom sink and sobbed into the hand towel to muffle the sound.

Sam wandered into the kitchen after he'd finished crying and had used eye drops to soothe the redness, following the scent of breakfast cooking, to see if Mina needed help with anything.

"I made breakfast," Mina announced with a smile. "No beard? Don't think I've ever seen you without it, have I?"

Sam shook his head. "I'm not hungry," he said.

This was true. He didn't feel hunger anymore. He felt sad, angry, hopeless, and now lustful for Mina, but never felt hungry anymore.

"Eat, Sam," Mina instructed him, pushing a glass of orange juice into his chest, and holding eye contact. "You need food."

Mina had stopped signing when she spoke, which Sam both hated and was grateful for, and the forceful tone of her voice took him by surprise. She'd never given him an order before, but over the last two weeks, she seemed to have come into her own, and he wondered if that was because she understood that she had to take charge of life because Sam no longer could. He missed the easy flow of Sarah's hands when she signed to him, he missed coming home from work and not having to use his voice, he missed being able to contain a full exchange in one glance and facial expression. Sometimes he caught himself responding to Mina speaking to him with his hands, but he did so less and less as time passed. It was enough that he'd allowed Mina to essentially replace the woman he was supposed to marry. She lived in her condo, slept in her bed, used her kitchen towels, so yes, he was grateful she'd not adopted her language too. Sam wondered if he'd ever be able to get over this guilt. If he'd ever be able to say goodbye to Sarah and love Mina without the looming fear that she was simply an easy replacement. He thought it was as likely as Sarah miraculously waking up.

CHAPTER 23

C olors didn't appear as Sarah remembered them when she opened her eyes. The world was muted and unrecognizable. The walls surrounding her were pale, an ugly color which she could not name, and above her were dingy and mottled white ceiling tiles. Sarah saw Sam sitting beside her, his skin was pale, and she knew he looked different but couldn't place exactly what. Sarah turned her focus to Mina next. She stood behind Sam, looking equally drab in a gray and black outfit with a matching black scarf tied into a turban around her hair. She rested a hand on Sam's shoulder, and Sam held his hand atop Mina's as she spoke to him, but Sarah couldn't read her lips. Sarah felt something when she saw them touch, but she couldn't place exactly what she was feeling. Finally, the two of them noticed Sarah's open eyes, and while Mina instantly began crying, Sam sat wide-eyed, appearing shocked but somehow still lifeless.

"You're awake!" Mina shouted as a nurse entered Sarah's room, responding to the call button Sam had pressed.

Mina rushed to Sarah's bedside, held her palm to her sister's cheek, and kissed her forehead. Sarah tried to move but couldn't. Even keeping her eyes open for this long was exhausting, and she fought falling back to sleep. Sarah's gaze shifted back to Sam, who held her hand now, his face resting on it, and Sarah felt his tears running over the back of her hand. She saw more people come into her room and watched them speak to her, or to someone, as though she could hear them, and as they poked and prodded her body, Sarah drifted back to sleep, too tired to keep her eyes open even through this examination.

When she woke again, Sam and Mina were still there, and again, Mina immediately began talking when she noticed her sister's eyes had opened.

"Do you... do you know what happened?" Mina asked, looking hopeful.

Sarah tried to understand what her sister had said to her but couldn't. She wasn't even sure where she was, why her body felt so odd, or why Sam seemed so sad. Sarah tried to move, but even the slightest movement sent blinding pain shooting from her jaw right out the top of her head. She tried to move her arm, to reach for whatever had just caused such pain, but even that was too exhausting, her arm too heavy. She tried to move her hand, her fingers, to sign and struggled with any sort of coordinated motion there as well. She paused to try and understand and felt her muscles burning. Finally, Sam moved. He reached for Sarah's hand and held it between both of his, tears running down his face as he shook his head, no.

"Thomas did this to you," Mina said once Sarah's attention had returned to her. "I'm sorry, Sarah. I'm so sorry."

Mina waited for Sarah to respond, and when she didn't, Mina ran from the room. Guilt kept her from understanding that her sister was confused, not angry. Sam kissed Sarah's hand and laid his head on her stomach. Sarah felt the bed shake with each sob he let out. As she slowly became more awake, the dull pain that had been lingering in Sarah's head grew stronger until she could feel nothing but pain.

The glass door to Sarah's room slid open, and Mina reappeared with a doctor no older than Sarah following closely behind. The doctor did a brief examination of Sarah, and Sam's head shot up off the bed, and he seamlessly moved into interpreter mode the moment the doctor began speaking.

"Sarah, I'm Doctor Collier. I've been overseeing your care. You've been through quite a lot."

Sarah didn't move her head, still reeling from how much it hurt the last time she'd done that.

"You were attacked in your home. Do you recall anything about that?" Dr. Collier asked.

She understood a question was being asked of her, though she didn't know what or why. It was as though she was searching for one specific, meaningful item in a messy pile of things she had never seen before. Nothing had meaning.

"There's nothing for you to be afraid of. The man that did this was arrested. The only thing you need to worry about is recovery. Would you like me to explain the extent of your injuries to you?" Doctor Collier asked.

Sarah knew what she wanted to say—a simple "why?" Why was everything so confusing? Why did she feel this way? Why was she in this place and not home? Why couldn't she make sense of the words in her head? Why? She couldn't recall how, though, so instead, she cried, which only caused her more pain.

"You suffered a severe head injury. You had a massive bleed in your brain, and paralysis is a result of that. You've had six surgeries in the past sixteen days, and it appears the last one was a success. You have a drain in your head to ease swelling. You may improve with therapy, but the damage was tremendous, and you may not recover fully." The doctor explained.

Sarah tried to make sense of something, but there was nothing. She didn't understand. She didn't understand anything, why she couldn't feel anything but her head, why it hurt so badly, why everyone looked so upset, nothing.

"Sarah," Doctor Collier began, "Are you in pain? I can set you up with a button for pain medication if you like. I suspect your head will be rather painful for a little while."

She thought about how much pain she was in, but none of what anyone said to her made any sense, so she only lay there and moved an eyebrow. Sarah looked to the window, and the light hurt her eyes, so she closed them and drifted back to sleep as various hospital staff came in and out of the room. When she woke again, the room was dark. Only a reading lamp beside her bed dimly lit the room. Mina had gone, but when Sam noticed her stirring, he came and sat beside her on the bed. Once again, Sarah thought one word—why—but failed to move the word from her mind to her hand.

"I'm sorry I wasn't there, Sarah. I'm sorry I didn't protect you. I should have been there, I'm sorry," Sam said, unsure if Sarah understood anything at all.

As badly as Sarah wanted to understand everything, staying awake was too hard. Sam stopped apologizing and told her to go back to sleep when he noticed Sarah again struggling to keep her eyes open. Letting her rest was so excruciatingly difficult. His world had disappeared in an instant, and now she was back, and he wanted nothing more than to catch up. Two weeks of waiting, of not knowing, forced apart from the woman his life was built around felt like a lifetime, and he had so much to tell her. Before, the two had shared everything, from life's minor annoyances to world-altering realizations, and Sam felt as though he'd been stockpiling all of it, keeping a mental checklist of things to tell Sarah as if she'd simply been gone away on a long trip.

It then occurred to Sam that the biggest change he would have to tell her of was that he'd been sleeping with her sister and he was grateful, when he looked back to Sarah, that she'd already fallen back to sleep and hadn't seen his face change with that realization.

"You sleep," Sam told her, "we can talk when you wake up." He kissed Sarah's hand that he was still holding, and she let her head sink into the pillow.

CHAPTER 24

S am woke coughing in his small bed situated in the corner of the
groundskeeper's house arranged like a studio apartment. The
smoke had just begun seeping through the microscopic cracks around
the two windows and the door, though he couldn't yet see it. One by
one, his senses woke as he did. His nose first, inhaling the unforget-
table odor of burning hay, then his eyes opened and instantly burned,
and then his ears tuned into the sound of the horses screaming from
the barn. Finally, his brain woke and put the three together.

The barn was on fire.

He jumped out of bed and pulled on the pair of jeans he'd draped
over the desk chair the evening before. He pulled on his boots and a
t-shirt, and before he could think of what he should do, he was out
of his small house and tearing open the sliding barn door to find the
fire already filling the back half of the barn. Sam ran down the aisle
and, one by one opened the stall doors and swatted each horse to
shoo it out of the barn. He screamed with the horses, "Git! Go on! Get
up!" more to drown out the terrified sounds of those he couldn't get
to than to serve any purpose. When that aisle of stalls was empty, he
looked to his horse in the first stall of the next aisle. He saw the terror
of Eddie's wide eyes as the huge gelding reared in his stall, and Sam
turned and walked out of the barn, leaving behind Eddie with thirteen other horses.

Sam's head rested uncomfortably where sweat had soaked into the pillow, and his discomfort in bed fed the pain he was in in his nightmare, so it didn't jolt him awake as it would most people. Instead, he slowly came to his senses, his hand resting on Mina's scar-laden bare chest, and as his senses came to him, he remembered he was in bed, safe, not in the barn on fire. He always had the same dream about the fire, and it was more like a video of what had really happened than a dramatized nightmare.

Fully awake, he couldn't shake the image of looking at his horse one last time before he walked away from him, leaving him to die in the fire. Had the nightmare not been so vivid and mostly true, he would have appreciated the absurdity of how the dream had distorted to fit his current life, stuck between Mina and Sarah.

He hadn't left Eddie to die in the fire. Instead, he'd chosen his own horse, who was much harder to reach than the others in the barn. He'd run past the stalls of nine other horses to get to Eddie in time, and in the end, Eddie still died. That's how he'd gotten a chest covered in burn scars and how he'd come to be haunted by the sounds of terrified horses screaming as they died. He had chosen Eddie over every other horse in the barn and failed anyway. He didn't need to be a shrink to assess the dream as being indicative of how he felt about being with Mina while Sarah lay in the hospital.

Before Sarah was attacked, he seldom had the nightmare anymore, but lately, it had become a regular occurrence again. He'd never shared the details of the fire—or the dream—with Sarah. He felt it was in poor taste to share that image of animals suffering with anyone that hadn't witnessed it themselves. But he told Mina about it because he knew she could relate to the torture and the suffering of having the worst moment of your life burned into your skin as a reminder every waking moment.

Mina woke to Sam shifting in her bed, which they now shared. Sam hadn't slept in his own bed since the night before Sarah was attacked.

"You have the dream again?" She asked.

"Yeah. But this time, I didn't save Eddie. Didn't even try. I looked right at him and walked away, outside to the other horses."

"You know that's not what's happening with Sarah, don't you? You're not abandoning her." Mina told him as she stroked his head.

Sam let his head, still damp with sweat, settle comfortably onto

Mina's chest.

Even after being arrested, Thomas was confident that he'd won, that his imprisonment was just a small setback. That is until he saw Mina. He'd killed her sister; he knew he had. There was no doubt in his mind that doing so would send Mina back to Radiance, where she belonged. He knew her, after all. He'd broken her so methodically that he knew exactly how to bring her back in line, and as he sat in his cell, Thomas envisioned Mina and Noah having returned to the community to await his own return.

There was no question that Thomas had attacked Sarah and that his intent was to kill her. When the police talked to others on the block, many had seen him wandering the block for far longer than a usual tourist does. Then there was the indisputable evidence of him bludgeoning Sarah with a rock on the security camera, a smile on his face as more and more blood-spattered it. He was being held without bail until his trial, during which Sam was positive he would be found guilty. The fact that none of them would ever have to encounter the man again was a small comfort to Sam.

Until Mina announced that she wanted to go see him in jail.

Sam knew he had to accompany Mina when she went to see Thomas. Sam wanted nothing more than to beat the man with his bare hands until he choked on his last breath, but he'd seen the way Mina had reacted to the mere mention of his name far too many times to let her go alone. Sam went with Mina expecting he'd be bringing her home a broken mess. He had no desire to see Thomas. He wasn't sure he'd be able to control himself if the monster wasn't separated from them by the little desk and glass he'd seen prisoners behind on TV. He had now irreparably damaged both women Sam loved, and Sam wanted him dead. He wanted him dead, and he wanted to do it himself. Sam's curiosity won out when Mina entered the visitation room. He couldn't help but stay and watch, silently rooting for Mina to be exactly who she'd been working toward becoming. Sarah. A woman, strong and unafraid.

There was no glass partition, no phone for prisoners to talk with their visitors through. Thomas sat with his hands cuffed and attached to the table and wore a smirk on his face meant to scare Mina into submission for the thousandth time. But Mina was reborn in that moment.

Mina took a seat across from Thomas. She sat and silently stared at him for a moment as she wove her fingers together and rested her hands calmly on the table in front of her.

"Do you remember," Mina began, speaking to Thomas in a slow and measured tone, "when you cut me and burned me, and you thought you had beaten me then?"

Thomas snorted a laugh but said nothing.

"You didn't win that day. I made love to a man just before I came here today. A man who makes me happier than you would ever be able to."

Thomas looked away briefly, swallowing his shame.

"Do you remember when I was afraid to leave the house because I was so humiliated by the bruises you told me I deserved? You always told me that I had no choice but to deal with it and that if I could just figure out how to be better, you would stop. You told me no one else would ever want me," Mina said, her tone still unwavering. "I have a family here, and they love me. They love my son. I own a business. I have a life here."

Thomas would no longer meet Mina's eyes.

"Did you like the ponytail I left on the counter for you? Did you save it? The only thing you have left to remember the wife who left you?" Mina asked him.

"Do you remember what you did to me when I came home from the hospital? Was that the only way you could feel like a man?" Mina asked Thomas, who sat on the metal bench disappearing into himself in the jail uniform that was far too big for his small frame, looking far more fearful than Mina had ever been. "I'm not afraid of you anymore. You will never leave here. You'll rot, and no one will ever miss you. And Noah? He will never know you existed."

Mina stood to leave but turned back and sat back down to rub salt in the wound. "I'm going to go back to Radiance, and I'm going to tell every single person there what a failure you are and tell them all the lies you told. When I'm done, you'll be nothing more than an embarrassment."

Mina smoothed her scarf, stood from the table, and stormed out of the room when the guard opened the door. Thomas would look at neither of them. Mina had accomplished exactly what she'd set out to.

"And Thomas…" Mina turned back to him again. "I'll be at every court appearance, and when they send you to Arizona to answer for killing Abraham, I'll be there too, so I can ask that they don't give you the courtesy of death. My face will be the very last one you see before you spend the rest of your life in prison. And I hear they love small, weak men like you there. You'll finally get what you deserve. I hope it was all worth it."

"Let's go home," Mina said to Sam as she breezed right by him. He followed, in awe.

When they reached the car in the parking lot, Sam tried to find words to express how impressed and proud he was.

"Mina, I—"

"I meant what I said to him. I love you, Sam. You make me happy, and this is what I want. I want you. I know it's terrible, but it's true."

"Don't," Sam interrupted her, "please don't."

Instead of letting Sam finish his thought, she wrapped her arms around his shoulders, and they kissed beside the car. Mina knew what that thought was, and she couldn't bear hearing the inevitable *"but Sarah…"*

Did Sam love Mina? Of course he did, he knew that, and it was a comfortable love that he was content to settle for when he believed Sarah would die. It comforted him when nothing else could, for which he was grateful. But Sarah, she was awake, real again. Loving Sarah felt right. Loving Mina felt good. Sarah's love felt like fate, if there was such a thing, while Mina's love came as a surprise twist in a film that left moviegoers conflicted but oddly comforted.

Should he choose right and easy, the path which he and everyone who knew him had long believed was his future, or new and soothing? He'd never been one for indecision, though he'd never quite found himself in such an impossible spot either. And so, he chose neither, for now, and would carry on as he had been.

CHAPTER 25

T he severity of her condition overwhelmed Sarah when, over the next several days, her fog lifted, and she discovered, bit by bit, every function that she could no longer perform.

She couldn't sign, instead having to rely on verbal speech, which she'd always despised. She couldn't shift her body in bed. She couldn't dress or undress herself, bathe herself. She couldn't even scratch her own head when it itched. Instead, she often hit herself in the face when she tried to reach for her head. Several times a day, one of three different people came into her room to do exercises they'd been doing while she was unconscious, which she couldn't help but feel violated by. The physical therapy assistants would move her arms and legs up and down, flexing them. They told her it was to ensure they didn't atrophy. She was given a stress ball to squeeze, and each time she attempted to use it, she dropped it because her fingers didn't respond as quickly as she needed them to. She was infuriated by her inability to do even the simplest of things, like holding the goddamn ball.

She got mad at stupid things, too, like having a catheter because she couldn't control her bladder anymore. She hated the nurse that came in to empty her bag of urine. The greatest violation of all, though, was that it had been Sam and Mina who dictated all of these things be done to her. They had allowed her autonomy to be slowly chipped away and replaced by things others had control of, and for what? So she could live in this constant state of confusion and pain while the world carried on as usual. Sarah didn't know how to exist in this body that needed others for its continued existence.

On the twelfth day after Sarah regained consciousness, the memory of what Thomas had done to her came rushing back. She'd had a drain sticking out of her skull, put in to monitor and manage swelling so the damage didn't get any worse, and after four days of no new fluid draining, it was time for it to be removed. There was no gentle way to remove it. Doctor Collier simply braced herself with one hand on Sarah's head and yanked it out with the other. The drain seemed to come out in slow motion, and as pain filled each part of her body, she could still feel the image of Thomas and his rock, beating her in the head, played in her mind. The strangeness of it was overwhelming. In the time before she became his victim, she'd grown accustomed to Mina having a physical reaction to memories of the things he'd done to her. She would cry, or vomit, or pee herself each time she allowed a memory in. Sarah came to understand this was the effect the monster had on people. But she had no reaction when she recalled, after days of trying to, what he'd done to her. This just was a thing that happened to her.

The day after the drain came out, Sarah got her new wheelchair, and she wanted no part of it. Under the watchful eye of a nurse, Sam lifted her from the hospital bed and carried her to the big black thing. He wouldn't look Sarah in the eye, and she watched her legs dangle lifelessly over his arm, the legs that used to carry her through marathons. The urge to do something that would force Sam to look at her overtook her, and she used the only tool at her disposal, her teeth. Sarah turned her head toward him and sunk them into his bicep.

It worked.

"Ouch! Shit, Sarah!" Sam dropped her into the chair. "What the hell?"

He looked at her like she'd lost her mind, and she was sickly pleased with the mark she'd left behind as he pulled up the sleeve of his t-shirt and rubbed the new purple bruise. Sarah knew precisely why she'd wanted to hurt Sam. For two weeks now, he'd been speaking for her, finishing sentences for her because she couldn't, all without ever really looking at her. He was her personal robot that carried out her will with no emotion at all.

Before, Sarah had adored the connection they shared. The fact that

Sam could finish her sentences, voice what she was thinking without her having to sign. It had been one of the many things that made people believe they were such a perfect couple. Like their minds had melded, and the thoughts that started in Sarah's mind finished in Sam's. But now, each time he spoke for her, it felt like he was stealing from her.

Sarah didn't know why she was so mad at Sam. She didn't blame what happened to her on him. It wasn't as though he'd planned on Thomas coming. He hadn't taken Mina and run, leaving Sarah at his mercy. But she needed to be mad at someone, and she knew it couldn't be Mina. She'd seen her sister twice since she'd woken up, and she didn't wonder why. Mina blamed herself, and Sarah was conflicted as to whether she thought Mina was right in doing so or not. She was conflicted about so many things. She still didn't quite understand what had happened to her or if she would ever get better. She never felt clear-headed, and very few things made sense anymore, least of all her relationship with Sam, who still wouldn't look at her.

It was remarkably difficult, Mina discovered, to fall into a normal routine with someone when your entire existence with them had grown from the unimaginable. Had Thomas not been such an awful man, such a violent and frightening man, she never would have come here to know her sister or Sam. Had Sarah not been abused and abandoned by their father, she never would have been able to show Mina how good living could feel. Had Mina not been so damaged beyond repair that she needed love and care in excess from Sam, a man, to be able to function in the world, she wouldn't know him as the man she had come to love. Had Sarah not been attacked and so badly hurt, she would have never known the pure joy that can come from sex when it's with someone you love. All of these horrible things had given Mina life, and the guilt she felt because of it was not something she could simply sit with, so she busied herself, always making sure she had something to do, something or someone to fuss over. She and Sam would never be a normal couple, though she doubted that she could ever be normal with anyone.

Mina felt guilty knowing Sam in all the intimate ways she did. That he hated pulp in his lemonade, and that he preferred strawberry lemonade to regular or any other variety, and even that lemonade was his favorite beverage. She knew the sound of the vacuum bothered him, so she always did it when he was out of the house, and she bought a tea strainer for his lemonade, and that in itself felt like an act of infidelity. But Mina knew that someone needed to care for him, put him back together after the devastation of Sarah's attack. They both needed each other to be exactly who they were, no matter how intrusive the guilt that came along with it.

It was the small things that made Sam and Mina grow even closer. Before the attack, Sam had easily become Mina's closest friend, which felt like a strange distinction given her relationship with Sarah. She had become everything Mina had ever dreamed of having in a sister, but while Sarah had come to know Mina deeply and understood every unspoken thing about her, it was with Sam that Mina preferred to spend her time and enjoy the inconsequential and mundane parts of life. The guilt came in knowing she'd loved Sam well before Sarah's attack. She'd been attracted to him since the first night they stayed up talking. But until now, she'd been able to deny and ignore her feelings because she had an intimacy with her sister.

Eventually, the awkwardness faded, along with the shame and guilt, and the two functioned as a couple seamlessly, caring for each other and caring for Noah as two parents. Sam still went to see Sarah every single day, though sometimes the world that had continued to turn without Sarah being an active part of it got in the way, and his visits felt hurried and obligatory on occasion.

Sarah had been awake for over two weeks and had yet to improve even the slightest bit. Every morning when she woke up, Sam was there smiling at her, and every day she needed to be reminded what had happened, where she was, why she couldn't go home. Sam could tell that even as he signed these things to her over and over, none of it registered, and each day, he explained a little bit less because reliving it hurt him more than it helped her.

By the end of the sixth week of Sarah's recovery, Sam had perfected his routine. He was there in the morning when she woke, and he stayed for an hour and a half. He watched a portion of her physical therapy session, which seemed to be about as helpful to her as his daily recitation of what had happened to her. Nothing at all was changing or getting better. When he left the hospital, Sam could at least feel like something of consequence was being achieved by his routine.

"This may be as good as it gets," Doctor Collier explained to Sam during one of his visits, "or, she may be recovering very slowly. Progress after a brain injury isn't measured the same way you and I measure our own progress. She's not recovering from the flu, Sam, be patient."

Both Sam and Mina made themselves believe that Sarah would accept how things had progressed between the two of them in her absence. They chose to believe that she loved them each enough to only want them to be happy, however that happiness came about.

Sarah now looked like a ghost to Sam. He remembered her best with her eyebrows drawn on perfectly, bold red lips, blushed cheeks, and her headscarf. Now she lay in the hospital bed pale and every touch of makeup long cleaned off her face, no trace of eyebrows penciled in and no false lashes glued on. He remembered the light scent of cocoa butter and honey from the balm she would rub into her scalp each day to keep it from drying out. He used to close his eyes and breathe it in when Sarah rested her head on his shoulder. It had been over two months since he'd been able to hold her and breathe her in. Two months since his world had become a state of limbo where nothing was certain, and everything felt wrong. Everything but Mina.

When Sam went to visit with Sarah, he didn't keep things from her. The nurses encouraged talking to her. They said she could hear him, even if none of it seemed to be registering, which made Sam laugh each time. *She's never heard a sound in her life before, but a massive traumatic brain injury would remedy that. Right.* He signed to her instead of speaking, for even though he knew Sarah was getting maybe a word or two at best, that remained the only natural way to say anything to her. He told her how big Noah was getting, he told her about how well their salon was doing, he even told her that while he missed her terribly, he thought he was really falling in love with Mina. Not in the weird guilt-riddled filling in for Sarah way he had been feeling, but in love with her really. And yet, he never could tell Sarah that he didn't love her anymore because it was simply not true. He could tell Sarah everything and absolve himself of guilt because most of the time, Sarah didn't recall any of it the next day.

Mina didn't come to see Sarah every day like Sam did. Her guilt was too great, both the guilt of thinking this was all her fault—it had been Thomas that did this, after all—and the guilt of taking the man she would have married had this all never happened, though Sam had been a willing participant in everything they'd done together. Mina visited her sister on Fridays. She always made sure to visit before going to Friday prayer at the masjid. She felt that this was somehow helpful, like she could take little bits of Sarah's cells into the masjid with her if she visited and held her hand for a while.

They rarely took Noah to see his aunt. He was far too young to understand what had happened to her, and he had adjusted to life without the woman he had become so attached to, and neither wanted to risk confusing the boy.

It didn't feel like a betrayal when, after four months, Sam and Mina moved on with life and accepted all of this as normal. Normal that the extent of Sarah's recovery had been that now she could ask for water and then forget she'd asked for it when someone brought it to her. They went out and did things as a couple, they had passionate sex completely free of guilt, and they were content to be considered a fitting couple among the friends they'd made, some of them the very same pairs of couple-friends Sarah and Sam had. It wasn't a betrayal. It was life. Sam couldn't say whether he had fallen out of love with Sarah, but his heart seemed to understand that he couldn't have her, and if he was going to ever be okay and happy, he would need to allow himself to love someone else.

CHAPTER 26

Finally, after six months of living in a rehabilitation hospital and counting progress one inch at a time, the day Sarah was to be released and allowed to return home had arrived.

As much as she despised the term, Sarah had grown used to her "new normal" because she believed it to be temporary. She could walk, albeit very slowly and briefly and only with the help of a walker, and she could once again sign, though not with the same ease she'd once taken for granted, her coordination and reflexes being just a hint of what they'd once been. The last ability to return to her, and the most difficult to have gone for so long without, was her rationality. The process of being able to experience something, take a beat to consider it, weigh the choices and consequences, and take measured action. The mere fact that this was a process at all had escaped her for forty-odd years, along with the dozens of mundane but remarkably intricate and involved things a person does without thought every second of their lives—the many things you don't know you have until you lose them.

She'd watched her own forward motion, however slow and infuriating it had been, just as she'd watched from a distance the undoing of all that had once been her and Sam, the perfect couple that everybody wanted to be, or at least emulate. Sarah's progress remained measured but unspoken until it wasn't. Just as she'd finally grown accustomed to living in the rehabilitation hospital, her doctor told her she would be going home in a week.

As with Sarah's progress, the state of her and Sam, or rather, Sam and Mina, remained unspoken—at least in Sarah's recollection—until it wasn't.

"I don't want to do this anymore, Sam," Sarah signed as they sat in her room in the ever-uncomfortable silence that always followed Sam having to wipe Sarah after she used the bathroom.

"Sarah, I don't know what else you want me to do," Sam admitted, exasperated from starting what he thought was the same argument they'd had a hundred times before in recent weeks. "You can't just shit and wear it. Somebody needs to wipe you, and I'm here, so—"

"Not that," Sarah signed and looked away, "I don't want you anymore, us. I don't want to do this."

Sarah meant what she'd said to him, as it had been coming for the months she'd been in the rehabilitation facility. Sam was her nanny, not her lover, her partner. *Once someone cleans you up after you've shit yourself, the romance is effectively dead*, she'd told herself.

"Sarah, I told you I don't care about this. It doesn't bother me. I'm happy to do it," Sam pleaded with her.

"Happy Sam? You're happy to be here every damn day, wiping my ass, changing my diapers? Is that why you've been sleeping with Mina? Because you're happy?" Sarah asked, her question feeling much angrier than she'd intended it to.

Sam took a sharp breath in and forgot to let it out until he began to feel dizzy. There was nothing he could say, he felt, to fix it. He should have told her a long time ago, and this was what he got for failing to do so. Before he could say a word in his defense, Sarah continued.

"I'm not mad, Sam, but I'm not stupid either. You think I couldn't tell?"

"You're not?" Sam asked.

"Come on, Sam. I don't understand what this has been like for you any better than you get what's it's been like for me. You needed Mina, and I need this. And if Mina is what you really want, then it's okay."

"I don't know what I want, Sarah. Mina was—"

"I know. Mina was a warm body when you needed one, and you didn't expect it to come to this. I don't think any of us expected to be where we are right now, did we?"

"I love you, Sarah, I never—"

"I love you too. It's not…" Sarah paused and laughed to herself over the words she was about to sign, the worst words anyone in love can receive. "It's not you, Sam. It's me."

Sam wiped tears from his cheeks with the palm of his hand, and Sarah appreciated that at least that hadn't changed. At least Sam still wiped away his tears in his weird way and not with his fingers like people normally did.

"Sam, I need this," Sarah continued. "At the very least, I need to be able to put a pin in us. I don't have it in me right now to recover from this shit and be the kind of partner I want to be for you. Plus, Dr. Phil said caregivers never last as romantic partners."

"Fuck Dr. Phil!" Sam signed in response, so quickly his arms created a breeze which Sarah felt on her cheeks.

"Sam, you're not listening. I'm not hurt or angry about you and Mina. I don't blame you for it. This isn't even about that."

"What's it about then? Let me help you. Let me be this person you need right now."

"*That*. That's what it's about. I need you, and there's no way around it. I can't be with someone I need. I don't want you to be my nurse and my husband. I want you to look at me like you used to, and you don't, Sam. You don't."

"How am I supposed to? Sarah, I thought you were dead. The doctors as much as told me to just go on and unplug you because you were gone, and now you're not. How the hell am I supposed to reconcile that? How can I look at you the same way after I…" There were so many ways Sam could have finished his question that he simply didn't finish it.

"That's my point, Sam! We're not the same. This is not the same! And I can't do two things at once right now. I can't recover and get you past that. I need to do me, and you…" Sarah snorted a laugh, "you need to do you and figure out what the hell you want because you can't have both of us."

"I can't have you at all, apparently," Sam bitterly rolled his eyes even though he couldn't say Sarah was wrong.

"Don't do that, Sam, I don't deserve that. You want to help me, and I'm trying to tell you how. Don't dismiss me."

Sam sucked in his lips and bit down on them. His tell, Sarah knew, that he was both losing his patience and at a loss for words.

Finally, Sam found words. "So, what then? We go home, and I'm just your nurse? Your buddy who's there to take care of you?"

"You see anybody else here to do it? Really, Sam, is there anybody else, aside from someone we can't afford to hire, to do what you're doing for me? I don't know if you've noticed, but our friends stopped visiting months ago, and we don't get one of these nurses as a parting gift. We're on our own, Sam. It's on you to keep me alive and getting better, and I know that's unfair, and it's not what either of us wants, but that's where we are."

Sam couldn't respond because he knew Sarah was right. He thought about how months before all this happened, she told him that she was going to start going to a barbershop for shaves because she didn't want to become his job and how he'd appreciated that because it had gotten old pretty quickly. When he stopped to consider what she was saying now, he knew she was right, and he couldn't argue.

Sam took a long breath in and let it out in a short, defeated huff. "Can we at least agree to revisit us? Check in sometimes, see where we're at?"

"Can you figure out what you want? Me or Mina, Sam. I promise I'm not mad about it, but I will *not* be whatever I am for you right now. You can't have both, and you can't carry on with her for now if you still want me in the future. That's going to have to be a risk you take."

"Yeah. I'll talk to Mina," Sam said without thinking. He didn't need to think about it. He knew his choice was Sarah. It had always been Sarah, and he would have to leave it to chance that he'd get to be her husband one day.

They sat in silence, though not a tense one but one of resolution, as they waited for Sarah to be formally discharged. Both were terrified and thrilled at the notion of Sarah finally coming home when they both had once believed she never would.

"Disappointed," the word finally made its way out of Mina's mouth.

She'd sat in silence for an uncomfortably long time in her therapist's chair after Mary had asked her how she felt about her sister returning home. And that was the moment she decided she was a monster, just like her father, just like Thomas.

Sarah had something she wanted, someone she wanted, and she knew she would get him back, of course she would. And so, she admitted to her disappointment at Sarah not dying after all. She'd have been lying if she said she wasn't aware Sam loved her differently. The love he had with Sarah, it was the kind people idolized and struggled for. The love Sam had given her? It was of convenience and comfort. She was there when Sam was too bitter, too heartbroken, to leave the house. She was there when he collapsed in the shower, his grief too great to allow him to stand. She was there to remind him to get up and showered and dressed because they had a business to run. And now, all of his attention would be going right back to Sarah. Mina was sickened by her jealousy, but she couldn't deny it was real, right there waiting for the best thing that had ever happened to her to come to an end. Or was he the best thing that had ever happened to her, she wondered?

"Mina," Mary began, "if there's anything I've seen you come to understand in the time you've been seeing me, it's that you have choices now. There are so many choices you can make. You don't have to just sit and wait for things to happen, you know?"

What Mary said hadn't occurred to Mina. She was grateful for the reminder, and she knew exactly the choice she had to make. It was the very same choice Sarah would make in their shared belief in what was meant to be.

Mina thanked Mary and said goodbye as she did at the end of every session. Though Mary knew that this time, the goodbye wasn't the usual until next time variety but the goodbye her clients always gave on their last session.

Mina returned home and collected Noah from Mrs. Kostas and hurried upstairs. She wanted to be gone before Sam and Sarah got home. She packed as little as she had when she left Radiance, though this time, it was yet another choice she'd made and not a choice that had been made for her out of necessity.

She stopped in the bathroom just off the entryway and studied her appearance as she considered how she should leave. She no longer recognized herself as the same woman she'd been a year and a half ago when she'd arrived in Chicago. Somehow, despite all that had happened, Mina had found exactly what she'd needed to become exactly the woman she'd hoped she would one day be.

On the bathroom counter, instead of a long ponytail that held within it ten years of terror and pain, she left a note.

> *I love you, both of you, and I'm grateful. You've given me life and choice. You know where we've gone, I'm sure, and we'll be awaiting a visit from Baba Sam and Mama Sarah as soon as you're able.*
>
> *Love,*
>
> *Mina (and Noah)*

Holding Noah on her hip, Mina knocked on the bright turquoise door. On the flight, Mina had prayed. Not that Reina welcome her with open arms and forgive her, but that she would be able to finally be the woman Reina loved and was deserving of.

After a moment, the door opened, and Mina was greeted by Reina's smile that in an instant, felt just as it always had, like home, like love, like a wide-open space reserved just for Mina with room for her to be just as she was, imperfect, a little selfish, and a bit afraid. All of the things which Mina thought she shouldn't be.

"I knew you'd come," was all Reina said as she wrapped her arms around both Mina and Noah and pulled them inside the house, without so much as a glance at the wall of Radiance that still stood behind them.

Manufactured by Amazon.ca
Bolton, ON

27269857R00111